Daily Express
Sept 24 '92.

Cracking tale of a top Tory on trial

AFTER John Mortimer, Lord Rawlinson, the former Attorney General, has written a novel inspired by the fate of Lord Aldington, who had to sue when he was falsely accused of war crimes.

While Lord Aldington still waits for his damages, Peter Rawlinson, now 73, should do handsomely from his second novel Hatred And Contempt (Chapmans, £14.99).

It's a cracker; a spellbinding read from the moment the fictional Lord Brackley, Tory ex-Cabinet Minister and supposed war hero, is accused in a pamphlet of being a coward, traitor and homosexual.

Enter beautiful, blonde solicitor Alexandra, who takes pity on the accuser and gets her lover, aggressive young QC Simon, to defend him.

The novel has great court drama, some commercial bonking and ingenious plot twists.

Move over Lord Archer, you have a rival.

PAPERBACKS

1 (1) THE LIAR, Stephen Fry (Mandarin £4.99)

HATRED AND CONTEMPT

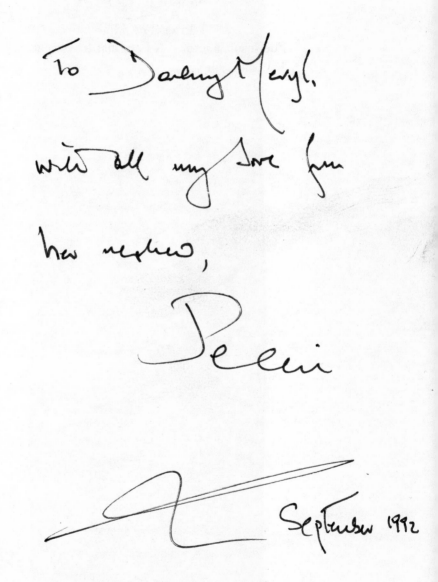

To Darling Meryl,

with all my love from

her nephew,

Peter

September 1992

Peter Rawlinson

HATRED AND CONTEMPT

CHAPMANS

Chapmans Publishers Ltd
141–143 Drury Lane
London WC2B 5TB

BRITISH LIBRARY CATALOGUING IN PUBLICATION DATA
Rawlinson, Peter
Hatred and contempt.
I. Title
823.914 [F]
ISBN 1–85592–066–2

First published by Chapmans 1992

Photoset by Rowland Phototypesetting Ltd
Bury St Edmunds, Suffolk

Printed and bound in Great Britain by
Clays Ltd, St Ives plc

For my children –
Mikaela, Dariel, Haidée,
Michael, Angela and Anthony.

'To bring into hatred, ridicule and contempt'
– the definition of libel

ONE

It was shortly after first light on a cold Thursday in January when the man served the writ.

He had arrived in the street just after 7.30, somewhat earlier than he had planned. But then he was usually early when he had a job to do. He had also been nervous about the amount of traffic on the drive from Ruislip and he knew that it was important that he should not be late.

They had told him that at eight o'clock each weekday morning the old man returned from his walk with his dog along the river by Battersea Park, close to where he lived in Pelham Lane, Fulham. It was, they said, a cul-de-sac, and the man would turn into it from the Fulham Road and go to the ground-floor flat at number 11. That was the time to find him at home. Remember, they had insisted, when you hand him the writ, make a show of it; frighten him if you can, so that he understands what he is up against. Above all, be sure to get a signature. We must have a signature.

The process-server had never before been instructed by these lawyers; they were a large firm with smart offices in Mayfair, not the kind often to have to serve a writ on an individual. They were the kind who dealt with other lawyers, enclosing the writ in formal letters. So he was flattered that to do this job they had come to him, to Les Price of Ruislip, former Detective Constable in the Metropolitan Police and now professional process-server.

When he had found Pelham Lane and parked his car round the corner, he walked down the Lane noting the numbers until he had come to number 11. Then he retraced his steps to the small newsagent's shop at the corner, where

1

he stood wrapped in his greatcoat against the cold, reading a newspaper and waiting. He was a tall man with sandy-coloured hair, a short, almost cropped moustache and a pronounced Adam's apple, which for the present was hidden behind a grey woollen scarf.

At eight o'clock precisely a figure passed him. He did not raise his eyes from his newspaper. The first he had seen was the dog, a black long-haired mongrel, a mixture between a Retriever and a Labrador, an old dog with grey around its mask. After the figure had passed, Price looked up and saw the back of an old man walking behind his dog, using a stick and moving a little unsteadily as though his knees troubled him. He was dressed in blue canvas trousers, with a black beret on his head, a khaki muffler and a short rain-proof jacket, a kind of camouflage-jacket such as is worn by the soldiers of today. The process-server could see the white of the old man's hair beneath the beret and when he turned to follow the dog up the steps from the street to enter the ground-floor flat of number 11, the white of the moustache.

When the old man had disappeared through his front door, Price followed down the street to number 11 and pressed the bell-button. He could hear the peal and then the bark of the dog. He rang a second time, peremptorily, keeping his finger on the button, listening to the sounds of the bell and of the barking. When the door was opened, he looked into the startling blue of the pale old eyes above the white moustache; and, unusually for him, he felt discon-certed. He had to remind himself that he was there to do a job.

'Mr Tarnovic?' he asked. 'Mr Tomas Tarnovic?'

The old man stared at him. He had taken off his jacket and Price could see his round-necked, military-style khaki sweater, with canvas epaulettes and patches at the elbows.

'Colonel Tarnovic,' the old man said quietly.

'If you wish. Colonel then. But Tomas Tarnovic?'

'Yes.'

'Then I've something for you.' Price pulled the documents from the inside pocket of his greatcoat and held them out so that they almost touched the other's chest. The old man looked down at them.

'What is it?' he asked.

'Legal documents, which I've been directed to serve upon you.'

The old man turned away. 'It is cold in the doorway. You had better come inside. Are you from the council?'

'No, I'm certainly not from the council. It's more serious than that. You have to sign for them to prove you've received them. These papers are very important.'

The words were those the process-server had planned to use in the car, but he had not said them with the menace that he had intended.

'Are they? Come in and shut the door behind you.'

Price hesitated and then stepped inside. They might be interested to know how the old man lived; it would do no harm if he were able to give them a description at first hand. He shut the front door behind him and went through the small lobby into the sitting-room.

It was a large room and cold, the chill only slightly taken off by the gas fire in the centre wall on his left. At the far end he could see through the glass top of a door a small patch of wild and unkempt garden. In a corner there was an alcove with the curtains half-drawn and behind them a camp-bed. Opposite the gas fire, another door was open and he could see and hear the steam of a kettle boiling on a hob in the kitchen.

The dog suddenly loped towards him and he backed hurriedly away. Price was used to being greeted by dogs, but this one was friendly, snuffling at the hand, which after a time he put down nervously to pat the dog's head.

'Have some tea.'

Price was not used to this. He said, 'This is not necessary – and it's not usual. I am not sure that it's even proper. I just have to give you the papers and get your signature.'

But the old man had disappeared into the kitchen and Price was left fondling the dog, now more confidently. He

3

looked around the large, untidy room, noting the book-shelves full of tattered volumes, most of them in foreign languages. In the gaps between the books were photo-graphs. He walked over and examined them. The largest, and the one in the most prominent place, was of a man in uniform, a tunic buttoned to the collar. He had a full, bushy beard and moustache and sad eyes behind steel-rimmed glasses. But for the military uniform, he looked like a pro-fessor. Written across the right-hand corner, in a spindly, looping hand was: 'Tomas, from his friend Draža. April 1941.'

Other photographs were of groups of armed men in shabby, rag-bag uniforms. In the background were moun-tains. One photograph, obviously much older, was of a steam-yacht with a tall funnel sailing between two islands. The last of the photographs he had time to study was of a blonde woman with her hand under her chin, a misty, faded photograph. She was very beautiful, the process-server thought.

On the wall behind him were two large oil paintings, one of yellow marigolds in a white vase, the paint thick and the colour vivid; the other of a bunch of anemones lying on a blue-and-white-checkered table-cloth, with bright pink petals and centres heavy in black. Unframed canvases stood against the wall. In front of him, hanging on two nails over the mantel of the gas fire, were a sabre and a curved steel helmet, both tarnished and rusted. On the floor, beside the canvases, were piles of yellowing newspapers and more books and sheafs of documents tied in bundles with string. An old typewriter and stacks of typescript stood on a table in the centre of the room.

The old man came back into the room carrying two mugs of tea.

'You know, this is most irregular. All I require is for you to sign the top paper in this bundle of documents. That's to record that you've received them. The others I'll leave with you. That's all I want.'

'You shall have everything that you want. But sit down.

It is a cold morning. I saw you at the corner. Drink your tea.'

They both sat.

'It's certainly damned cold.' Price sipped the tea.

'What is your name?'

'Mr Price, Les Price.'

'How old are you?'

'I'm thirty-six.'

'That is a good age. When I was that age I was a prisoner of war. Have you ever been a soldier?'

Price laughed. 'No. But I've been a policeman.'

'That is not the same thing,' said the old man severely. 'You are tall. You might have made a good soldier.'

Price, flattered, drank noisily from his mug. Then the old man said, 'Tell me, are you happy?'

The process-server almost choked on his tea. 'Happy?' He thought of Annie at home in Ruislip. There had been the devil of a row that morning, one of their very best. He had been out drinking the night before and had got back late. In the morning he had caught it.

'That's a funny question to ask. Of course I'm happy.' He tried to laugh. 'At least I think so. I haven't really thought about it.' He put down his mug. This was ridiculous. 'Of course I'm happy. And happy in my work, which this morning is to give you these papers. Now look here, Mr Tarnovic, you're being very polite, but I'm here on serious business and not to discuss my happiness. What I've given you —' he pointed to the table between them where he had laid the documents on top of one of a pile of typescripts, 'those papers I've put there are very important. When I've gone, take a good look at them. It'll be in your interest to study them very, very carefully.'

He wasn't making much of a show, he thought, not much of the menace that he had been told to convey. But the old man somehow upset him.

Price tried again, tried this time to sound more authoritative. 'You should take them to your solicitors. You should show the papers I've served on you to your lawyers – straightaway.'

The old man looked at him over the rim of his tea-mug and the process-server went on hurriedly. 'But it's a matter for you, entirely a matter for you.' They had not told him to say anything about lawyers. Perhaps they didn't want the old man to consult lawyers. 'What you do is your business. I'm only here to do my duty and give them to you.'

He stopped again and then concluded lamely, 'It's only because you have been so polite that I am advising you.'

'The poet Byron, you know, said that to have small ears was a mark of breeding. You have small ears. But you have an unimportant moustache and pouches under your eyes and many lines beside your mouth. No, I do not think that you can be very happy.'

This, the process-server felt, had to stop. He took a pen from his pocket and the top paper from the bundle. He unscrewed the pen.

'Look here, Mr Tarnovic –'

'Colonel Tarnovic,' said the old man very gently. 'I am always Colonel when the business is official.'

'Of course, I beg your pardon. Colonel Tarnovic. But please sign here. Then I'll be off and you can take the papers to your lawyers.' He stretched out his hand with the pen and the paper and leaned across the table.

'I do not have business with lawyers. I have never liked lawyers.'

'Well, Colonel, I'm afraid that when you have read that little package,' Les Price now felt on surer ground, 'you're going to have plenty of business with lawyers – whether you like 'em or not. And when you're finished, or rather when they have finished, you may like 'em a lot less than you do now.'

He laughed again and then stopped, embarrassed. 'You'll get me into trouble if you don't sign.'

The old man was still staring at him, both his hands clasped around his mug of tea. Although the gas fire burned beneath the mantel and the ancient sabre and helmet on

6

the wall above, the room was cold. For a time neither spoke. The process-server was still holding out his pen and the receipt. The only sound in the room was the hissing of the fire. Then the dog came and settled his head on the lap of the old man, who put down his tea and laid one hand on the dog's head. With the other he beckoned.

'I would not wish to get you into trouble. Come round here.'

It was a command and when it had been obeyed, the old man slowly took a heavy spectacle-case from his trouser pocket. With a pair of gold-rimmed glasses on his nose, he took the pen and with the paper balanced precariously on a pile of manuscripts in front of him, he signed with a flourish.

Price stuffed the paper into his breast pocket. 'Well, that's it, then,' he said nervously. 'I'll be off now. Thanks for the tea. Quite irregular, but acceptable, most acceptable on this cold morning. No need to see me out.'

The old man had not stirred.

'So long then. See you in Court, as they say.'

Price forced himself to try another laugh as he went through the lobby to the front door. Before he closed it, he looked back to where the old man sat still and silent, staring at him with those pale, weak eyes. The papers were still on the pile of typescripts where Price had put them.

Outside Price blew vigorously on his fingers and trotted round the corner to his car. Early as it was, he would go straight to Clifford Street and report. 'Mission accomplished.' As he drove he thought that he had better dress up the tale a little. He would say that when he had served the writ, he'd given the old fellow a damn good fright. After all, that was what they wanted. But he'd been an odd one, that old man, and no mistake. It was funny what he had said about his ears. He would tell Annie when he got home. She'd have a good laugh.

In his room the old man picked up the papers which had been left with him and tossed them across the table, where they fell carelessly among the pile of manuscripts and where

7

they were left to lie undisturbed – and unread. He finished his tea slowly, his hand still on the dog, who after a time left him and ambled off to subside on to the rug in front of the gas fire. The old man put a fresh sheet of paper into the typewriter and began to type.

TWO

Price pushed through the glass door to the offices of Baker and Turnbull in Clifford Street.

'I've come to see Mr Roger Bentall,' he said to the concierge. 'I hope it's not too early. Tell him it's Mr Price.'

He took the lift to the third floor and was told by the secretary to wait. After half an hour he was shown into Roger Bentall's office.

When he entered, Bentall remained seated. He was a small, neat man in his late forties, with a sallow complexion, shiny dark hair and large horn-rimmed spectacles, which disguised his grey, almost colourless eyes. In his expensively-tailored dark suit, his bespoke cream shirt and discreet tie, he fitted snugly behind his large and ornate Regency desk. Price was impressed.

'Well?' said Bentall. He did not invite Price to sit down or remove his overcoat.

'All done, sir. Not a hitch. And I did as you wanted. I frightened the old bugger all right.'

Roger Bentall winced slightly and tapped his pen on the pad in front of him. 'Did he say anything?' he asked.

'Not much. He just looked rather bewildered. He's pretty frail.'

'Did you get into the room?'

'I did. It's a squalid little place, just one room and a kitchen.'

'Did he read the papers when you gave them to him?'

'He gave them a glance. But he was shaken, I could see that.'

'Did he appear to have expected them?'

9

Price paused. He remembered the old man's disinterest, but that wouldn't do. 'He went into what I'd say was a state of shock. He was really shaken up. You can see by his signature.'

Price handed over the receipt. Bentall studied the signature made by Tomas Tarnovic when the paper had been balanced precariously on a pile of pamphlets. He opened a drawer in his desk with a key from his watch-chain and placed the receipt inside. He then locked the drawer.

'Very well,' he said. 'The cashier should be here by now. Draw your money from her.'

Price lingered. He did not often get the chance of instructions from the Senior Partner of so important a firm and he thought of the other wares in which this man might be interested.

'If ever you need anything in the way of enquiries or information, I've a partner who works with me. He was also in the Met.'

Bentall was looking at him steadily.

'The Metropolitan Police. He and I take on private clients who sometimes want to know a thing or two which may not be so easily come by. And, of course, we've excellent contacts. Sometimes it's important to get information and my partner is very experienced, especially in electronic supervision, if you get my meaning.'

Bentall still said nothing.

'Well, I thought you might like to know, sir. Just in case you ever need, how shall I put it, intimate information or anything like that. You know where to find me. Good-day, sir, good-day.'

Secretive bastard, Price thought as he went down in the lift. But the lawyer had wanted the pressure put on that old fellow all right and he'd been interested in what I'd said about Ned and his electronics – even if he had said nothing.

Price drew his money, collected his car and drove back to Ruislip. He would not be surprised to hear again from that particular individual.

10

In his office Bentall spoke on the intercom. 'Get me Lord Brackley. He will be in Yorkshire.'

While he waited, he unlocked the drawer and examined the receipt which Price had brought to him, studying again the signature – Tomas Tarnovic. It was certainly a very shaky hand.

The telephone rang.

'Lord Brackley,' he said, 'the writ was served this morning. My man told me that the fellow was very shaken when he was handed it. We won't hear any more from him, take my word for it. But all the same, we shall apply to the Court for an injunction to stop him repeating his lies. After that, if he publishes any more, he'll be in danger of imprisonment.' Bentall paused and listened to the other. Then he said, 'I understand. It is most unpleasant, particularly as I'm afraid that he circulated it to every MP, many in the Lords and everyone in government. We're still getting reports from those who received it.' He paused again. 'Yes, I've seen some of the Press, but they can't repeat what is in the pamphlet, only that it is about you. We had to act. I am quite sure of that.' He was interrupted and sat, nodding his head gravely. 'Of course. The accusations are infamous. The fellow must be mad, but you really couldn't have ignored it. No one will believe a word of it, but you had to be seen to be taking action. Now you have and that will be an end of it. I'll let you know about the application to the Court. Give my regards to Lady Brackley.'

He replaced the receiver and sat for a moment looking out of the window at the roofs of the houses in the street opposite. Then he again spoke on the intercom. 'Get me Sir Leonard Gordon at the Ministry of Defence.' Gordon was the Permanent Secretary, the senior civil servant at the Ministry.

Bentall waited. Then: 'Sir Leonard? It's Roger Bentall here, of Baker and Turnbull. I'm calling about Lord Brackley and that wretched pamphlet which was sent to you and many others. I thought I should tell you that this morning we served a writ. Of course, the fellow is a crank and he

11

was very shaken when the writ was served on him. We shall apply for an injunction to silence him and that should be the end of the matter.'

Bentall sat listening. Then he went on. 'I know it all happened nearly fifty years ago, but it's a very wicked libel. And, of course, the Press are now sniffing around. But they'll have to be careful. At least we could get some hefty damages out of them – which we certainly can't out of this madman.'

Bentall paused. Then: 'Yes, Lord Brackley's book must have triggered it off. However, I'm quite sure that we've now heard the last of it. I will keep you in touch. Goodbye.'

Back in Fulham, Tomas Tarnovic spent two hours at his typewriter. At eleven o'clock he let the dog into the small garden and then settled him with water and a couple of biscuits. He put on his camouflage-jacket and beret, and taking several pages of a typescript from the table, he put them into a plastic carrier bag and set out. He took a bus across the river to the Imperial War Museum. At four in the afternoon he left the Museum and began to walk westward. After an hour he came to a house in Lees Square in Lambeth and rang the bell.

The door was opened by an elderly woman, her white hair scraped back and fastened at the nape of her neck. She held herself very straight and was dressed wholly in black.

'How is Alexei?'

'The same.'

'Give him my best wishes. Does he want to see me?'

'No.'

'If he ever asks, let me know and I shall come immediately.' But he knew that Alexei would not ask. Alexei was dying and he did not want his old friends to see him as he now was. Alexei wanted them to remember him as he had been, in his prime.

The woman looked at him. 'Kosta is in. You know where.'

She turned and went into a side room, closing the door behind her. Tomas went to the end of the corridor and entered a small room in the centre of which stood a large copying machine. The man behind it looked up.

'I heard the bell,' he said. 'I thought it would be you.'

He was a man of about fifty, square, strongly-built, with close-cropped iron-grey hair and a pale, swarthy complexion. He was in shirt-sleeves and was wearing an apron. He came around the side of the copier, wiping his hands on a rag and taking off his steel-rimmed spectacles.

'You've brought the new text?'

'Yes.' The old man sat himself in a plain wooden chair, the carrier bag on his lap. 'When can you do it?'

'You can have it on Sunday.'

'How is your father?' The old man needed time to recover. It had been a long walk from the Museum.

'About the same. They say that he won't last out the winter. Mother knows. You saw her?'

'Yes. I shall miss him when he goes. There aren't many of us left.'

'Father knows what you're doing. He's heard about the Englishman's book, but he says you'll only get yourself into trouble and you ought to let sleeping dogs lie. But then, you always were an obstinate old bastard – Father says.'

The old man smiled. 'That is a very insubordinate remark.'

'You may not worry, but what about me? I am doing the printing. Could they get after me as well as you?'

'They won't know about you. They will only know about me.'

Tomas thought about the visit of the process-server, but there was no need to trouble the printer with that.

'The Englishman will think that he is too grand to trouble himself with an old fool like me. They won't bother about me and my pamphlets.'

'I hope you're right.'

Tomas took the typescript from the bag. 'Here it is.'

Kosta took the pages and began to look through them.

13

He took a pencil from the large pocket of his grimy apron. 'What's this correction here?' He brought the paper to Tomas. 'Here.' He pointed. 'Is that 1942 or 1943?'

The old man took out his glasses and studied the page. 'It is 1943.'

'It's all so long ago. Who cares now?'

'The Englishman, Brackley, he will care.'

He handed the page back and the other went on reading. When he had finished, Kosta said, 'You can collect them on Sunday.'

'Good. Then I can post them on Monday.'

'You're doing the envelopes yourself?' The printer walked back behind the press, the typescript in his hand.

'Yes.'

'It must cost a fortune in stamps.'

When Tomas got home, he took the dog for his walk and fed him. Then he settled down and began to address the envelopes. Most were easy enough, just the names of Ministers, which he had got from the library and these he addressed to Government departments in Whitehall; the peers and MPs to the House of Lords or Commons in Westminster.

It was late when he finished and climbed wearily on to his camp-bed. Before he slept, he did not think about what he had been writing earlier in the day. He did not think about Price and the papers that Price had brought to him that morning. He thought only about what he would be doing the next day. For tomorrow was Saturday, his happy day, which he spent at the studio of his friend Felix the painter. Afterwards, there would be the Club of the Exiles, where for an hour or two he really was a colonel and, to some, a hero.

The first thing Tomas noticed when he arrived next morning at Felix's studio was the new girl. She was working at the easel next to the one which was always reserved for him in the corner at the far end of the room. He was, as usual, later than the seven others who had come punctually at half-past nine and who were already hard at work. Six were women; one a thin, middle-aged man whom Felix was teaching to draw a square piece of white paper lying on the wooden surface of a low table. Felix was seated on a painter's stool, a 'donkey', with a drawing pad in front of him, while the man, looking a little resentful at being presented with such a difficult exercise, stood behind his teacher watching the demonstration.

'The slope of that line is wrong and unless you get that correct, nothing'll come right. The angle is much sharper than you have it. You must use the plumb line.' He looked up and saw Tomas. 'Good-morning, Tomas,' he said.

Felix was a young man, thin, too thin one of his more motherly pupils felt, with dark curly hair and a smile which aroused memories and even flutters in the breasts of some of his Saturday class.

The students who were standing at work on their canvases paused and looked towards the door of the studio. 'Good-morning, Tomas,' they chorused, while Tomas stood bowing to each of them in turn. It was a Saturday morning ritual to which they were all accustomed. Tomas, an old fishing-bag which carried his painting kit over his shoulder, threaded his way noisily but carefully between the painters and the easels until he had reached his own. The new girl was younger than the others and tall, with ash-blonde hair which fell across her oval face. Over her faded jeans she was wearing a long shirt with blue-and-white stripes, which reached to below her waist. Tomas, stumbling a little, deposited his bag with a clatter on the table behind his own easel and threw his jacket over the chair which Felix had provided for him so that he could rest when he grew tired. The girl raised her brush from the canvas on which she was working and stood back. She turned towards him and he looked into her blue-green eyes.

'Welcome to this very special corner. Only the élite are allowed here,' he said bowing. 'I am Tomas.'

'I'm Alexandra.'

15

She smiled and he thought of someone whom he had not seen for half a lifetime. He sank on to this chair. 'That is my favourite name. I have not seen you here before.'

'No, it's my first day. Are you a regular?'

'I am. Felix has tried for several years to teach me, but I get no better.' He got to his feet and began to unpack his tubes of paint and lay them out on the table. 'Felix is very polite and only rarely expresses his despair. Now and then he wanders over to this corner, where he hides me away, and stands behind me when I am at work, looking at what I am doing. Then he sighs and walks away sadly.'

Felix had heard him from across the room. 'Do not believe him, Alexandra. He paints very boldly, like the wild man that he is. But he's also very stubborn. And be careful of him. He will try to seduce you.'

At this several of the painters on the other side of the room peered around their easels.

Alexandra said, 'I shall be on my guard.'

Tomas was trying to place a canvas on his easel, but he was having difficulty in loosening the butterfly screws in order to adjust its height.

'Here,' she said, 'let me help you.' She put down her palette and brush and went behind Tomas's easel, turning the screws and adjusting the crossbar. She was watched by some of the women.

'Thank you,' he said. 'I have become very clumsy.'

She came to the front and fixed the board in place for him. 'Is that all right?'

'Perfect.'

He looked across at the work which she had begun. It was the start of a still-life study of chrysanthemums in a green vase, which stood on a multicoloured cloth beside a copper jug on a table in the centre of the room. She had already roughed in the outline, drawing in thin, pale green paint.

'I can see that you are an expert. You have had training?'

'I was taught a little as a child, but I've never been to art school. Felix persuaded me to take it up again.'

16

Tomas began to squeeze out the colours on to the edge of his palette. 'I love to paint, even when Felix is bullying me. It makes me forget to worry.'

'Do you have many worries?'

'I have many memories.'

Felix approached. 'There's too much noise coming from this corner of the room. You must leave Alexandra alone, Tomas, and get started. You're late as usual.'

'I know. But I have my duties with Tito and for some reason, I seem to have been busy. Doing nothing as usual.'

'Well, start to do something now.'

'I shall, I shall. Do not bully me, Felix.'

Felix put his arm around the old man's shoulders. 'You're an old villain,' he said and walked back to the motherly painter, studying her canvas. He took her brush and scrabbled with it in the paint of her palette, demonstrating how to mix the richer, redder brown which she needed. Her glance flitted from the brush mixing the paint on the palette to Felix's profile.

After an hour they broke for coffee and went down to the kitchen in the basement of the studio. Tomas was the last down the steep stairs. The women were already seated, drinking from mugs, chatting to Felix. There was no seat for Tomas and when he appeared in the doorway, Alexandra got up from the sofa.

'Sit here,' she said and then sat at his feet on the floor. Felix gave him a mug of black coffee.

'Who is Tito?' she asked.

'My dog, and he is almost as old as I am.'

'Why is he called Tito?'

'I do not really know. I would never have called him that, but I inherited him from a friend and he had already been christened.'

'My father once met Tito, the Yugoslav leader – not your Tito.'

Tomas was staring into his mug of coffee. He did not reply.

'My father was in the Navy and he told me a story about

17

the War and being sent to ferry some of the guerrillas up the Adriatic coast.' She paused as though she expected some response, but Tomas remained silent. She went on. 'He had to bring his ship close in to the coast and signal with a lamp. Then he heard the splash of oars and a dinghy appeared out of the darkness. When it came alongside, Marshal Tito had to scale a rope-ladder and my father stretched down his arm and pulled him over the side.'

Again she paused. The women were laughing with Felix at the other end of the room. Tomas was sipping his coffee.

'My father said it was the only time he'd met any of the great men of his war.' She looked at the old face above her, the tired eyes and the white moustache. He was not looking at her. 'My father's now an admiral,' she added lamely.

Tomas pulled a red handkerchief from his pocket and wiped his moustache. He put down his mug and struggled to his feet. 'I must get back to those flowers. I am finding them exceedingly difficult.' He made his way through the door and very slowly up the steep stairs to the studio above. Alexandra followed him. She knew that what she had said had displeased him, but she had only told the story because his dog was called Tito and she had thought that with his white military moustache, he must have once been a soldier. If he had been, he would have fought in her father's war and then he might have been interested. But evidently not.

Upstairs they painted in silence. The Saturday students only stayed until half-past twelve, when they packed up and went, save for Tomas. He always stayed on and Felix gave him a glass of red wine and some bread, and he remained painting all afternoon, resting often in the chair beside his easel. On this Saturday, Felix told Tomas that the new girl Alexandra also wanted to stay, and so she and Felix and Tomas sat on the 'donkeys' in the studio and drank Felix's wine. Then Tomas and Alexandra went back to their easels. Felix stayed with them for a time, advising and suggesting, disappearing at intervals into his office, but returning to see if they needed help – and 'to chaperon Alexandra and keep an eye on the old rascal'.

What Alexandra had said downstairs in the studio kitchen had apparently been forgotten and when they were alone and painting together, Tomas began to speak French, telling her that the pair of them were like Berthe Morisot and her brother-in-law Édouard Manet; because, Tomas claimed, Berthe, like Alexandra, was the better painter of the pair. Then he began to talk of his youth, when he was a boy seventy years ago staying in France and bicycling in the Lubéron; and of even earlier memories when he was a child with his mother on his uncle's steam-yacht sailing into the harbour of the island of Capri in the last summer before the guns had begun in 1914 and the old world had died. He said that there were no tourists in those days and that the hills and meadows of the island were quite empty of people and vivid with wild flowers. His uncle, Miloje, he said, had a black beard like the beards of the King-Emperor in London and of the cousin Emperor in St Petersburg.

When he told her this, Tomas sat down heavily on the hard wooden chair, his paint brushes still in his hand. She said nothing, listening and painting.

'I remember,' he said, 'being with him at the top of a cliff and my Uncle Miloje held me up in his arms so that I could look down and see the Roman baths in the sea below us. And then, as we walked back to the town through the flowers on the hillside, he told me stories of how in order to amuse the wicked Emperor Tiberius, little children were flung down on to the rocks hundreds of metres below. It was a savage tale to tell a child and that night, in my bed in the stateroom of the yacht, I had a nightmare and woke screaming, and my nurse held me and sang me to sleep as the yacht steamed through the night towards Sardinia.'

He went back to his painting and they were both silent. Soon he sat again and dozed until just before four o'clock, he woke and began to clean his palette and wash his brushes.

When they were standing with Felix outside his front door at the top of the steps to the street, ready to leave, Felix said to Alexandra, 'Now that I've got you painting again, will I see you next week?'

19

'Only if my friend will be here to tell me stories.' She smiled at Tomas.

'Now that you have joined us nothing in the world could stop me.'

'You've made a hit, Alexandra,' said Felix.

'Can I give you a lift?' she asked Tomas.

'Thank you no, I must walk. Walking is good for me.' He took Alexandra's hand and bent over it, lifting it to his mouth, but not touching it with his lips. 'Alexandra,' he said. 'Sacha.'

She watched him as, with his bag over his shoulder, he walked unsteadily down the street. 'He's a darling,' she said to Felix. 'But I thought something I'd said had upset him.'

'He's a Slav and we're all very temperamental. I'm afraid he's growing very old and sometimes he gets confused. He and my father were great friends. I knew you'd like him.'

'I did, very much. And I'd like to hear more of his stories.'

'Let's have dinner this evening.'

'Sorry, I have work. I must finish it before Monday. But I did so enjoy the day, quite apart from meeting your old friend. It was lovely to start to paint again.'

'You career women. You're all so difficult to love. You must come back next week. You did very well today.'

She kissed him lightly on the cheek and ran down the steps to her car. Felix watched her go.

When he got home, Tomas fed Tito and let him out in the garden. Then he lay on the camp-bed and slept. At half-past six he had a bath and then dressed carefully in his dark blue double-breasted suit, now old and shiny at the elbows and slightly frayed at the cuffs. He put on a white shirt, which he had washed and pressed earlier in the week, and a dark blue tie, and taking up his jacket and beret, he set out for Queen's Gate and the Club of the Exiles.

It was bitterly cold, but the walk warmed him. When he had hung up his beret and jacket in the cloakroom, he was short of breath and he needed to sit. He went straight into the bar. As usual nowadays, it was nearly empty. He sat at a table and the white-coated barman, Starjevic, came to him, a glass on a silver salver.

'*Comme d'habitude*, mon colonel,' he said.

Tomas sipped the sweet vermouth and looked about him. There were only two men standing by the bar. One turned and looked at him and then bowed. Tomas inclined his head and the other turned back to his friend. When Tomas had finished his aperitif, he went to the dining-room. It was empty, save for a group of six at a table in the centre of the great room with its chandelier and ornate cornice. He went to his usual corner table. As he sat, he saw that the host of the party of six was the Chairman of the club, Milan Misic, a stout, bald-headed man whose father had once been Tomas's ADC. There must have been a committee meeting, Tomas thought. He ordered his dinner and half a bottle of wine.

An elderly man and a woman in the Chairman's group rose and came across the room. Tomas got to his feet when they approached, his napkin in one hand.

'Sit, Excellency, please sit,' said the woman. Tomas took her hand and raised it to his lips, but remained standing. 'We just wanted to greet you and to enquire how you are. We're not often in London now.'

'I am very well,' he said. 'I keep myself very fit. You live in Scotland, do you not?'

The man replied, 'We do, Colonel. We seldom come south.' He looked round the room. 'The club is very empty. It is very sad. Some must have gone home and, of course, many of our generation have died.'

'But not us,' said Tomas.

'I remember the first days, before you came to London,' said the man wistfully.

'Milan told us that they have made you a life member because you come so faithfully,' said the woman.

'It is sad here now,' the man repeated.

Before they went back to join their party, Tomas again

21

kissed the woman's hand and then sank thankfully back into his seat.

When the two had rejoined their friends, the bald-headed Chairman, whose stomach bulged over the waistband of his trousers, said, 'The place cannot last long. We had a committee meeting before dinner and none have stayed to dine. We shall have to close in the summer. The only one who will miss the place will be himself over there.' The Chairman nodded in Tomas's direction. 'He comes every Saturday night. He has a free dinner, courtesy of the club.'

'And quite right, too,' said the woman whose hand Tomas had kissed. 'He suffered a great deal. When he was young, he was a great friend of Draža Mihailović. I heard that he was a hero in the War,' she said looking at her husband.

'Perhaps he was,' said the bald-headed Chairman. 'A long time ago.'

Tomas walked home to Fulham, the icy wind cutting through his jacket. Apart from the barman, the waiter and the couple who had come across to his table, he had spoken with no one.

He let Tito into the small patch of garden and lit the gas fire. When the dog scratched to come in, Tomas opened the door, then shut and bolted it. He sat before the fire and the dog came and put his head on Tomas's lap and Tomas held it, looking into the dog's sorrowful eyes.

'Someone spoke your name today. But she was not speaking about you. She was speaking of the Communist.'

As he lay in his camp-bed waiting for sleep, he thought with pleasure of his 'happy day', now over; and especially of the girl with those blue-green eyes, who had reminded him of that other girl also called Alexandra; Sacha, the girl he had loved so many years ago and whom he had never seen after the Germans had taken her away on the dreadful morning which had been the start of his purgatory.

22

THREE

In Yorkshire the snow began to fall in earnest on Monday night. In the early hours of Tuesday Edwards woke. The room felt less cold and he knew that the snow had come. He slipped out of bed and watched the snowflakes falling softly and silently on to the stable-yard below. He and the guv'nor were due to leave for London at eight o'clock that morning and the journey now would not be easy. He swore softly, went to the bedside table and advanced his alarm one hour. Then he got back into bed beside the warm and ample body of Alice and slept.

At six o'clock he went downstairs to the stable beneath his and Alice's flat. It served as the garage for the household's four cars and he opened up the door and started the Rolls, letting the engine turn gently while he pulled on a pair of Wellington boots. He took his leather fleece-lined jacket off the peg and, picking up a long-handled torch, inspected the yard.

He stood at the open door shining the beam of the torch on the snow, which lay in front of him like the waters of a lake. It was still snowing as heavily as it had been when he had woken and peered out of the bedroom window. He walked out, disturbing the smooth surface. There must already be about three inches. That would be no problem in the drive which wound through the estate; the Rolls could manage that with ease. The trouble might start at the Lodge when they had to turn into the narrow lane where the hills began and it was up and down for eight miles before the main road. Only after another fifteen miles would they reach the motorway to London, where by then the road ought to be reasonably clear. It was certainly no morning to take a seventy-eight-year-old man who had recently been unwell on a long car journey.

But Edwards knew the guv'nor. He would not easily be persuaded to postpone the trip if the reason for it was important and from what Edwards had overheard when driving him on Sunday, he had guessed that it was. He heard Alice moving in the kitchen above and he went back inside the garage and called up the wooden stairs.

'Alice, turn on the weather forecast, will you? I want to get a report on the roads.'

'I've just heard it. Snow in the North, but fairly clear as you get south. He'll be mad to try and go this morning. I am sure she won't let him.'

'I'm not so sure,' Edwards called back gloomily. 'He's a wilful old bugger.'

Over in the big house, George Brackley stirred, turning restlessly from one side to the other, jerking and twisting in his sleep. Then he woke and lay on his back, staring up in the dark at the canopy over his great four-poster. As his eyes began to focus, he felt the usual sense of relief with which nowadays he greeted each awakening. There would be another day before him – unless he was suddenly struck down as he got up from the bed. He imagined the sudden piercing pain, picturing himself pitching headfirst on to the floor, lying there in the cold of the vast bedroom until they found him when they brought him his early-morning tea.

They would run to call Grace. She would mind when he died. A few others might care, but it would not be for long. They would read about it and write to Grace and talk about him at the bar at the House of Lords, the Bishops' Bar they called it. Later they would come in their dark suits and black ties and enjoy the hymns during the Memorial Service at St Margaret's – or if they thought he had deserved it, Westminster Abbey.

The doctors had warned him that it could happen at any time, especially after the attack last year. He had not told Grace, although she probably suspected.

He pushed back the white hair from his forehead and stroked the white stubble on his chin. He looked at the illuminated face of the bedside clock. They would bring his tea in an hour. He stretched out in the warm bed. He was alive; it was another morning. But it was not only because he had survived another night that he was glad. He was glad to be free of the dream which now constantly troubled him and which made his sleep so uneasy.

It was the same dream he had dreamt every night for the past fortnight, the dream he had not dreamt for fifty years. A dream of battle, of tracer fire in the night sky and of men dropping on the mountainside as the guns picked them off. Of cowled figures with their rifles at the entrance to the cave as he clambered through the snow, sliding and falling.

It was the dream he had dreamt when the fighting was finished and War was over and he was safe. He had not dreamt that dream last year when he had been writing about the War in his autobiography. The dream had only returned when they had brought to him the pamphlet, the photostat leaflet stapled together, which had been sent to all his friends, signed 'Tomas Tarnovic, formerly Colonel in the Royal Yugoslavian Army'.

The name had meant nothing to him. Who was this Tomas? He could remember no Tomas – but then he had never been able to master those foreign names, not even when he had been living among them. When he had read what Tarnovic had written, he had searched his memory trying to picture the faces, but the images would not return. The men, the figures, remained shadows, except for one – the Commandant. Of him he had at least an impression – the Commandant with his black, pointed beard and sad eyes. The places he remembered vividly: the high ridge of mountains to which they had climbed from the dropping-ground the night they arrived by parachute; the cave with the snow lying on the ground outside, just as the snow was now lying on his garden and on his park outside his house in Yorkshire; the snow that he had struggled through when he had left the cave and set off across the mountains, the

25

vast expanse of whiteness beneath the grey sky. He remembered a small patch of yellow tobacco-stained spittle on the snow where someone had spat. But of the faces there remained only that of the Commandant, and that only faint – except for those eyes, those tired eyes. Much later back in Cairo, James had confirmed that all those men had been killed. So who was Tomas Tarnovic?

Very slowly George Brackley swung his legs out of the bed, his feet feeling in the dark for his crimson velvet slippers with his initials embossed in gold. When his feet were in them, he sat on the edge of the bed and switched on the light. His back ached, as it always did early in the morning. He stretched out for his silk dressing gown and struggling into it, went across the room to draw the curtains and look at the snowflakes falling past the window and on to the lawn.

It would make for a damnable drive, but he had to go; he had to see Roger Bentall, the solicitor. Bentall had said on the telephone that this fellow Tarnovic would be easily dealt with; it was not uncommon for people to surface and blackguard public figures. But they had better meet, so the trip to London could not be postponed.

Later when he had dressed, he sent a message to Edwards. They would take the Land Rover, not the Rolls. In the hall Grace made him put a padded waistcoat over his dark suit before she helped him into his topcoat and wound a woollen scarf around his neck. As she did so she said, 'You have had nothing to eat.'

'I don't want anything. I've had some tea.'

'Must you really go?'

'Yes.' He bent and kissed her cheek. She was more than twenty years younger than he and still beautiful, her dark hair untouched by grey – although, as she told him, that was due to art.

'You are very stubborn.'

'I always have been. Don't worry. We shall be all right. Edwards will look after me. It is only here that it is snowing. It's clear further south.'

She handed him his cane.

'At nine o'clock, will you telephone Bentall for me and tell him meet me at the Lords for luncheon, Peers' Entrance, at one o'clock? And book me, please, a table.' She watched Painter, the butler, holding an umbrella above him against the snow, helping him into the car. She waved as they drove away.

The going was not as bad as Edwards had feared. They drove in silence, George Brackley staring out of the window at the snow-covered fields, his dream of war still haunting him. There had been so many days of snow during that time in that far-off country to which he had never returned. Tomas Tarnovic, sometime Colonel in the Royal Yugoslavian Army. Could Tarnovic be the Commandant of whom he had written in his book? But those men were all dead. What was it that the psychologists claimed? That the human mind rejected and expelled memories which could not be borne? And memories of war were usually best buried. But now they would need to be revived, for Tomas Tarnovic was telling the world a story very different from that which George Brackley had told, seeking to destroy the reputation of Lord Brackley of Brandsby, former Cabinet Minister, former war hero.

He settled back in the warm car. His back was still aching, but not as badly as it had when he had first risen from his bed. He had lived with the pain for fifty years. According to Horace Telfer in Harley Street, it had been the knocks he had suffered during the falls from parachuting and the wounds he had received in the fighting in the mountains, honourable wounds for which he had been decorated. In your old age, the doctor had told him, you are paying the price for the adventures of your youth.

He kept his eyes on the leaden sky and the white landscape, his mind still full of war. Not good cover against German spotter planes, he thought. The cloud was not low enough. What had those planes been called? Fieseler

Storchs? Was that it? And there was no forest to hide in like the forest of those days of long ago, no caves, no tall firs, no high mountains – only the hills of the Yorkshire countryside through which Edwards was driving him.

'I'm going slowly, my lord, but the worst is nearly over. We shall soon be on the main road and then the going will be easier.'

'You're doing splendidly, Edwards.'

It was after half-past twelve when Edwards pulled the Land Rover into the courtyard of the House of Lords.

'Collect me at 3.30,' Brackley said as he entered the swing-doors of the Peers' Entrance.

Roger Bentall arrived at one o'clock precisely. They walked up the stairs together.

'The Royal Gallery.' Brackley waved his stick and pointed as they passed. 'Never show it to the Frogs when they come here. It has a mural of Trafalgar down the whole length of one wall and of Waterloo on the other.'

When they were seated at their table, tucked around the corner of the L-shaped dining-room, and inspecting the menu, George Brackley said, 'I hope you're not expecting much in the way of food. It's nursery food, you know. Tapioca pudding, I expect.'

After the waitress had left them, he enquired, 'Well? Tell me the developments.'

'As I told you, we served the writ. The writ will frighten him off. You'll hear no more from him now.'

'Are you sure?'

'I am certain. These cranks are all the same. A whiff of gunpowder settles them. It has been most unpleasant, I know.'

'I suppose we had to take action? We couldn't have ignored it?'

'Not after he'd circulated it so widely. There are enough people talking about it already. The only way to stop the gossip was to issue a writ.'

Brackley crumbled the bread on his side-plate. 'Was it my autobiography which set him off?'

28

'It must have been. Unless someone has put him up to it. It's possible, of course, that he may have had in mind getting some money out of you.'

Brackley looked at Bentall. 'Shall we do that? Shall we pay him off? Could we make, say, a contribution to help an old comrade – if, of course, he was an old comrade?'

Bentall looked at his host. 'No, Lord Brackley. That would be most unwise. No, have no fear. We shall hear no more of him now.'

'What is this injunction you spoke about?'

'We apply to the Court to get an order forbidding him to repeat the libel and I shall see that is well and truly broadcast. The world has to know that as soon as you learnt what the fellow had written about you, you took action. Lies like these have to be nailed, and quickly.'

At the end of their meal George Brackley took Roger Bentall back to the top of the stairs. 'I shall go into the Chamber. I want to show my face. Forgive me not coming down, but after that long drive my back is playing me up.'

'Of course. As I said at lunch, I'll need an affidavit from you. I'll telephone and send my assistant round with a Commissioner of Oaths so that you can swear it.'

'I shall wait to hear from you.'

In the Chamber of the House, Question Time had begun as George Brackley limped in and took his seat on the Government side, on the bench in the front row nearest to the bar, the bench reserved for ex-ministers and Privy Councillors of the Government party. Those already seated shifted to make room for him. He noticed that some in the House turned and looked at him, but no one spoke to him, not even his friend Harry Cranston, the former Foreign Secretary, who was seated beside him.

When Questions were over and he was still in his seat, the Chief Whip slipped on to the bench beside him. 'Can we have a word, George?' he whispered. 'Outside.'

George Brackley followed him out into the Peers' Lobby.

'I'm afraid there has been another of these.' The Chief Whip handed him a pamphlet. 'It arrived this morning. As far as I can judge it has been sent to everyone, as was the first. It's much the same as the other, but longer and, I'm afraid, nastier. All about the War, you know. So long ago, but, nevertheless, most unpleasant. I expect you'll want to do something, so I thought that I should tell you. I'm terribly sorry, George.'

On that same morning, while George Brackley was being driven through the snow to meet his solicitor, Roger Bentall, in the House of Lords, Crichton Smith MP had collected his post and messages and taken them into the Library. He sat himself at a table with his back to the terrace and the river below, a heavily-built man with a florid face, iron-grey hair and bushy eyebrows, dressed in the tweed suits he always affected at Westminster – a uniform at odds with his own urban background and different from that which he wore on visits to his industrial constituency in the North-East of England. But his taste for rich food, fine wines and betting on horses had recently aroused the hostility of some in his local party, who were plotting to have him deselected at the next election and replaced by an earnest young lecturer from the local polytechnic. But Crichton Smith had been the Member for a quarter of a century and he was confident that with the support of his cronies in the unions and his bookmaker friends, he would be able to see them off. His speciality in the House was national defence and he usually had a good Press, certainly in the nationals. To the media, generally, he had become what they called 'a House of Commons character'.

But he had few friends, on account of his unpleasantly sharp tongue. For he invariably took as a personal slight even the most mild put-down on the floor of the House or in a party committee and he harboured grievances, carrying them from the floor of the Chamber into the tearoom and smoking-room outside.

On this wintry morning in London, he had just returned from a Parliamentary jaunt to the sunshine of Hong Kong, a trip he had much enjoyed. Now he had to get back to the mundane business of his constituency correspondence. Before he did so, he lit a cheroot and began to read the newspapers, starting with the *Sporting Life*.

When he was through with the newspapers, he looked rapidly at his post. He pinned together the letters which required an answer, tossing everything else into the waste-paper basket beside him. Finally, he turned to the telephone messages written on the flimsy white paper used by the Members' Telephone Exchange. Most he crumpled and threw away, but one pleased him. It was only an hour old and it was from Jumbo Lancaster of the political staff of the *Star*. If Crichton would like to have luncheon that day, the message ran, he was to come to El Vino's in Fleet Street at 12.30. There was no need to call back; just turn up if he was free. Crichton brightened. He would like that. And he got on more cheerfully with his mail.

At a quarter to one, Crichton Smith pushed through the swing-doors of El Vino's and turned at once to his right to the table where, for fifteen years, Jumbo had held court, a tradition he resolutely maintained even after all the news-papers had deserted 'The Street' and moved away to Kensington, or across the river, or to the Docklands. There Jumbo sat, a vast barrel-shaped man, his cheeks as round and as monstrous, Crichton used to tell him, as had been those of the eighteenth-century historian, Edward Gibbon. But there was little of Gibbon's orotund prose in Jumbo's political articles, which were sharp and often exceedingly offensive, especially about the members of the present Government whom Jumbo fervently hoped would be defeated at the next general election. He prided himself on keeping well-informed, better informed than any other correspondent in the Parliamentary Press Lobby, especially about the peccadillos and private lives of all the prominent politicians. He cultivated an army of informants, dispensing gargantuan hospitality designed to loosen tongues and encourage indiscretions.

'Glad to see you, Crichton. Come and join us,' Jumbo

31

boomed. He waved the glass in his hand over the bottle of champagne on the table in front of him. Beside him sat a single companion. Usually there were several at Jumbo Lancaster's regular court who, in accordance with the rules Jumbo laid down, were all expected to contribute a bottle to the regular pre-lunch session.

Jumbo poured some of the wine into an empty glass. He knew I would come, thought Crichton.

'You know Walter, on our racing desk?'

'Of course he does,' said Walter. 'We meet often enough. The last time was at Sandown. How are you, Crichton?'

Crichton pulled up a chair and sat. 'Better for being here and even better when I've had this.' He drank some of the champagne.

'What's the news from Westminster?'

'Nothing much, but I've been abroad, in Hong Kong. I only got back last night.'

'Any gossip about the date of the election?'

'The usual. Some go for October, some for next spring, others for next year.'

'Well, that covers the field,' said Walter.

'And you?' asked Jumbo.

'The autumn of next year. The Government will plan to hold on.'

'I've heard,' said Jumbo, 'that some in your constituency are planning to ditch you.'

'A few of the bearded intellectuals. They've wanted that for years.'

Jumbo has not asked me here to discuss the date of the election, nor my constituency, thought Crichton as Jumbo refilled Crichton's glass. He has brought Walter with him to chat me up about racing, while he fills me up with his champagne. There's no such thing as a free lunch and especially not in politics, he reflected. But at least it would be a decent lunch.

Jumbo certainly did want something, but he would bide his time until after when more wine had flowed, Walter had gone and he and Crichton were alone. Later would be at the restaurant, Boulestin, off the Strand, at about the same time as George Brackley and Roger Bentall were sitting down to their more modest lunch in the House of Lords.

When they began to eat, Jumbo said casually, 'Do you remember that row you had with old George Brackley in the House many years ago when you were very green?'

'I've never forgotten it – and never forgiven it.'

'He was Secretary of State for Defence at the time, wasn't he?'

'He was. It must be over fifteen years ago, a debate about the strength of the Army in Germany. I thought I'd caught him out on his figures, but the young fool in the Ministry who had leaked them to me had got them wrong. Brackley savaged me.'

'He always gave the impression of being a rather amiable old buffer.'

'That was George Brackley's Parliamentary act. He could be very nasty when he wanted.'

'And you never forgave him for what he did to you?'

'No, I never did. Whenever I could I went for him and I got him fumbling pretty often. But that's years ago. He must have been out of government now for over five years.'

'He's still very influential in their party.' Jumbo poured some more claret. 'There's a story going around about him. Some ghost has emerged from his past. People are receiving a leaflet about him when he was in the Army in World War Two. Have you heard about it?'

'No. But as I said I've been abroad and I always chuck out the circulars.'

'This fellow is putting around a yarn about Brackley's war record, accusing him of treachery and cowardice when he was in the Balkans.'

'That's intriguing, but the War's pretty ancient history.'

'Maybe. But it might prove useful for your lot. I'd be interested to know if Brackley is going to sue.'

'He'd be a damn fool if he does. Far better to ignore it.'

'Perhaps he can't afford to ignore it. A lot of MPs have received the circular. I'd like to get hold of one.'

'I'll get you one this afternoon when I get back to the House.'

'Do that. I thought you might be amused, remembering your love for that old hero.'

'I certainly would be if they discovered after all these years that old Brackley was a fraud.'

I bet you would, thought Jumbo. I bet you would, you malevolent bastard. And so would I.

On the day following those luncheons, Les Price returned to Pelham Lane in Fulham. On this visit he behaved very differently from how he had the week before. When Tomas opened the door to him, Price tapped Tomas menacingly on the chest with the papers he was holding.

'Another "billy-do" for you, General. You're in right trouble now, old cock, I can tell you.' He thrust the papers into Tomas's hand. 'No need for any signature this time. Just a delivery. Cheerio, you old sod. See you in quod, as they say.' He laughed and skipped down the steps and into the street.

Tomas went back into his room. He tossed the papers on to the table, where they fell beside the unopened and unread documents which Price had served the week before. The two bundles wrapped in their legal red tape lay side by side on the dark wood of the table-top.

Tomas sat down in front of the fire. He had written what he had wanted. Now he would wait for what he also wanted, what he had planned – his day in Court.

FOUR

Although there was an electric fire burning on either side of the dais in Felix's studio on the following Saturday, the model was blue with cold and the temperature in the studio had made the skin of her belly and thighs mottled and pimply. The girl was young, hardly out of her teens, and her figure was stumpy, with heavy, rounded breasts and short, sturdy legs, which were tucked underneath her as she reclined on a pale yellow coverlet, her back against a dark-brown curtain which hung from the wall. Her long black hair, which fell below her shoulders, was cut in a fringe above a pair of black, mischievous eyes which, while her body remained professionally still, swivelled continuously around the silent studio.

After a few minutes, however, she abruptly broke the pose and asked plaintively for more heat, hugging her arms in front of her breasts. The middle-aged women in their smocks over their jerseys looked at her, irritated by the interruption. They watched Felix as he plugged in a third fire. The model settled down again and the students returned to their easels.

During the pause when the extra fire had been produced, Tomas, in the far corner, had sunk down into his chair. He had hardly spoken since making his usual late entry, save to greet Alexandra as he had unpacked his paints from his bag. He looked pale and unwell. Once or twice he coughed, painfully.

Alexandra had herself nearly not come this morning, for earlier in the week her stepmother had suggested that she should go down to Wiltshire for the weekend. But she

35

had been reluctant. It would have meant enduring one of Jessica's Saturday night dinner parties, which Alexandra found even more exhausting than a day at her desk in the office. So she told her stepmother that she would let them know. Later in the week Felix had telephoned; next Saturday he was having his life-class and it would be a good test for her. Also, he had said, she had to come and help him keep an eye on old Tomas.

'He has fallen for you, Alexandra.'

'And I for him.'

So she had called Jessica back and said she would drive down on Sunday for luncheon, provided the weather was not too bad. From the silence at the other end of the telephone she knew that Jessica was registering her usual disapproval of her stepdaughter and her life as a newly-qualified solicitor living alone in London. Jessica wanted her to marry an eligible merchant banker in the next county and make grandchildren for the Admiral.

'Are you feeling all right, Tomas?' Felix had appeared in their corner. The model's eyes swivelled round, watching them.

'Yes, Felix, thank you, although I think I may be starting a cold.' Then louder, 'I like your little model. She's nice and plump.' The model smirked, her eyes still on the two men.

When they broke for coffee, the model wrapped herself in a faded silk dressing gown and joined the circle of women disciples around Felix. Alexandra brought Tomas his mug and, as she had the week before, settled at his feet.

'How's Tito?'

'He is very well.'

'You're looking a little tired.'

'It is this cold which I have picked up. I think I caught it when I was walking Tito one night.'

'You shouldn't do that in this weather.'

'But I have to.' He coughed again, then he said, 'I dreamt last night of school.'

'Where was that?'

'In England, in Somerset. In my family we were always sent to England to school. That is why I speak English so well.'

'You certainly do.'

He remained silent for a moment and then said, 'Nearly seventy years ago! I liked that school. I made a lot of friends there. The Headmaster was a great character. He collected animals. He liked me because I liked his animals. He had quite a menagerie, peacocks strutting about the lawn by the shrubberies in front of the main entrance. He even had a kangaroo which an Australian Old Boy had given him. It did not last long.'

'What happened to it?'

'It was found down a quarry with its neck broken. That's what I dreamt about last night. The kangaroo, with its broken neck.'

'Where was your home?'

'In Belgrade. We are Serbs. We had the house in the city, almost a palace, and others on the coast and in the mountains. It is absurd when I think of it now.' He tried to rise from the low sofa and Alexandra helped him to his feet. He kept his arm on hers. 'Would you mind helping me up the stairs? I am a little shaky today and they are steep.'

During the rest of the morning he spent much of the time on his chair. At 12.30 the model rose and stretched like a cat, standing on tiptoe, naked, her arms high above her head. She is making a statement to the women who have been painting her, thought Alexandra. They paid no attention, but gathered together their kit as the model made a slow exit behind a screen and emerged dressed in jeans and a tight orange sweater.

'Ta-raa, everyone,' she said, and blew a kiss at Tomas. The women packed up and left, one by one.

When they had all gone, Alexandra said to Felix, 'So there's nothing for us to paint this afternoon?'

'I thought I'd put back the still life which you hadn't finished last week. The vase and the chrysanthemums. The flowers are a bit faded but . . .'

It was then that they heard the crash.

'Oh, my God!' said Felix. 'It's Tomas!'

He had fallen across the table, knocking over his easel which fell against others bringing them down so that they lay broken and splintered on the floor of the studio. Canvases, paints and pools of turpentine were scattered among the broken pieces of wood. Alexandra and Felix rushed to where Tomas lay across the overturned table on the floor. They lifted him and put him into his chair. He was very pale and there was blood on his forehead.

'It is all right,' he said. 'It's all right.'

'Get some water, Felix.'

'I'd rather have wine,' said Tomas.

'Keep still.' Alexandra loosened his collar. Felix returned with a glass of water. Alexandra dabbed at the cut on the old man's forehead with her handkerchief. 'It's not deep,' she said, 'but you're badly bruised. I'm going to take you home.' She and Felix knelt and picked up some of the tubes of paint and packed them into his bag.

'I'll come with you,' said Felix.

'No, stay here and clean up. I'll telephone when I have him home. There may be some delayed shock.'

'I have no telephone, but I am quite all right,' said Tomas. He began to shake and Alexandra took the wine from him.

'Come on. I'll get you home.'

They got him to her car. As she drove, Tomas closed his eyes and she put her hand on his arm and shook him gently. 'You must direct me.'

'Of course. It is not far. This is very kind of you. I hope I did no damage.'

'Only a little. Felix will straighten it out.'

'He is a good fellow. He is like a son to me – or, I should say, like a grandson.'

In the narrow street in Fulham, she managed to park directly opposite Tomas's door. She helped him out of the car and up the steps. 'Where is your key?' It took time for him to find it in the inner pocket of his jacket.

Inside Tito came up to them.

'He has hurt himself,' said Alexandra to the dog. 'So don't get in the way.' She saw the camp-bed in the alcove. 'You must lie down,' she said and led him across the room. He sat on the bed and she knelt and loosened the laces of his boots. 'Lift your feet, one at a time.' She pulled them off. 'You must get into bed.'

'I shall.' He smiled. 'I shall if you will kindly withdraw and make us some tea. And would you be so kind as to light the fire?'

She went out of the alcove and drew the curtain. 'Call me if you need help.'

'Tito,' he said, 'come and talk to me while I undress.'

After she had lit the fire, she went into the small kitchen and lit the gas ring and put on the kettle. Then she went back to the alcove. 'Are you all right?'

'Perfectly. I am sorry to have been such a nuisance.'

She brought him the tea and stood watching him drink.

'May I ask one further kindness?'

'Of course.'

'Would you let Tito into the garden? He has not been out since this morning.'

It was still very cold and after she had let the dog out, she closed the door and watched through the window. Tito took his time and she wandered round the room looking at the photographs of the soldiers and the helmet and the sabre hanging above the fireplace. So she had been right when she had thought that he must have been a soldier and had told him that story about her father and Marshal Tito, the Partisan leader; the story which, for some reason, had so displeased him.

After a few minutes she heard the dog scratching at the door and she let him in.

'I am much better,' Tomas said when she went to him.

'Do you want to see a doctor?'

'Certainly not. It is Saturday. I have to go out this evening. I always go out on a Saturday.'

'You will do nothing of the kind. Not on this Saturday. You must stay in bed and rest. Have you any aspirin?'

'Yes, in the bathroom.'

When she had given them to him, he closed his eyes. The dog came and lay beside the bed. He lowered his hand and stroked the dog's head. 'I usually rest when I come back from Felix's.'

'Sleep,' she said. 'I'll sit by the fire until you doze off.'

She looked down at the two of them. The two old friends, she thought. Then she drew the curtains of the alcove and walked towards a chair in front of the fire. As she passed the table, she saw the two bundles tied with the red tape, which the process-server had served on him. She could see at once what they were. She stopped and picked them up. 'In the High Court of Justice. Writ and Statement of Claim. Between *The Right Honourable the Lord Brackley of Brandsby, Plaintiff* v. *Tomas Tarnovic, Defendant.*'

She half-turned and looked towards the alcove. The room was silent, save for the hissing of the gas fire. Then she walked over to the chair by the fire and sat. She untied the tape and began to read.

The writ had been issued by Messrs Baker and Turnbull of Clifford Street W1, which Alexandra knew was one of the largest and most important firms of solicitors in the West End of London. The Plaintiff was described as 'George, Baron Brackley of Brandsby; a Member of Her Majesty's Privy Council; a Companion of Honour; a Companion of the Distinguished Service Order; a Holder of the Military Cross; and of countless foreign decorations'; the Defendant as Tomas Tarnovic of 11, Pelham Lane, Fulham, London SW15.

The claim was for damages for libel contained in a leaflet entitled *War Hero? A Liar*, written by the Defendant, Tomas Tarnovic, which alleged that the Plaintiff was a liar; a homosexual; a traitor; and a coward.

'The said words were grossly defamatory of the Plaintiff and calculated to bring him into hatred, ridicule, and contempt; and the Plaintiff hereby claims damages for libel.'

Alexandra stared at the document in amazement. Then she read the words of the writ again. A claim for damages for libel brought against the old man now lying asleep in his shabby apartment a few yards from where she sat! And, what was more, a claim brought by someone who sounded exceedingly important! What on earth could the old man have written to cause Lord Brackley to sue? With the writ was a letter from the solicitors and this she began to read. Their client, the solicitors wrote, was a distinguished retired public servant who had held high office in the service of the Crown and who as a young man in the Second World War had been awarded many of the highest decorations for gallantry in the field. He had been wickedly libelled in a leaflet entitled *War Hero? A Liar*, written, published and circulated by the Defendant, Tomas Tarnovic. In respect of these libels, Lord Brackley demanded an immediate public withdrawal, an apology and damages. They intended, the lawyers wrote, to make an application to the High Court on behalf of Lord Brackley for an immediate injunction to stop any repetition of these infamous libels on a very gal-lant and public-spirited Englishman.

Beneath this letter was a second, dated a week after the first and phrased in even sharper, more threatening terms. It asserted that after the original writ had been served and after notice of the commencement of proceedings by Lord Brackley, Tomas Tarnovic had deliberately repeated and expanded the original libel in a second leaflet entitled *The Full Story of the Conduct of George Brackley in the Mountains of Eastern Serbia in 1943*. Accordingly the original claim would now be amended to add the further matters com-plained of and include a claim for aggravated damages.

Alexandra, flabbergasted, laid the two letters and the writ on her lap. What could the old man have been up to? What had he written – and why?

She saw that the claim referred to a leaflet, so she turned and looked back to the table from which she had taken the writ. At its far end, next to the battered typewriter, she saw two small piles of papers. She got up from the chair and crossed the room to the table. The papers were stacks of leaflets, plainly printed on copying paper, the pages stapled together. On the top leaflet of the nearest pile she read the title, the title referred to in the writ: *War Hero? A Liar. By Tomas Tarnovic, late Colonel in the Royal Yugoslavian Army.* The second pile was of another leaflet: *The Full Story of the Conduct of George Brackley in the Mountains of Eastern Serbia in 1943. By Tomas Tarnovic.* She took them both back to the armchair by the fire and began to read.

I am writing this, *the first and slimmer leaflet began*, because of the lies which have been published by George Brackley in a book of memoirs called *A Time to Remember*, in which he wrote about his experiences in Yugoslavia in World War Two and glorified himself as a brave British officer.

When he wrote his book, Brackley must have thought that all who knew the truth about him were dead. But one survived, and I propose to tell the world the true story of the treachery and cowardice of George Brackley. In 1941, during the Second World War when the Germans occupied my country, General Draža Mihailović, in the name of the exiled King Peter who had escaped to London, raised his standard in the mountains near to Ravna Gorna and took up arms to continue the fight against the invader.

He and his gallant men, the Royalists, lived in the forests and the mountains, descending to the plains to harass and attack the occupying army. In response, the Germans mounted sweeps through the mountains in order 'to cleanse the area of bandits' – as they called their operations against the Royalist patriots. In retaliation, they seized hostages from the villages and shot them without mercy. But the General and his loyal troops, with few arms and little ammunition, managed to survive. Later, but, of course, only after the Nazis had invaded Soviet Russia, a Croatian ex-criminal, Josip Broz, or Tito as he later came to call himself, set up a separate force of Communists called Partisans. He was not interested in the national honour or in freedom. All he wanted was to make sure that at the end of the War he would be able to establish a Communist dictatorship in Yugoslavia.

Immediately be began a civil war by using his Communists to attack General Mihailović and the Royalists. Because of false information deliberately fed to the Allied leaders by Communist sympathisers in Cairo, massive supplies of arms were sent by the British, not to the legitimate patriot movement under Mihailović, but to the Communist Partisans under Tito. As a result, at the end of the War he was able to destroy General Draža Mihailović and my country fell under the tyranny of a Communist dictatorship.

But in the beginning, in 1942 and 1943, the Allies did drop by parachute some supplies and a few liaison officers with wireless operators to General Mihailović and his Royalists. One of these was Captain George Brackley. But this British officer came not as an ally but as an enemy. For Brackley was no friend to the Royalists. He was a secret Communist, determined to aid the enemies of those he had pretended to come and help.

George Brackley did not know it, but I had encountered him in 1939 when I was serving at our embassy in London as Military Attaché. I was paying a visit to my young cousin, Stepan Stepanic, who was then an undergraduate at the University of Cambridge and we were strolling through the grounds of King's College, when a young man stopped Stepan and began to speak to him. Stepan broke away as soon as he could and I asked Stepan who he was. Stepan said he was called George Brackley and was one of a decadent, extreme left-wing group which always sided politically with the Communists and was always pestering Stepan to join them. I warned my young cousin to keep clear of such people and he promised that he would.

Four years later this same Communist sympathiser, George Brackley, parachuted into the mountains as one of the British officers sent by British HQ in Cairo. Significantly, he was not sent to join his friends, Tito's Communist Partisans, but to General Mihailović's Royalists. His secret instructions from his Communist friends were to betray the men who were to meet and shelter him. And that is what George Brackley did.

When he dropped by parachute with his wireless operator, they were warmly welcomed and at once escorted to the headquarters, then established in a series of caves high up in the mountains. The track which led to these headquarters was not known even to the villagers in the valley below. It remained a closely-guarded secret – until the secret was betrayed by Captain George Brackley.

At headquarters he and his youthful wireless operator were allotted one of the caves where they kept the WT set and where they slept, together and alone. The orderly later reported that the men were sniggering that the two Britishers were sharing one sleeping-bag.

Immediately after their arrival, Brackley began asking questions about where the sentries were posted, the number of look-outs and the strength and armament of the group. He said he needed to know this so he could signal Cairo for Allied HQ to send supplies and weapons. Later he put this information to good use when, after he had demonstrated his cowardice in battle, he deserted and betrayed to his real friends, the Communist Partisans, those who had so warmly welcomed him as a friend and an ally. In short, George Brackley was not a hero. He was a pervert, a coward and a traitor.

I dare George Brackley to challenge the truth of what I have written about his cowardice and treachery. If he says that it is untrue, let him take me to the

44

English Court. Let an English Court decide between us. But I know that he will not dare – because he knows that what I have written is the truth.

Here this leaflet abruptly ended. When Alexandra had finished reading it, she lowered it on to her lap and turned in amazement towards the alcove where Tomas was sleeping. No wonder, she thought, no wonder that George Brackley had issued a writ.

Then she began the second and lengthier leaflet, *The Full Story of the Conduct of George Brackley in the Mountains of Eastern Serbia in 1943*.

After a brief introduction resetting the scene, the leaflet went on:

Just before George Brackley and his young wireless operator had parachuted into the mountains, General Mihailović had instructed all his units to carry out certain operations against targets selected by British Headquarters in Cairo. The British had chosen these targets in order to test General Mihailović and the Royal Yugoslavian Army, because certain quarters in Cairo were accusing them of collaborating with the Germans. If he failed the test, then Cairo had warned General Mihailović that all Allied supplies to him would cease immediately. It was therefore vital that these Royalist operations should be successful. Their success, however, depended upon the part to be played by the British officers attached to them – and one of these was Captain George Brackley.

In the Orgulica area, the tasks allotted were first to destroy a part of the local railway line between Grdelica and the town of Vladicki Han; and second to destroy an important bridge. Brackley's role was to lay and blow the charges.

The following night Brackley was taken to the point where he was to blow the line. But the charges failed to explode. The flank guards warned that a patrol from

45

a German mountain battalion had been sighted; Brackley was told to lay another quickly. However, he took so long that the attempt had to be abandoned and the order was given to withdraw. But they had been seen and from hence forward the Germans established regular patrols along this section of the line. The operation had been a failure and it could not be repeated.

The men were angry. On the march back to headquarters, the British wireless operator explained to those who could speak English that the officer must have made some error with the fuse which was slow-burning and fired by a detonator taped to Primacord. But one of the men replied that the real reason why the Britisher could not do his work was that his hands were shaking with fear. Others muttered about sabotage, but they were silenced for the command knew that the Britisher was needed for the second and more important operation, the blowing of the bridge.

From the alcove, Alexandra thought she heard Tomas stir. She rose and, with the leaflets in her hand, crossed the room and drew back the curtain. But Tomas was asleep, turning in his narrow camp-bed. She watched him for a moment and then redrew the curtain and went back to her chair.

Two days later the order was given to carry out the attack on the bridge, which was guarded by a block-house manned by Bulgars, who were then the allies of the Germans. After the guard had been neutralised, Brackley was to lay the charges and blow the bridge. He was warned that this time he must not fail.

Once again the men assembled in the snow outside the caves high in the mountains and set off down to the plain to launch the attack. It was a fierce battle while it lasted, but the attack took longer than had been planned and by the time the last of the Bulgar defenders had been silenced, the look-outs warned that a German column, alerted by the noise of the firing,

46

was now approaching in armoured troop carriers.

Brackley was called for to set and fire the charges, but he was nowhere to be found. His young wireless operator had been killed in the assault on the block-house, but no one had see Brackley. By now the Germans had reached the bridge and the order had to be given to withdraw while a rearguard covered the retreat. As the men scrambled back towards the foot-hills Brackley was found hiding in the scrub. He was white and shaking and he said that in the darkness during the approach he had fallen down a ravine and was concussed. He said he had lost consciousness and had then lost contact with the column. Some of the men wanted to shoot him on the spot, but the officers restrained them. The second operation ordered by Cairo had failed.

Alexandra stopped reading, staring into the gas fire warming her feet in the cold room, trying to picture the battle around the bridge and the retreat of the angry men up the mountain to the cave. The leaflet slipped from her lap and as she bent to pick it up, the dog appeared beside her. She fondled his head and the dog went back to his vigil beside his master; Alexandra to her reading.

That night, the command discussed the conduct of Captain Brackley and it was decided to confront him on the following morning. But just after dawn, the sentry sighted Brackley slipping away through the snow down the path until he disappeared into the mountains. He could not be followed because German spotter aircraft had begun reconnoitring the mountain ridge and it was feared that the Germans were planning a sweep. But when the attack came, it was not by the Germans; it was by the Communist Partisans. They were led by Captain George Brackley, who had brought them up the secret path to the headquarters in the caves. The sentries were surprised and the Royalists systematically massacred.

But one man managed to survive and so the true story of George Brackley's cowardice and betrayal can be told. It has not been told before because within days that sole survivor fell into the hands of the Germans. He had escaped death from Brackley's gang of murderers – only to find himself in hell. For he was sent with others in cattle trucks to slave labour in Norway. Those who survived the terrible conditions of Trondheim were later sent to the East for more slave labour and when the Russians came, all that happened was that the prisoners exchanged slave masters. After many years in the mines of Siberia and more years of wandering, I finally came to England ten years ago and I have lived here ever since.

Just before last Christmas a friend told me about a book, part of which was about the war in the mountains in 1943. The book was *A Time To Remember* by George Brackley, the traitor who had betrayed those who had welcomed him as an ally and a friend.

Brackley's account of his exploits is a pack of lies. The truth is that he showed himself to be a coward in battle and deliberately sabotaged the operations of those brave patriots. Then he betrayed them to their enemies. Now, years later, he thought he could get glory for himself by writing lies about them, because he believed all had died in the massacre he had planned.

I am told that Brackley has become a famous man. All the more reason that his countrymen should know the truth about him. This is what I am now doing – exposing him for the fraud, the coward and the traitor that he is. Let him sue me if he dare. But he won't dare. Because George Brackley is a coward.

For several minutes Alexandra sat quite still, turning over in her mind the extraordinary accusations which Tomas had levelled against the man who was now the famous Lord

Brackley. Then she read both leaflets again, carefully and slowly. 'Let him sue me', Tomas had written, 'if he dare.'

Well, Lord Brackley had dared. In her hand she held the writ, Lord Brackley's answer to Tomas's challenge. So Tomas had got what he apparently wanted, what he had deliberately provoked – an action at law. But when he had taunted George Brackley into suing him, had he conceived what that would involve? Had he understood what a lawsuit for libel meant? Had he realised what he would have to do to face it and to fight it?

She examined the date of the writ and the letters. They had been written and served several days ago and the old man had just left them lying there on the table, the tape around them undisturbed. But they could not be ignored. They had to be answered, for Tomas Tarnovic was now being summoned in the High Court by a powerful and wealthy man backed by a leading firm of lawyers. Tomas Tarnovic having literally invited Lord Brackley to sue, could not now do nothing.

Alexandra rose to her feet and went again to the alcove, gently pulling back the curtain. The dog raised his head sleepily and his tail thumped on the mat beside the camp-bed. Tomas did not stir. As he slept, the lines on his old face were smoothed away, almost as if in death. He looked innocent and peaceful. But however calm his present repose, Tomas, she knew, was now in serious trouble. For if he did nothing, Lord Brackley's solicitors could sign judgement against him and he could be stripped of every-thing he possessed.

She knew that she had had no right to read Tomas's private papers. But she had, and she was glad that she had. For someone would have to help him.

She went back into the sitting-room. Tomorrow, Sunday, she had to go to see her father, but she would be back by the evening. She replaced the documents on the table from which she had taken them. The two leaflets she put in her bag and then she took a pencil and wrote: 'I have to go. Hope that you are better in the morning. I shall come to you at about seven o'clock tomorrow evening. We must talk then. Without fail. Alexandra.'

She left the note beside the legal documents around which she had replaced the ominous circle of red tape and quietly let herself out the front door.

FIVE

'We're going to have an early lunch so that you and your father can have a walk,' said her stepmother, Jessica. 'I expect that you won't want to be late starting back. Unless, of course, you can stay the night?'

Jessica was a short, bird-like woman with iron-grey hair, some years younger than her husband. There was the hint of reproof in her voice usual when she spoke to her step-daughter.

'I can't. I have to get back. I have to work tonight.'

'You working women,' said her father, one arm around his daughter. 'You put us idle old things to shame.'

Alexandra was glad there would be time to have their walk. They would be alone together, as they had been when she was a child.

At luncheon there were only the three of them, sitting at the long table in the large dining-room in the red-brick, Queen Anne house in which Alexandra had been born and brought up, the only child of a father widowed when Alexandra had been ten. Then two years later, Jessica had come. The child had hated seeing her stepmother presiding over the home in which her mother had died and she had pleaded to be allowed to go away to boarding-school. Her father had looked at the determined little face and had agreed. So Alexandra had gone to boarding-school younger than usual, pouring all her energy and passion into fierce possessive friendships. The holidays were uneasy, the father often away at sea or at the Admiralty in London and Jessica was always as glad as Alexandra when the time came for the child to return to school. Later, Alexandra had won a place at Exeter

University and had read law. After graduating, she had moved to her own flat in London, bought with the money her mother had left her, and visited home rarely. Latterly, the tension had eased between Jessica and herself; a truce had developed and Alexandra began to look with less resentment at the stepmother who so astutely looked after her father's comforts and so capably managed his home.

She watched Jessica's neat, bird-like movements as she sat at the end of the table eating the food which she had prepared with such care. After they had finished luncheon, Alexandra in the boots and windcheater she had brought in the car, and with her father similarly clad and armed with an ash stick, they set out across the lawn and along the ride which led through the beechwoods. The trees overhead were gaunt and naked in the pale winter sunshine and the fallen leaves still crusted with frost. It reminded Alexandra of walks in her childhood, when she had thought of such leaves as breakfast cereal coated with sugar as she crunched them under her boots. She slipped her arm through her father's.

'I've started to paint again.'

'I'm very glad. You were first-rate when you were at school. You should never have given it up.'

'I know. Now I've started again and I'm loving it. I go to a friend's studio every Saturday. It's wonderfully relaxing after a week in the office.'

'Are you enjoying the work in your new office?'

'Very much; much more than when I was an articled clerk. This firm is much smaller, just two partners and another assistant solicitor. I do the conveyancing. It's fun.'

'I can't imagine the law as fun. Still, I suppose it is in the blood. After all, your grandfather was a lawyer. I suppose it was he that made you choose the law.'

'You know it was. He used to tell me about his cases, remember? But he was more than a lawyer, Daddy. He was a judge.'

'Not a very grand one. He always said he might have gone further in the law if he'd not inherited this place.

Anyway, he settled happily enough for the County Court Bench. I think it was because he could get home early and could hunt twice a week. I suppose he was pretty lazy, not like his granddaughter.'

'It's different being a County Court Judge today, much more work.'

'I expect there is. Your grandfather was very content. He never wanted me to go into the law. That's why he sent me to Dartmouth.'

'And turned you into an old sea salt.'

'Not too much of the old. I am not that ancient.'

'Well, a salt then. And a grand sea salt, grander than grandfather was as a judge.'

They had come out of the woods and were skirting a ploughed field, keeping to the strip of grass at the edge.

'Daddy, who is Lord Brackley?'

'George Brackley? The former minister? I served under him when he was at the Ministry of Defence and I was at the Admiralty. Why do you ask?'

'Just something that has come up at work. When was he a Government minister?'

'Some years ago. He was the Secretary for Defence and a damn good one, too. But he's been long retired. They could do with a few more like him.'

'Was he in the War?'

'Of course. I think he was in Special Operations, SOE they called it. He's just published a book of memoirs. Rather good. I enjoyed it.'

The strip of grass had narrowed and they were walking in single file. At the end of the field they mounted a stile, crossed a meadow and turned back into the woods.

'Do you remember the story you used to tell about picking up a man called Marshal Tito? Was he a Communist?'

'Yes. His troops were called the Partisans.'

'Were there others fighting the Germans in Yugoslavia who were not Communists?'

'A few, to begin with. But they began collaborating with the Nazis. So the Allies supported Tito, dropping him

53

supplies and sending in liaison officers. After the War, he broke with Stalin and the Russians.'

'Was Lord Brackley one of the people we sent?'

'Yes. He wrote about it in his book. Why are you so interested in him?'

'It's nothing really. Just that his name came up in some papers which I had to read and I seemed to have heard about him, but I couldn't remember where.'

'Probably when he was in public life. He used to be very prominent.'

They were through the woods now and skirting the lake.

'Odd your reading about him in a lawyer's office. Has he come into any money? He doesn't need any. His wife is an American heiress. Rich as Croesus.'

Alexandra again took her father's arm. 'No. It was just a reference to him in some papers and I was curious.'

They walked on in silence until they were approaching the garden. Her father said, 'Jessica thinks it's time you got married.'

Alexandra laughed. 'Jessica is very old-fashioned. I'm very good at my job and I enjoy it. I'll marry when the right man comes along and then you'll get the grandsons you want so much. And they can become sailors and follow in their grandfather's footsteps, like I followed in mine.'

'By then there will be no ships left for them to go to sea in, even if they wanted to. The damn politicians will see to that. But I'd like someone to have this place – after me, and after you.'

'You will, Daddy. Just give me a little time.'

He put his arm around her and they went into the house. He stood at the door, watching as the car disappeared down the drive. When she was out of sight, the Admiral went to his study and sat for a long time staring into the fire. Then he reached for the telephone and began to dial.

At a quarter past seven Tomas let Alexandra into his flat. Over his pyjamas he had on a thick woollen dressing gown tied with a cord around his waist. He looked frail – and very old.

'Come in,' he said, bowing. 'I wish to thank my Good Samaritan and express my apologies for my behaviour yesterday.'

'You had a fainting fit. It can happen to anyone. Are you better?'

'I should be. I slept until this afternoon. Well, in fact, I woke in the morning and I let Tito out. Then I went back to bed and fell asleep again.'

'Quite right.'

He pulled up another chair for her beside his in front of the gas fire. 'Where have you come from?'

'I have been in the country, visiting my family.'

'Then you will be tired and you will need some refreshment. I shall make some tea.'

She sat waiting for him. She saw that the documents were still on the table where she had left them the night before.

When he had handed her the tea, he said, 'You must have some *rakija*. It is plum brandy. We used to drink it at home.' He poured her a glass and sat himself in the chair beside her.

She sipped the drink and pulled a face and drank some of the tea. 'It's very strong.'

'A drink fit for heroes.'

Then she said, 'Tomas, what are those papers?'

'Which papers?' He did not look at her.

'The legal papers on the table.'

'Those? I really don't know.'

'Tomas, someone must have come and given them to you. I expect that whoever it was asked you to sign for them?'

'How did you know? But you are quite right. A tall man came, with remarkably small ears and a scrubby little moustache.' He pulled at his own, brushing up the ends.

'He came twice and each time he gave you some papers.'

'He did. However did you know?'

'Tomas, I am a lawyer.'

55

'No, you are not. You are a painter.'

'I'm a lawyer, Tomas. That is what I do for a living.'

'You don't look like a lawyer. You are beautiful and lawyers are not beautiful. I like you and I do not like lawyers. I have nothing to do with lawyers.'

'Well, you will now, Tomas. For you are in trouble, serious trouble.'

The old man looked at her gravely. 'I did what I had to do.' He rose from his chair and stretching above the fireplace, placed his hand on the hilt of the rusty sabre. 'This is not mine. It was my father's. Someone gave it to the club and they have let me keep it.'

'Last night I read the leaflets you wrote. You have written some terrible things.'

'No. I have written the truth.'

'But the truth can be very terrible.'

He was silent. Then he said, 'Are they not well written? Do I not write good English?'

'You do.'

He looked down at her sitting in her chair, the light falling on her ash-blonde head.

'You are very sensible,' he said, 'for someone so young and so beautiful.'

'The only way you can get out of this trouble is to apologise and withdraw.'

'I shall never do that.'

'Have you any money?'

'I have a little. My cousin Stepan in America left it to me when he died. I miss him, although his wife did not like me very much.'

'Then they could take everything from you.'

'Who will?'

'The man who is suing you. Lord Brackley.'

'Who will let him?'

'The Court, the jury. They will give him damages and when you cannot pay, they will take everything you have.'

'No, that will not happen. But if it does, I do not care. I wish to say what I have to say – in Court.'

Tomas wandered over to the side of the room and picked up one of the photographs. 'These photographs are not of me. There are none of me. This one is of my General, General Draža Mihailović, whom the Communist, Tito, murdered. And the others are of the General's troops who fought in the mountains. Most were killed.'

'That is why you could never prove the truth of what you have written.'

He came back and stood in front of the fire. 'I shall tell the judge my story and he will believe me.'

She rose from her chair and put her arms around him, hugging him to her so that she felt how frail was his body, how little of him there was. 'Oh, Tomas, Tomas. You must understand. They'll take everything from you.'

'If they do, they do. But I shall have my day in Court. You must not worry. But I like what you did, taking me in your arms. If that is what you do when you worry, then you must keep worrying.'

'Tomas,' she repeated. 'Oh, Tomas.'

He now had his arm around her. 'I know, I know. I am very silly. But I will never apologise and I will never withdraw. I will tell them the truth and they will believe me. You must not worry about me. I am not worth it and I do not wish to see your lovely face looking sad.' He was leading her to the door. 'Now I must sleep again. I get very tired.'

She broke away from him and went back to the table. She picked up the writ and the solicitors' letters in their two bundles tied with their red tape.

'What are you doing?'

'I'm taking these. I shall do what I can.'

'You are kind to think of me. But it will make no difference. And remember, I shall never apologise. I want – how do you call it in English? – my day in Court.'

She bent forward and kissed him on the cheek. Then she left.

SIX

On her way to her law office in Fetter Lane Alexandra, dressed in her office uniform of white blouse and dark tailored skirt and jacket under a heavy black overcoat with a red scarf at her throat, stopped at the bookshop, Hatchard's, in Piccadilly, and asked for two copies of *A Time To Remember* by George Brackley.

When the young assistant handed them to her, he said, 'It's selling very nicely. I'm told it's quite interesting.' He would like to have talked more to this girl with her blue-green eyes and her blonde hair swept back and tied at the nape of her neck in a bow, and he tried to think of something else to say. But she smiled, paid in cash and left.

Later in the morning, Alexandra went to the office of the Senior Partner, John Arrun.

'John, can we talk for a moment? I have a problem.'

'Haven't we all, Alex.'

She did not like to be called Alex, but she had not yet summoned up the courage to tell him. John Arrun was a tall man in his early fifties, with an angular face and a quizzical expression which often irritated her, but it was he who had taken her on when she knew that her looks were a positive disadvantage in an office, especially a lawyer's office.

John Arrun himself was an experienced solicitor. He had been articled in his youth to Sir Henry Baker, a former President of the Law Society and the then Senior Partner in Baker and Turnbull. After a few years with a medium-sized firm in Kensington, he and two friends had started their own firm and built up a sizeable practice. When he had taken on Alexandra as an assistant solicitor, he knew her looks would create mayhem among the male staff, but he had gone ahead and had put her to work on the conveyancing side of the practice. At first he had supervised all that she did, but she was thorough and painstaking and it was not long before he was confident enough to leave her in sole charge of this department of the firm's business.

'Is your problem personal or professional?'

'It's a bit of both.'

'Then you really do have a problem. How can I help?'

'Well, I met a man . . .'

Arrun sighed. 'I knew it would be a man.'

She stopped herself from snapping at him. 'He's an old man, in his eighties,' she said quietly. 'I met him with a friend and when he became ill, I took him home. While I was there, I saw lying on his table some documents and I looked at them.'

'Should you have?'

'Well, at the time the old man was sleeping and I could see that one was a writ. He was ill, so I picked up the papers and looked at them.'

Arrun had clasped his hands together on the desk in front of him. He did not look at her and said softly, 'You had no right.'

Alexandra blushed. 'I know, but I am glad that I did. There were also two letters addressed to him from Baker and Turnbull.'

'Baker and Turnbull? Formidable people. Why should they be suing an old man of eighty?'

'It's a writ for libel.'

Arrun looked at his fingers and then pushed aside a folder which had been lying on his desk. 'Then I trust that your old friend is exceedingly rich.'

'No, that's the problem.'

'His problem. But surely not yours?'

'He's old – and a foreigner. I want to help him.'

Arrun got up and started to patrol the room, stopping at

59

the chimney-piece, making a show of winding the clock. 'Do you know anything about the law of libel?'

'No.'

'Or about litigation?'

'No. As you know, I do property work.'

'So how can you help? And if, as you say, he's not rich, how could he afford to instruct any lawyer to represent him in a libel action?'

'I don't think he could. Anyhow, he doesn't seem to understand that he's in trouble. Or if he does, he doesn't seem to care.'

'If the putative client doesn't care, why should you?'

'Because he is so old and he's a stranger and he's in trouble.'

'Who is suing him?'

'Lord Brackley.'

Arrun swung round. 'Lord Brackley!'

'Yes. The old man has circulated a pamphlet about Lord Brackley's behaviour in the War, in World War Two.'

'In the War?' Arrun's tone was incredulous. 'Lord Brackley's behaviour in the War?' He marched back to his desk and literally dropped into his chair. 'My dear Alex, fifty years ago Brackley was a war hero. That might mean nothing to your generation and not so much even to mine, but it does to quite a lot of people who're still alive. Further, Brackley was exceedingly prominent in public life until he retired and he is still very influential in the party. He plays a leading role in every Army charity and he's seen by millions on television sitting with the Royals in the Albert Hall at the Poppy Day Remembrance Service. To the soldiers he's almost a legend.'

'I know,' she said miserably. 'My father told me.'

'And this is the man suing your friend for libel. What has your friend been writing about him?'

Alexandra bit her lip. Then she said, 'That what Brackley has written in his memoirs about the War were lies and that he's a coward and betrayed the people he was sent to help and . . .' She paused.

'There's more? Is that not enough?'

'And that he was a Communist and a homosexual.'

Arrun put both hands to his face. Then he lowered them. 'Is the fellow mad?'

'I don't think he is. He says that Brackley betrayed his friends when they were fighting in Yugoslavia in the mountains in, I think, 1943 and he swears this is true. And,' she paused and then said defiantly, 'and I believe him.'

Arrun looked at her. 'You believe him!'

'Yes. So I want to help him. I want to do something about the writ and then — '

'And then,' he said flatly, 'persuade him to withdraw and apologise. That will be the way to help him.'

She did not reply, remembering Tomas's words – that he would never, never apologise.

Arrun went on: 'You know that there is no Legal Aid in libel cases?'

'No, I didn't.'

'Has he any money at all?'

'Very little, I imagine. But I still want to help him.'

'At your expense? At the firm's expense?' He saw how miserable she looked and his eye rested, as it always did, on the ash-blonde hair and at the curve of her chin. There was a silence. Then he sighed again and said, 'Must you really get involved?'

'I must. He is quite helpless.'

He shook his head and sighed. 'Very well. You may enter an appearance to the writ and place the firm on the record as representing him. Then put in some general holding defence – that the words are not defamatory or something of that sort, although from what you tell me, how you will be able to do that, God alone knows. But — ' he raised his hand, 'but you do this only in order to gain time and then you use the time to make the old fool apologise. Let's hope that Brackley will be satisfied with an apology and a withdrawal. You had better go to Counsel straightaway. Do you know Simon Harrington?'

'No.'

'He's quite young and has only recently taken silk. He owes a lot to my support in his early days, so he ought to be reasonable over fees, especially if you tell him the tale you have told me. I'll arrange with his clerk for you to see him at his chambers. Get him to tell you how best to extricate the old fool at the least expense to him – and to us.'

Alexandra rose. 'Thank you,' she said.

'But remember. We can't take it further than entering an appearance to the writ and perhaps putting in a holding defence. This firm's not big enough to carry the costs of a trial defending an insane old foreigner who has gone around libelling one of the country's heroes. It'll be up to you to get your friend to apologise – and quickly. Otherwise he will be on his own.'

'Miss Alexandra Layton from Arrun and Co. is here to see you.'

Simon Harrington QC looked up from the papers he was studying at his desk. He had just returned to chambers from Court, where he was in the middle of a tax appeal which was not going well. He had been on his feet arguing the appeal to a hostile Bench from 10.30 that morning and he had much work to do before the next day's hearing.

'You remember, sir. Mr Arrun telephoned before we went to Court this morning. They want some advice about a libel matter. Apparently, it's pretty straightforward.'

'Oh, God,' said Simon. 'I'd forgotten. The last thing I need at the moment is to have to listen to some story about a libel case. Must I?'

'Yes, sir, I fear you must. Mr Arrun was a good friend to you and to these chambers. He still is.'

'What's this Layton woman like, Mathew?'

His clerk put his hand to his bald head. With his portly figure and his black jacket and striped trousers, he looked like an undertaker and spoke like a bishop. 'Not what we are accustomed to, sir. Not at all what we are accustomed to. But, if I may say so, she is very striking-looking.'

'Well, that's something. Show her in.'

When Alexandra came through the door, Simon saw what Mathew meant. This girl was most certainly not what they were accustomed to when instructing solicitors came to number 12 King's Bench Walk.

He leaned over the desk and extended his hand. 'Please sit down, Miss Layton,' he said.

Alexandra sat. She saw in front of her a man in his early forties, tall and very slim, with brown eyes, a pale complexion, a rather pointed face and firm chin. There were lines at the corner of his eyes and beside his mouth and dark patches beneath his eyes. A lock of dark hair kept falling over his face, which he swept back with his hand. He was, she thought, very handsome – and he probably knew it.

'John Arrun spoke to me this morning. I understand that you've come about a writ for libel which has been served on an old man who is a friend of yours.'

'He's not really a friend. At least, I've only just met him.'

'Where did you meet him?'

She paused. 'Well, I go to a studio each Saturday.' She could see an eyebrow rise faintly. 'To paint,' she added. 'It's my hobby.'

'I envy you.'

'Oh, I'm not very expert. I have only just taken it up again.'

'As a relief from practising law? Very sensible. I play the piano.' She pictured him bent over the keyboard with the lock of hair falling over his eyes. Then he said curtly, as if regretting what he had told her, 'But you haven't come here to talk about our hobbies. Is it your friend the painter who's in trouble?'

'No. At least –'

He interrupted her. 'Who then is in trouble if it is not the painter?'

'No, it's not the painter who has the studio. He is one of the students.'

'So your friend is a student, like you; but elderly, unlike you?'·

What he said and how he said it annoyed her, but she made herself smile and replied, 'I'm not a witness under cross-examination, Mr Harrington.'

He pushed back his lock of hair. 'I'm sorry. Please tell me the story.'

'I first met him two Saturdays ago when we painted and talked together. This Saturday he suddenly became ill at the studio and I took him home. When I was there I found these.'

She handed him the writ and the letters from Baker and Turnbull. He took them from her without a word. While he read them, she looked around the room. She had never been to barristers' chambers before. She saw two heavy mahogany bookcases filled with the bound volumes of the *Law Reports* behind the glass doors. On the walls were two seventeenth-century oils of ships moored at a quay in a harbour. Above the chimney-piece of the gas fire hung a modern water-colour of flowers in a glass vase. On a table beside the desk she noticed a photograph of a young woman.

By now it was almost dusk and through the window behind Harrington's desk, she could see the lights in the wintry garden of the Temple and beyond the trees lining the river which led to Westminster.

'What does it all mean? Why has this man, this . . .' he looked again at the writ, 'this Tomas Tarnovic written these extraordinary things about Lord Brackley? If he has written what the solicitors allege, it is, as you'll appreciate, extremely defamatory.'

'I know.'

Simon Harrington rose from the desk and went to the bookshelf to his left and took out the red volume of *Who's Who*. He turned the pages and stood reading. Then he closed it with a snap and replaced it in the shelf.

'I was checking the entry for Lord Brackley. His war record could hardly be bettered. You know about his later career in politics?'

'Yes. He has just written a book of memoirs. I have it here.' She handed it to him across the desk. He noticed her eyes. She is beautiful, he thought as he took it from her.

'I think,' she went on, 'that what Lord Brackley wrote in his book prompted Tomas Tarnovic to circulate his pamphlets.'

'Why do you say that?'

'Because of what Tomas Tarnovic has written.'

'Then that is what I need to read.'

'I took these leaflets from his table.'

Again she leaned over the desk and he placed them beside the book *A Time to Remember* with the photograph of a silver-haired George Brackley smiling confidently from the shiny cover. This, Simon thought wearily, is going to involve more than just an hour in conference. If it had been any other solicitor than this girl, he would have ended the matter there and then by saying he was too busy.

'To whom were the leaflets circulated?'

'I believe to many people in public life.'

'Does your friend know that you have the leaflets and the legal documents? I ask because John Arrun told me that Mr . . .' he looked again at the writ, 'Mr Tarnovic is himself wholly unconcerned over the writ and, indeed, that he's not even very interested.'

'That's the trouble. He doesn't seem to care. He is . . .' and she paused, 'he is a very sweet old man.'

He did not immediately reply, but played with the lid of the silver ink-well on his desk, letting it fall and then opening it again. Finally, he closed it with a snap. Then he said almost to himself, but loud enough for her to hear, 'A sweet old man being sued for damages for libel who could not care a damn; and an eager young lawyer who does.'

If he had not been overtired and worried about the work which already lay ahead of him that night, he would never have spoken as he had. As soon as he had uttered the words, he regretted them. Alexandra coloured.

'I'm sorry.' He brushed the recalcitrant lock of hair off his forehead. 'I should not have said that. It's just that I was thinking of the old man who cares so little and you who care so much.'

She got to her feet. 'John Arrun told me to come to you, but even if you won't help, I am going to act for Mr Tarnovic whether he has the means or not.'

'Miss Layton, please.' He too was standing. 'I didn't mean to offend you. I cannot properly advise until I've read the documents, especially Mr Tarnovic's pamphlets and Lord Brackley's book. If you still wish me to, I shall read the papers you have given to me as soon as I can.'

'Tonight?' she replied. 'It is urgent.'

'Is it that urgent?' When shall I ever have the time? he thought.

'It is. The papers have been lying in the old man's flat for days.'

He groaned inwardly, but he had been rude. It would be the small hours of the morning before he could start the reading. In any event, it was probably all nonsense – an old man accusing Lord Brackley of cowardice and betrayal fifty years ago!

'Very well. As I am in Court again tomorrow, can you come back at 4.30 in the afternoon?'

Her blue-green eyes met his brown eyes across the desk. 'Yes. I shall be here.'

He came round and took her by the arm. 'I will certainly try and help.'

He dropped his hand and she turned to the door.

'Thank you. It may be absurd, but there is something very special about the old man.'

Simon went before her to the door. With his hand on the doorknob, he said, 'I'll see you tomorrow at 4.30 when I am back from Court. I'll tell my clerk, Mathew, to expect you.'

She did not look at him as he showed her out.

When she had gone, he stood at the bow window looking down, waiting for her to appear under the light on the steps leading up to the entrance to the eighteenth-century building. He saw her emerge and walk down the steps. She turned up King's Bench Walk towards the north end of the Temple and stopped for a moment as though she had forgotten something. The light from the standard lamp on the corner of the garden shone on her hair. Then she was gone. She is very remarkable, he thought.

SEVEN

Later that night, Simon Harrington sat in the drawing-room of his first-floor flat in Onslow Square. It was a large room, handsomely furnished; a gas log-fire burned cheerfully in the grate. The low stool in front of the fireplace was covered with political and historical magazines; books were piled on occasional tables around the room. In one corner was a grand piano; on it a single photograph in a silver frame. It was the same photograph of the young woman which Alexandra had noticed in his chambers during her visit that afternoon. On the floor around the arm-chair in which Simon was sitting was a large briefcase and beside it several thick bundles of legal papers – the tax brief on which he had been working all evening. Beside them, now tied by red tape, were the papers which Alexandra had brought to him that afternoon. On top of this pile was George Brackley's autobiography.

It was approaching midnight when Simon finally put aside the papers on the tax appeal and picked up the book. He leafed through it, looking at the pictures. The first was of the child with his parents, the father in the stiff collar and narrow-cut suit of the early twenties; then the school-boy sitting cross-legged in the foreground of a school cricket eleven. The next group of photographs began with Second-Lieutenant Brackley in uniform, followed by one of him standing in the snow, surrounded by a group of armed men in ragged uniforms. In the background were the mountains; and a final wartime picture of the youthful Colonel after an investiture holding up to the camera a decoration, as he stood with his mother at the sandbagged gates of Buckingham Palace. Later came photographs of the author as the Parliamentary Candidate on the hustings and a formal Cabinet photograph with Brackley sitting in the front row. Other plates showed him with two successive Prime Ministers at Chequers and one with the then President of the United States and fellow Defence Ministers at meetings of NATO. The photographs ended with some of the author's home, Brandsby Hall in Yorkshire, and of his wife, Grace Brackley as a bride at the time of their marriage; then in hunting kit on her hunter, and last in full evening dress at an official reception at Lancaster House.

Simon turned back to the start of the book and leafed through the early chapters on childhood and school and the few pages devoted to Brackley's time at Cambridge, until he came to the chapters about the War. There were three in all; the first was entitled 'The Battle in France in 1940'; the second, 'My Arrival in the Mountains in 1943'; and the third, 'With the Partisans; the Triumph of Tito'.

Simon took a sip of claret from the glass on the table beside him and began to read about Brackley's experiences with the British Expeditionary Force in France in 1940 and the retreat to Dunkirk, the campaign in which Lieutenant Brackley had been awarded his first decoration for gallantry, the Military Cross.

Before he started on the next chapter, 'My Arrival in the Mountains in 1943', Simon laid the book aside and reread both of Tarnovic's two pamphlets. Then he went back to Brackley's book, underlining and sidelining as he read.

At the end of 1940 I was on leave and like many in those days if they happened to be in London on a Saturday evening, I went for a drink at the Berkeley Hotel, then in Piccadilly. I was wondering how to pass the evening, when an old university acquaintance called Tommy Laker came in and joined me. After a few drinks, Tommy suggested that I dine with him at his club. There was an air raid in progress and as we walked through the black-out down St James's Street, we had to dodge the shrapnel from the anti-aircraft guns and when we heard the whine of a salvo of bombs which sounded uncomfortably close, dart down area steps.

After dinner, we went up to the roof of Tommy's club and watched the fires burning in the docks away to the east. I recall wondering how the bombing could ever be brought to an end before the whole of London was destroyed.

I had told Tommy that I was bored with training and waiting for action and anxious to get back into the fray. I was still very young!

How young? thought Simon. He checked the note he had made from *Who's Who* in chambers. Brackley had been born in 1916 and had been at Cambridge in the mid-thirties. So in 1941 he would have been twenty-five.

The long and the short of that dramatic but convivial evening was that Tommy, who was involved in some clandestine organisation, arranged for me to have an interview at his HQ in Baker Street, to which a few days later I was summoned and interviewed by an odd, bald-headed man in plain clothes, in a bleak, sparsely-furnished room lit by a single naked electric light bulb dangling from the ceiling. I succeeded in persuading him that I was fit material for Special Operations and was sent on a series of courses: first at a country house in Surrey; then an assault course in the Highlands of Scotland; and finally back to another country house in Hampshire.

It was early 1942 when I embarked for Cairo, instructed to report to the local SOE – or MO4 as it was then called and which later came to be known as Force 133. I was sent to Camp 102 at Rouat David, near Haifa, in Palestine, for parachute training and to learn to handle explosives and German as well as British automatic weapons. We were also taught to kill

70

with a knife. There followed a sketchy crash language course in Serbo-Croat. Eventually, in 1943 I was ordered to drop into the mountains in south-east Serbia to join a band of the guerrillas who had taken up arms against the German and Italian invaders.

At that time there was much debate among the planners in MO4 and in diplomatic circles at Allied HQ over which of the guerrilla groups in the forests and mountains in Bosnia and Serbia and Montenegro were proving the most effective in fighting the Germans and Italians. There were the Cetniks under the Minister of Defence in the Royal Yugoslav Army, General Mihailović; and the Partisans under Josip Broz, later known as Marshal Tito. However, those of us on active operations paid little attention to the political issues. We would have a job to do as liaison and explosive officers attached to whatever group we had been dispatched. As it turned out, I soon discovered that Mihailović's men were useless – and, what was worse, that he and they were collaborating with the Germans. Tito's Partisans was the only force actively committed to fighting the Nazis and the Fascists.

With his pencil Simon sidelined this passage and underlined the reference to the 'debate' among the planners in Cairo.

Eventually in November 1943, I and my wireless operator, a Sergeant Alan Hopkinson from Chichester in Sussex, were sent by train and lorry along the North African littoral to Derna in Tripolitania to await final orders for our drop into Yugoslavia. Within days of our arrival in the mountains, my companion, the unfortunate Alan Hopkinson, was dead – not killed in action, but murdered.

When he read this, Simon turned back to Tarnovic's pamphlet. In this the wireless operator had shared Brackley's sleeping-bag and been killed in the assault on the block-house on the bridge.

It was a fine evening in November 1943 when, with our bulky wireless equipment stowed beside us, we boarded a Halifax bomber with an unpressurised cabin, which was to carry us across the Mediterranean to the mountains of eastern Serbia.

During the flight, I looked down at the sea glittering beneath us in the moonlight and then when we crossed the Dalmatian coast, at the dark landmass of what was then Yugoslavia. I felt the same mixture of fear and elation which every soldier feels before battle and although I had experienced my baptism of fire in the retreat to Dunkirk, I wondered how I would face up to the dangers and hardships of a different war in the mountains.

At last I saw far below us the cross of fire which marked our dropping-zone. At the signal from the RAF crewman, I settled the harness of my parachute. The hatch was opened; I kept my eye on the dispatcher's hand. As it fell, so fell I.

First a rush of air and the sensation of falling which seemed interminable, but which in reality lasted only a few seconds during the struggle to pull on the rip-cord; then the eerie sensation as, with my companion close to me, I floated above the mysterious land in which I was to travel and live and fight for the next twelve months. We landed easily, far more easily than many landings I had made in training, Hopkinson only a few yards from me. Within seconds figures emerged from the darkness, laughing and shouting noisily. I was greeted with a warm embrace, a beard pressed to my cheek and with it my first but not last scent of what I was soon to recognise as *rakija*, the local and extremely potent plum brandy, the comforter of those who lived and fought in the forests and mountains.

Our welcomers crowded around us; everything

seemed confused and disorganised. With difficulty we managed to dispatch some to locate and collect our precious wireless set. After much jostling and arguing, with the bottle of plum brandy constantly circulating and with no one apparently in command, the brush-wood fire which had been our signal was stamped out and we were eventually led away. We marched for three hours in single file from the flat dropping-zone up into the foothills and then into the mountains themselves. From my experience on the following night, I suspect that even on this first evening the guides lost the way, as our progress was halting and interrupted by frequent halts for argument and plum brandy. After following a steep path which led through thick snow-covered undergrowth, we finally emerged exhausted on to a narrow plateau of rock. The guide pushed through a tarpaulin cover and we followed him into a cave, or rather a series of caves, in the last of which we were greeted by the man who was the Commander of the group which we had come to join.

Simon tore a small strip of paper from his notebook and slipped it as a marker into the book.

He was a man, older than myself but only by a few years, bearded, with a natural dignity of manner. He had an attractive, cultivated air, which concealed, as I subsequently discovered, a fatal flaw of habitual indecision, a failing especially dangerous for a commander of an irregular unit engaged in guerrilla warfare. He spoke English well. I never learnt his name, but he was addressed by his men as the Commandant and so I followed suit. Compared to those who had collected us from the dropping-zone, his manner was reserved and not particularly welcoming. However, he offered me some of the inevitable plum brandy and when I declined food, he showed me a corner of one of the warren of caves where he said that I could sleep.

73

Sergeant Hopkinson with the WT set was shown to another cave, which he shared with the Commandant's orderlies.

My anxiety arising from the chaos at the dropping-zone and the march to the caves increased when, next day, I witnessed the casual and ineffectual manner of command exercised by this strange and introverted man. My impression was strengthened that I and Hopkinson were not particularly welcome to the command, as if our arrival heralded active operations against the Germans which, as I again later discovered, was what the Cetniks under the overall command of General Mihailović had been regularly seeking to avoid. They were more interested in forming accommodations with the Germans by which each side left the other in peace.

Later Hopkinson told me that one of the orderlies who was bunking with him and who spoke some English had said surlily that any operations which we carried out would do little damage to the Germans and would arouse massive retaliation and the shooting of hostages. This bore out what I had heard in Cairo – namely that the only real fighting against the Germans was being carried out by Tito's Partisans.

Once again Simon heavily sidelined the passage he had just read.

The next day, I was informed by the Second-in-Command that the following evening it was planned to blow up a stretch of the railway line in the plain near to Grdelica. I welcomed this since this was what we had come to do, but in the event, the operation itself turned out to be a farce.

We set off in a column soon after dark; at the start Hopkinson and I marched near to the Commandant, but soon he was called to the head of the column to resolve some squabbling and argument. When at last we reached the plain, I was informed that neither the

74

Commandant nor the leading files could make out where we were. Hopkinson and I rested in some scrub waiting for the confusion to be sorted out, but after about an hour of waiting and listening to the sounds of argument and dispute, we were told that the operation had been cancelled and that the column was to return to HQ. The Cetniks did not appear to be disappointed at the failure of the operation, but to me the incompetent leadership boded ill for any future operations with this group.

Here Simon laid down the book and turned to Tarnovic's version of the first operation after Brackley's arrival. According to Tomas, the railway line had been reached, but Brackley had failed to fire the charges. Simon returned to the book.

The next morning, the Commandant came to me. He offered no explanation of the fiasco of the previous evening, but merely announced that the same operation would be repeated that night and he warned me to prepare.

In Tomas's version, Simon noted, the second operation was the attack on the bridge and the assault on the blockhouse manned by the Bulgarians, when Hopkinson had been killed and Brackley had been discovered cowering in the scrub.

I remember that when the Commandant told me this, he had an open book in his hand and I could see that it was a volume of the poems of Mallarmé. I wondered at the extraordinary personality of this man, who seemed more like an ineffectual college professor than a fighting soldier.

By now I was filled with acute anxiety, since I doubted the chance of any successful operation under his command and I bitterly regretted that I had been

75

assigned to assist this disorganised and ill-led band. I tried to get a message through to Cairo but failed and I waited for the evening with a foreboding which, in the event, proved to be fully justified. I told Hopkinson that if the farce of the previous night was repeated, we should leave these people and make our way to join a proper fighting unit with Tito's Partisans.

At nightfall the column once again set off amid the inevitable scenes of confusion and muddle. We followed the same route, with Hopkinson and myself this time marching with the Second-in-Command. When we had reached the plain, the Second-in-Command warned me that we were approaching the appointed place where I was to blow the railway line and that the men would provide me with covering fire. He would give me the word when to go forward and lay the charges.

At that moment, a series of flares from Verey pistols soared into the night sky, mushrooming high above us, casting a violent light over the whole of the column. For a moment all stood as though transfixed and then the column broke with men fleeing in every direction. As they did so, the enemy's Spandaus opened up. We had been ambushed.

By the light of the German flares I could see men falling. Ahead I thought that I saw the Commandant standing apparently transfixed and totally bewildered. There were shouts, which I took to be calls to retreat back into the hills, but everywhere men were caught in the crossfire of the German machine guns.

Hopkinson and I had dropped to the ground in the snow and I watched the tracer bullets cutting into groups of running men. Then mortar shells started bursting near to us and I could hear screaming above the noise of the Spandaus and the mortars.

'When there's a break in the light from the flares, make for the path and then to the caves,' I shouted to Hopkinson. As I did so, I saw in front of me a pair of

German soldiers, one an officer. I fired a burst from my M-3 Sten sub-machine gun and both fell. When the light of the flares momentarily died, I led Hopkinson over rocks and through the scrub until we found a hiding place away from the site of the ambush. The firing continued, but I knew that there was nothing that we could do. The column had been effectively destroyed. During a pause in the firing we stumbled back the way we had come and by luck came upon the path and struck up the mountainside. After a time the firing in the plain below us ceased except for an occasional single shot.

'They're shooting the wounded,' said Hopkinson.

At last we reached the plateau. There were no sentries; the place was deserted. I pushed through the tarpaulin and entered the HQ cave. It was empty, dimly lit by a single oil-lamp on a table. I went to a bend in the cave where the Commander kept his maps on a wooden shelf fixed roughly to the wall. I put my pack on the shelf and laid my M-3 sub-machine gun against the rock wall and came back to Hopkinson with the maps.

'Not many can have survived,' he said.

I spread the maps on the table and said, 'There's nothing that we can do here.' I began to compare the Commandant's maps with the one supplied to me in Cairo. 'We'll have to make a break for it and try to cross the Sandzak and join the Partisans.'

'What about the WT set?' he asked.

'We'll have to carry it ourselves.' As I said this, the tarpaulin was pulled aside and two Cetniks came into the cave with their rifles pointing directly at us as we stood behind the table.

They came towards us smiling but not friendly and stopped on the far side of the table. One of them pushed the maps on to the floor with the barrel of his rifle.

He said in English, 'What are you doing here?'

77

'We got away from the ambush,' I replied.

'You are deserters,' he said.

'You're a liar,' I said angrily. 'The whole column has been destroyed because of the incompetence of the command. We're lucky to have escaped with our lives. Where is the Commandant?'

'Dead, like the others. We were betrayed.' The man jerked his head towards Hopkinson. 'Come with me.'

'Why?' I said. 'What do you want with him?'

But the man merely gestured with his rifle at Hopkinson and said, 'Take me to the wireless.'

Hopkinson looked at me. There was nothing that either of us could do. I nodded and Hopkinson walked to the entrance of the cave and the Cetnik who had spoken followed him, his rifle in the small of Hopkinson's back. When they had disappeared, the other man squatted in front of me, his rifle still pointing at my head. For several minutes we stared at each other in silence. Then I said in Serbo-Croat, 'Do you want gold?' The man looked at me and spat. I repeated my question. Then he smiled and nodded. I pointed to the bend in the cave where I had placed my pack on the shelf. 'I have gold sovereigns. I will get them for you.'

I began slowly to walk towards it. I heard the man behind me rise to his feet. I reached for the pack and deliberately fumbled so that it dropped on to the rock floor. I bent as though to pick it up and grabbing the M-3, turned and fired. The man fell. I ran to the lamp on the table and blew it out and then went to the mouth of the cave, pulling aside the tarpaulin and expecting that the other Cetnik would come at the sound of the firing.

'Hopkinson,' I shouted. But there was no reply.

Taking my torch from my pocket I slipped outside. Everything was very still and silent. I crouched by the rock and then moved slowly along the narrow plateau and came to the entrance of the cave where Hopkinson had been quartered.

I shone the torch and in the beam I saw Hopkinson lying face down, slumped over the wireless set which stood on a table. I went to him and tried to turn him. As I did so I saw that his throat had been slit from ear to ear. The pockets of his uniform had been ripped, his pack emptied, the WT set smashed.

I stayed on guard at the entrance of the cave until first light, but I heard and saw nothing. Hopkinson's murderer had gone.

When dawn had broken, I heard high above me the sound of a German spotter plane, a Fieseler Storch, circling over the crest of the mountain. I slipped inside the cave until the sound of the aircraft had died away and then went outside to reconnoitre. The place was still deserted, but I knew that it would not be for long. Now that it was daylight the Germans would be coming.

I found some bread and wine in the Commandant's cave and then set off through the snow along the crest of the mountain. I had not long started before I saw the first German patrol far below me clambering up the mountain. I turned south away from them, scrambling over the rocks and hiding whenever there was sufficient cover. Sometimes up to my waist in snow, I struggled on during the hours of daylight. Later in the morning I crouched under a rock as German Stukas dive-bombed the crest. I lay up all the following night, by now almost dead from the fierce cold. Finally, the next day I reached the foothills and towards nightfall, the plain. At first light I moved on, until the following night I came to a homestead, almost a hovel, a single-storeyed house with no chimney and only a hole in the peak of the roof. I decided that I must seek help. I was too near death from frostbite to care about the risk that I was taking and I banged on the door.

I was lucky. The peasants sheltered me for several days while I recovered my strength. They had heard of the ambush. All the Cetniks, they said, had been killed. They were not sorry, they said, for the Cetniks were thieves and robbers. Later they told me that after the bombing by the Stukas, German troops had been seen on the summit. They would have found the body of Hopkinson and the WT set in the caves and they would know that there was a British liaison team in the area.

I asked the people where the nearest Partisan unit was located. They directed me and shared with me what little food they had and after studying the maps, I once again set out. After four days' march and similar hardships, I at last found the Partisans. After the bloody confusion of that interlude with Mihailović's Cetniks, it was with relief that I found myself with a disciplined military unit, organised to fight a professional war against the Germans. Thankfully, I was done with Mihailović's men, their incompetence and their collaboration with the enemy. For the next twelve months I fought with the true Yugoslav resistance, which had been forged by their great leader, Marshal Tito, into a patriotic army which, with the help of the Allies, finally drove the Germans from their land and liberated their country.

Here the chapter concluded. Simon put down the book. By now it was very late. He was in Court in a few hours' time and he had to get some sleep. He would read the next chapter about Brackley's experiences with the Partisans later, but before retiring to bed he again took up Tarnovic's pamphlets and with Brackley's account still fresh in his mind he reread them, noting and comparing the difference.

According to the Tarnovic pamphlets, Brackley and Hopkinson had shared the single sleeping-bag; on the first operation Brackley had deliberately failed to fire the charges; on the second Brackley had cowered in the scrub during the raid on the bridge; after Hopkinson had been killed, Brackley had deserted to join the Partisans.

Simon remained in his chair, his eye on the flame of the

false fire burning cheerfully beside him. There could be no reconciliation between the two versions. One or other was false. One or other was invention. But which? Merely to pose the question struck him as absurd. What jury could be persuaded that Brackley was a villain and a fraud?

But why should Tarnovic write as he had? The girl believed him. There was something special about him she had said. But on what had that been based? On the old man's charm and her intuition? Neither would amount to much in a Court of law.

No, whatever the girl might think, the only proper course for a lawyer was to advise Tomas Tarnovic to withdraw his accusations, make an immediate apology, and beg Lord Brackley for mercy. To persuade him to do this was the only way in which the girl could help him.

Tomorrow he would tell her. Tomorrow? He looked at the clock. Today, later today. He bent and gathered together his papers and packed up his briefcase thinking all the while of her. The thought of seeing her again made him glad.

He placed the briefcase on the top of the piano from where he would take it when he left for work in four hours' time. As he did so, he looked at the photograph in its silver frame. Then he turned off the lights and went out of the room to bed.

EIGHT

Alexandra knocked and entered the Clerks' Room in Simon's chambers at King's Bench Walk in the Temple.

'Mr Harrington is delayed, Miss Layton,' said Mathew, Simon's Head Clerk. 'The Court of Appeal is sitting an extra half-hour to finish the appeal. He has asked me to show you into his room and serve you some tea.'

She followed Mathew across the corridor and into Simon's room. Mathew waved her to a large red leather club armchair and left her. She looked around the room, her eye falling again on the photograph beside the desk. She rose and went over to examine it more closely, picking it up and studying it. The woman, she thought, was very good-looking. Alexandra replaced it on the table and was back in the armchair when Mathew returned with a cup of tea on a tray.

'Thank you,' she said.

'Mr Harrington is on his way. He should be here in a minute or two.'

A few minutes later Simon burst into the room. 'I'm sorry to have kept you.' He went straight to his desk; he did not shake her hand and she did not rise.

'Your clerk told me that they were sitting on to finish your case. I hope that you were successful.'

'I was not.' He spoke savagely and tossed the lock of black hair off his forehead. He undid the button of his dark jacket and pulled his pocket-watch from the chain looped through his buttonhole above his top pocket. He laid the watch and chain on the desk and then threw himself into his chair.

'The damn fools dismissed the Appeal, with costs.'

She smiled. 'And were the damn fools wrong?'

'Yes,' he said. Then he grinned. 'No, not really. To let you into a secret, they were probably right. But I don't like to lose.' He looked at her; the grin disappeared. 'But now to the case of Tomas Tarnovic. That is certainly a queer kettle of fish.'

'Have you read Brackley's book?'

'Last night, or rather in the small hours of this morning. I have also read Tomas Tarnovic.'

'What do you make of it?'

'Obviously one of them is lying.'

She was about to interrupt him, but he raised his hand to stop her. 'I know, I know. And it's not your Tomas who is the liar.'

She coloured slightly and leaned forward out of the deep armchair. 'He's not my Tomas, as you put it.'

'Oh yes, he is. And very lucky he is to be your Tomas. He has a champion, and in some cases that's more than half the battle.' She subsided, almost disappearing into the chair.

'Have they given you tea?'

'Yes, thank you.'

'Well, what are we to do now?'

She looked at him, surprised. 'I expected you to tell me. John Arrun said you were the expert.'

'So I am. Well then, let me tell you. We have two totally different versions of a wartime incident involving a few days of battle in a far-off country nearly fifty years ago. Your client says one thing; the famous Lord Brackley another. It does not require me to tell you that what your client says, or rather has written, is defamatory and that the damages for a libel of such gravity could be astronomical. The only defence to the claim would be to prove that what Mr Tarnovic has written is true and you have produced neither witness statements nor documents to substantiate Mr Tarnovic's fantastic story.'

'I haven't any.'

'Exactly. So we're left with the two stories. What do you

want me to do? Call up spirits from the vasty deep to prove he's telling the truth when he circulates a pamphlet in which he accuses one of England's leading public men of being a liar and a coward and a bugger?' He looked across the desk at her and she stared back steadily into his dark eyes. 'So there is not a shred of evidence to back up your friend's story.'

'I wish you'd stop calling him my friend.'

'Well, he is, isn't he? You have befriended him and you believe him. Why do you believe him?'

Alexandra looked down at her hands while he watched her. Why did she believe Tomas? Then she said, 'There's something about him. I can't explain what it is, but I just feel that he's not the type of man who would invent terrible things about someone else. To me there's no reason why he should've done what he has done unless his story is true.'

He was studying her face and did not immediately reply. Then he said quietly, gently, 'No reason? What about pride or resentment or jealousy, or even the fantasy of an old warrior brooding over the battles he had fought or the battles he had avoided? Those might be reasons. And what about Lord Brackley? Is he the type of man who would invent a false story?'

'I don't know Lord Brackley. I do know, if only a little, Tomas Tarnovic.'

Simon rose from behind the desk and began to prowl up and down the room, taking up his watch on its thin gold chain and playing with it. She kept her eyes on the tall figure, wondering if this meant that he wanted to get rid of her and be done with the whole problem of Tomas Tarnovic.

'He tells a remarkable tale. It's well written, in clear English.'

'He was at school in England.'

'Then there's that incident with his cousin at Cambridge.' He turned to her. 'You have heard of "The Apostles"?' She nodded. He stopped by her chair and looked down at her. 'It could be the key,' he said softly and she knew then that he was dismissing neither her nor Tomas. 'The Fifth Man, or was it the Sixth or the Twenty-sixth? The dead Guy Liddell, the Deputy of MI6 and the dead Roger Hollis, the Chief himself – both have been accused. But Brackley? Lord Brackley, sometime Secretary for Defence? That would be new.' He flopped into his chair. 'And absurd – the ranting of a disturbed old foreigner who has got angered by a book of which he didn't approve.'

She watched as the lock of hair fell and was swept back. He dropped the watch back into his top pocket and threaded the chain through his buttonhole. Suddenly he added, 'Where is he now?'

'Who? Tomas?'

'Of course. Who else?'

'He will be at Fulham. He's not well.'

'How ill is he?'

'He had a fall on Saturday. I told you yesterday.'

'Did he hit his head?'

'Yes.'

'Perhaps it may have knocked some sense into him.' He rose from the desk. 'Come on,' he said.

'Come on where?'

'To Fulham, of course.' He was at the door, opened it and bellowed, 'Mathew, get me my coat. I'm going to see a client.'

He turned and grabbed Alexandra by the hand, heaving her out of the chair. 'Have you a car?'

'At home – in Drayton Gardens.'

'That's on the way. We'll get a taxi and pick up your car and you can take me to your Tomas.'

He literally pulled her through the door of his room and out on to the landing, seizing his coat from Mathew and galloping down the stairs, only releasing her hand as they got to the foot of the staircase by the outer door of the building. He began to pull on his overcoat.

'Mine is still upstairs.'

85

'Hell,' he said and ran back up the staircase, leaving her shivering in the cold evening air, waiting for him.

When Tomas opened the door he was fully dressed but wearing his thick woollen dressing gown. He had his stick in his hand. There was a strip of clean plaster over the cut on his forehead just below the line of his white hair.

'My good Samaritan!' he said to Alexandra. 'Come in, Sacha.' Then he saw Simon. 'And your friend.'

They followed him into the flat and Tomas shut the door behind them. The dog came at once to Simon who bent and took Tito's head in his two hands.

'What's his name?'

'Tito,' said Tomas.

Simon straightened. 'A strange name for a dog of yours.'

Tomas looked at him. 'It was the name of a Roman Emperor. It was not my choice.' He turned to Alexandra. 'Come and sit by the fire. The doctor you sent came this morning. He seemed very nervous as though I were some beast in a raree show.'

Simon picked up the reference. 'What Byron said of the English in Switzerland after he had fled from London. They looked at him as though at a raree show.' Simon had his hand on the dog. 'And Byron had a servant with a name like that of your friend here, not Tito but Tita, who fought with the Sergeant-Major.'

Tomas had seated himself in his chair. He did not look at Simon. 'My great-great-grandfather knew George Byron in Pisa.' Then, to Alexandra, 'Your doctor put some spirit and this plaster on my head and gave me some tablets. He kept eyeing my sabre and seemed happy to get away. You must have been telling tales about me.'

'No, but I warned him that you were very stubborn and would probably prove disobedient.'

Simon was patrolling around the room, studying the books and the photographs. He stopped before the photograph of the bearded man with the steel-rimmed spectacles.

'Draža Mihailović,' he said. 'Executed by Marshal Tito in 1947.'

Tomas said to Alexandra, 'Who is your friend?'

'He's a lawyer like me, only a more important one. I've brought him so that he can talk with you about the papers which were served on you.'

Tomas turned to look at Simon, who stared back at him and then abruptly drew up a chair and brought it close to Tomas.

'You have written some very wicked things about a very important and well-respected Englishman. Why?'

Tomas looked straight at Simon. 'That is my business.'

'What is your business now is that Lord Brackley intends to take you to Court, strip you of everything that you possess and demonstrate to the world that you're a liar.'

Tomas turned away from Simon and looked at Alexandra. 'Your friend is very fierce. But, like many lawyers, especially important lawyers, he is wrong. George Brackley knows that what I have written is the truth. George Brackley will not prove that I am a liar.'

'Lord Brackley has to prove nothing. In a libel action where the Defendant says that what he has written is true, he is the one who has to prove his case. So it is you who have to prove that Lord Brackley is what you have written about him – that he is or was a bugger, is a liar, was a coward and is or was a Communist agent who, on the orders of his Communist friends, deliberately came to your HQ in Serbia with the intention of betraying you. Only if you can prove all that in an English Court of law will Lord Brackley fail to brand you, Tomas Tarnovic, as the liar.'

Simon went on, 'And now, may I ask, how do you imagine that you can prove your accusations against Lord Brackley?'

Tomas turned to look at Alexandra and then back to Simon, eyeing him up and down. At last he said, 'By telling the truth. By telling your English Court what really happened when Brackley came to my country. And when I do, the English Court will believe me.'

'Do you seriously imagine that an English Court, twelve Englishmen and women, will believe what you have written about a well-known and well-respected Englishman just because you, a foreigner, say so?'

'Yes. Because it is the truth.'

'And when Lord Brackley swears that it is lies, why should you think that the English Court will prefer your story to his?'

'Because when he tells his story, those who hear him will know that what he is saying is false.'

'How?'

'Because of the way in which he will tell it. And as he tells his lies, I shall be sitting there looking at him and he will be remembering what really happened during those days and nights in the mountains and the Court will know that he is lying.'

'What evidence do you have to support you?'

'None that I know of. Some witnesses may come forward when they read of it, if they are alive.'

'And if they are dead?'

'Then they will not come forward. See,' he said to Alexandra, 'how foolish can be the most important of lawyers.'

Simon laughed and rose to his feet and walked over to the fireplace. 'If you want to avoid all this trouble and continue with your peaceful life in your comfortable room with your possessions still about you,' Simon laid a finger gently on the rusted sabre above the mantel, 'and with your old dog at your feet.' Here he bent and fondled Tito, who lay on his back looking up at him. 'If you want to keep all this, you may still have a chance. But only if you apologise immediately and withdraw what you've been saying and writing. Then I might be able to persuade Lord Brackley's lawyers to be merciful.'

Tomas thumped with the point of his stick on the floor. The dog rose from where he had been lying in front of the fire and came to him.

'I shall go to Court. I wish to go to Court. I tell you, young man, that I shall never withdraw and I shall never apologise. The Court will have to decide between George Brackley and myself and I have no doubt of the result.' There was silence in the room.

'Do you understand what that means?' said Simon.

'What does it mean?'

'It means that the case will go ahead and the probability is that you'll lose and you'll be ordered to pay a vast sum in damages and when you can't pay, Lord Brackley will strip you of every penny you possess.'

Tomas struck the floor again with his stick. 'I do not care what he does if the Court was so — ' he paused, searching for the word, 'so corrupt as to reject the truth. But I repeat, I shall never withdraw and I shall never apologise to George Brackley. What I have written is the truth. And the English Court will believe me.' His eyes were now sparkling and his face flushed as he stared at Simon.

'I know this country. I was at school here. My father and his father were at school here. I served in our embassy here. I shall die here. The English Court will believe that what I have written about George Brackley is the truth. I have come this far and nothing will stop me from having my say – in public.'

Simon had been standing, towering over the old man, looking down at him. 'All that I can do is to warn you of the consequences which will follow if, as you insist, you have your say – and if your say is to repeat what you have written.'

'The English, for all their crimes, are a fair people. They will see that justice is done.'

'The crimes of the English? Be careful, Colonel Tarnovic. That is a controversial subject; one to avoid in the presence of an English jury. One man's crimes can be another man's heroics.' Simon swung away abruptly and walked over to the shelf and picked up again the photograph of General Mihailović.

The old man said, almost to himself, 'Whatever you say, I shall never withdraw what I have written.'

Simon put the photograph back and said, 'Very well,

you refuse to withdraw, you refuse to apologise, you are determined to go to Court. So be it. Those are your definite instructions to your lawyers.'

'This is my battle,' said Tomas. 'I do not like lawyers. I shall do this alone.'

'You may not like lawyers. But just now you need them. Believe me, you need us badly.'

'I do not want lawyers. All I want is to have my say – and in public.'

'If that's what you are determined to do, your lawyers can't stop you. All they can do is to try to help. Without them you may never get what you are so anxious to have – which, as I understand it, is your say in public.'

Tomas looked at him, but Simon turned away. Then Tomas said quietly, 'I cannot afford lawyers. I have very little money.'

Simon turned back to face him. 'Even if you have little money, Colonel Tarnovic, you surely have some of the excellent plum brandy of your country. Will you offer some of that to the lawyers who have decided to represent you – whether you pay them or not?'

Tomas looked up at him. Simon brushed the lock back from his forehead. As though to match Simon's gesture, Tomas put up his hand and brushed his white moustache and smiled, a slow smile which seemed to light his whole face.

'Of course. I always have plum brandy. George Brackley has not got his hands upon that.'

'Not yet,' replied Simon and the old man smiled again.

When Tomas had shown them out, Simon turned to Alexandra and said, 'We must talk further. You must have dinner with me.'

'Must?'

'Please. We must talk. Let's go to my club in St James's Street. It will be quiet there and we can talk. I will show you where it is.'

90

In the dining-room, with the portraits of eighteenth-century English noblemen around them, they ordered their dinner and began to eat, at first in silence.

'You were right,' Simon said at last. 'He is remarkable. I think that in the end, after we had drunk and he understood that I'd been testing him, he accepted me at least as a champion. So you and he have persuaded me that although there's not a shred of evidence to support his monstrous accusations, they might be true.'

'Are you sorry that we have?'

'No, not after talking with him.' He pushed aside his plate. He was certainly not sorry. For now, he was thinking, he would be working with her. 'When I read the pamphlets and Brackley's book, I was sure that it was our duty as lawyers to persuade him to apologise and withdraw. That's what I have tried to do, but it's obvious that he is so passionate about it all that he won't. Like you, I find it very difficult to believe that he has invented the tale. So either it is true, or he is mad, or it's some extraordinary fantasy. He does not appear to be mad and if it's some fantasy, why would he have stayed silent during all these years? Unless it was Brackley's book which provoked him and he decided that he could not let what Brackley wrote pass unanswered.'

'He kept saying that he must have his say, his day in Court. But do you think that he understands what that involves?'

'I don't know, but if you hadn't come into his life, I believe that he would have tried to go to the Court alone.'

'Would he do better on his own?'

'No. A libel action is too complex and Brackley is too powerful. If Colonel Tarnovic wants his day in Court, he will need us to get him there.'

'How can we do that?'

'First we must lodge a defence on his behalf, a plea of Justification – which means that in answer to the claim, he says formally that what he has written about Brackley is true. That will stop them from applying for an injunction to silence him.'

91

'How can we do that?'

'I'll get Junior Counsel in my chambers, Perry Fanshaw, to draft the formal document. What you have to do is to take a proof from Tomas – that is, you must get Tomas to give you in writing, signed by him, a complete statement setting out his story and telling us who, if anyone, can support it. It must include where he has been and what he's been doing during all the past fifty years.' He saw the concern in her eyes. 'The defence of Justification is a complete answer to a claim for damages for libel. But as I told Tomas, the burden will be on him to prove the truth of his accusations.'

'How can he possibly afford the expense?'

He looked at her. 'I'm game – if you are.' He drank from his glass. 'And if you are game, then he has a solicitor, you; and Counsel, me. We can make a start by searching the historical records and try to find anyone still alive who was in the mountains in 1943 and who might know what happened.'

'The only friend whom I know he has is the painter, Felix.'

'Ask him to help.'

'Brackley has all the friends in the world. And all the money.'

'And we have neither. But, as I said, we've warned him. If later we can't come up with anything to support his story, I shall try again to persuade him to withdraw – in that way we might save something for him. But if I am any judge, Colonel Tomas Tarnovic will go to his grave before he does that.' She saw how serious he was as he went on: 'So you must get his statement and I get Perry to draft the defence. Then we must look at the wartime records in Kew of MO4 in Cairo and of SOE in the Balkans. We must try to find out who knew Brackley when he was in the Middle East in 1942 and in 1943 before he parachuted into Yugoslavia. We have to discover if there's anyone who might have been fighting with Tomas in the mountains.'

'It will take time, my time – which means the firm's time. Will John Arrun agree?'

He was looking at her intensely. 'I'll talk to John Arrun and try to persuade him to let you work on Tomas's case. As I said, I'm prepared to appear for him without a fee.' His eyes were still on hers.

'So I'm to begin with Tomas's signed statement.'

'Yes. Until we have it, we've really no right to enter a plea of Justification. Then Perry will settle the formal defence and you must persuade Felix to enquire around at that club to which Tomas used to go. He can also take you to Tomas's printer.' He was still looking at her intently. 'I repeat, are you game? Are you sure you are game?'

'Of course I am. I started it all.'

'Yes, you did.'

She watched the hand brush back the lock of hair.

'What do I call you?'

'Alexandra.'

'And I'm Simon. Together we'll begin the quest for the truth about Colonel Tomas Tarnovic and Lord Brackley and what really happened between them in the mountains fifty years ago.'

'You make it sound almost romantic.'

'It is. The more improbable the truth, the more romantic it is. Shall we drink to it?'

She raised her glass to his and when they had both drunk he stretched out his hand and took hers. She let it lie in his for a moment and then withdrew it, thinking all the time about the girl in the photograph.

NINE

George Brackley was unwell – he had taken a slight chill on his visit to London the week before and was confined to the house. But Roger Bentall needed to talk with his client and had decided that he must make a trip north. He had caught the ten o'clock morning train to York. Edwards, Brackley's chauffeur, would meet him and drive him to Brandsby. He would be back in London in the evening.

Bentall was not looking forward to the conference. When the second pamphlet had appeared, Lord Brackley had commented tartly that Bentall's opinion that they would hear no more of the matter after the issue of the writ had been, to say the very least, over-optimistic. Then yesterday evening there had been placed in Bentall's hands a letter announcing that in the case of *Brackley* v. *Tarnovic*, Messrs Arrun and Co. were entering an appearance to the writ on behalf of the Defendant and that the defence would be a plea of Justification.

The letter came as a bombshell. He had been so certain that the pamphlets were the work of a crank. It was not uncommon for people in public life to have insults circulated about them and the threat of an application to the Court for an Order to restrain a libel was usually sufficient to stop it. In the Brackley case, because of the prominence of the recipients of the pamphlets and the interest of the political Press, Roger Bentall had insisted that Lord Brackley issue a writ. They would then make a speedy application to the Court and Lord Brackley would hear no more. Bentall had been so categorical in his advice that when he read the letter from Arrun and Company announcing that

94

Lord Brackley's writ was going to be defended on the grounds that what Tarnovic had written about Lord Brackley was true, he was stunned. For some time he sat at his desk with the letter in his hand. If Tarnovic and his lawyers persisted in this defence, Lord Brackley would have to face a full-dress libel action amid a glare of publicity, an ordeal Bentall had so confidently advised would never happen. Now, not only was Lord Brackley's reputation at stake, so also was his own.

In the course of his legal career, Roger Bentall had made many enemies – people he had worsted in disputes or bruised by his abrasive personality. That he had miscalculated so badly with this important client would be received in some quarters with much satisfaction. It had been a hard road to the top, starting with scholarships to a grammar school in the Midlands and to a provincial university, followed by articles with a humdrum firm of solicitors in Birmingham. Then he had risked everything and emigrated to London, where he got employment in a smallish firm in the City. That had been the making of his success, for he had quickly built up a reputation as an extremely sharp and astute commercial lawyer. Success was crowned when he was recruited by the old and well-established firm of Baker and Turnbull to head their newly-created commercial department.

Within a few years, and despite the opposition of some of the older and more conventional partners, he had been elected Senior Partner. He had immediately removed his personal office away from the firm's traditional home in Lincoln's Inn Fields to new premises in Clifford Street in the West End of London. It symbolised the transformation he instituted in the character of the firm, with its new emphasis on corporate as opposed to personal clients. But Roger Bentall had been careful to cultivate and retain the most prominent of the firm's landed clientele. One of these was Lord Brackley who, impressed by the young lawyer, had introduced him into the organisational arm of the National Union in the political party in whose Cabinets Lord

95

Brackley had served with such distinction. It was not long before Roger Bentall had become an influential figure and was soon taken into the confidence of the party chieftains. For his part, Roger Bentall knew that while his professional work might earn him a fortune, his unpaid work with the National Union could bring the knighthood which he and his wife Pauline so greatly coveted.

That Lord Brackley might now face a full-scale libel action, which he had expressly warned his lawyer to avoid, was good reason for Roger Bentall's concern. As he read and reread the letter, he reflected on Arrun and Co., the modest firm now challenging the important firm of Baker and Turnbull and he grew increasingly angry. He told his secretary to get John Arrun on the telephone.

'Is that John Arrun? It is? I have in my hands a letter from you in the matter of Brackley and Tarnovic.'

'Yes.'

'Well, what the devil does this mean? What on earth are you doing being mixed up with this lunatic Tarnovic who has been writing this rubbish about Lord Brackley?'

When John Arrun had heard that Roger Bentall wanted to speak with him, he had been prepared to be a shade apologetic about the involvement of his firm for, despite assurances from Alexandra and Simon, he himself doubted not the propriety but the wisdom of accepting instructions on behalf of this elderly and eccentric foreigner. But he certainly was not prepared to accept the tirade which Bentall now loosed upon him.

'Tarnovic is either out of his mind or he is a crook who has set out to abuse a man who has served his country with gallantry and distinction. Now you are lending your name, which has hitherto been a respectable name, to assist a wicked campaign to destroy the reputation of a very fine Englishman.'

'One minute —' Arrun had begun, but Bentall had interrupted him.

'You write in your letter, which I have in my hand under the reference AL, whoever that may be —'

'Those are the initials of the assistant solicitor in my firm who has the conduct of this matter.'

'So I presumed. What he is announcing — '

'It happens to be a she.'

'He or she, I couldn't care less. What you're announcing is that your firm will be defending this case by pleading that what has been written about Lord Brackley is true. Do you really mean that?'

'That is what the letter was intended to make plain.'

'You know what that means? It means that you and your female associate, if you ever dare to bring your client to Court, have compounded the wickedness of the original libel and you'll face the risk of greatly increased damages.'

'I'm well aware of the consequence of the failure of a plea of Justification in the law of libel.'

'I consider it disgraceful that such a defence should ever have been lodged. I warn you that we shall strip your client of every penny he possesses. The damages will be astronomical.'

'Mr Bentall, you have no need to instruct me over the consequences which could follow the failure of such a defence — '

'And your firm will share in your client's infamy. You and your woman assistant ought to be ashamed of getting involved in such a despicable piece of litigation.'

The more angrily Bentall stormed, the icier became John Arrun.

'My firm has received explicit instructions to defend this claim and I'm making no apology for doing my professional duty.'

'Your professional duty! You should have refused to receive instructions rather than be mixed up with such a disgraceful defence. It is merely an exercise in muck-raking by a crook or a lunatic with a political grievance. He has no money to pay the damages when he loses, as of course he will, quite apart from the disgraceful pressure it will impose upon an elderly man with a fine reputation. You know very well that Lord Brackley will never get a penny back of the costs he will have to incur, nor of the vast damages which will be awarded to him when he wins.'

'I don't need to be instructed about my professional duty by you. I was taught as a young solicitor by your former Senior Partner, Sir Henry Baker, when I was articled to your firm many years before you joined it, that however high ran the feelings between the parties, it is the duty of professional advisers to remain polite.'

'It is not a professional duty to lend the name of a hitherto respectable firm to what amounts to a blackmailing defence. For that's what it is. Nothing more than sheer blackmail. I've no doubt that at the proper time the judge and the jury will come to understand that and I've equally no doubt that at the proper time they'll express their contempt not only for your client, but also for his advisers.'

'I repeat that as lawyers to the parties, we should confine our discussions to the procedures of the forthcoming trial. It is inappropriate for us to abuse each other and to comment on the merits of the case.'

'Merits! There is no merit in your client's case. It's nothing but naked blackmail. Well, I can promise you that we shall show no mercy and we shall enforce the Order for damages and costs which Lord Brackley will secure to the utmost limit. And your firm will be a party to your client's disgrace.'

'You are rude and arrogant. I have heard quite enough from you. Good-day.' And John Arrun had replaced the receiver. He lay back in his chair, seething. He had heard of Bentall's reputation, but had not dealt personally with him before. The exchange had outraged him.

He could not deny, however, experiencing a twinge of apprehension. For John Arrun still wondered to himself how rational was the Defendant, although Simon insisted that he had seen Colonel Tomas Tarnovic and was convinced that Tomas was genuine.

'Tomas Tarnovic, John, is determined to "have his day in Court", with or without the help of lawyers. At least we can get him into the courtroom and give him a chance when he gets there.'

Simon had gone on to say that because the old man had no resources and ought to be given a fair chance in his battle against so powerful an opponent he, Simon, was prepared to do the case for love and not for money. It was not long after that conversation that John Arrun understood the aptness of Simon Harrington's choice of those particular words.

So he had agreed to allow Alexandra to search for evidence to support Tomas's case on the understanding that if in the end no evidence could be found to support Tarnovic's case, Simon would 'read the Riot Act' and persuade Tomas to withdraw. Now Bentall's offensiveness on the telephone had dispelled John Arrun's reservations.

In the train rattling north, taking him to what must prove to be an uncomfortable conference with his influential client and political patron, Roger Bentall had his own share of unease. As soon as he had put the phone down after speaking to Arrun, he had begun to make his preparations. First he confirmed the retainer of Sir Leslie Turner QC, the doyen of the libel Bar, as Counsel for Lord Brackley. Next he tried to speak with Bagot Gray, who ran an international investigative business usually retained in takeover battles where one side or the other wished to obtain information about the source of funds of the predator or the standing of the predator's directors. Despite the expense, Bentall decided that he would employ Gray to mount an investigation into the background and past life of Tomas Tarnovic.

'Mr Gray,' he was informed, 'is in Tokyo. He'll not be back for a week.' Bentall arranged for Gray to call him on Gray's return to London.

But that was not all. The case of *Brackley* v. *Tarnovic* had now become for Roger Bentall a battle not only for Lord Brackley, but also for himself. Brackley's political enemies might wish to see Brackley humiliated; so also might Roger Bentall's enemies wish him humbled.

From his office, Bentall picked up the telephone and dialled the number in Ruislip given to him by Price.

On his way to the office at 8.30 on the morning he was due to travel to Yorkshire, Bentall instructed his chauffeur to stop the car on the bridge over the Serpentine in Hyde Park.

'I'll walk across the Park to the office. Pick me up at Clifford Street to take me to the station.'

The car had driven off and Roger Bentall began to walk east along the south side of the Serpentine, until he reached a bench half-way along the lake. There he sat and waited. But not for long; a figure emerged from the shrubbery at the end of the lake and joined him. Bentall handed Price an envelope and the two remained in conversation for several minutes. Then Bentall rose and continued his walk to his office, from which a little later he was driven to King's Cross station to catch the ten o'clock train to York.

It was after half-past twelve when Roger Bentall arrived at Brandsby. Brackley was in his study, seated in front of the fire, a rug over his knees.

'Thank you for coming, Bentall. I gathered that you wanted to talk and I wasn't up to coming to London. I haven't shaken off the cold I picked up on my last trip.'

'I was sorry to hear that you were not well.'

'It's nothing. But I was advised not to travel. I know that you'll want to get back to London today, so I've arranged an early luncheon. We can talk this afternoon and then if you leave here by 4.30, you can comfortably catch the 5.28. You'll be in London soon after eight.'

'That will suit me very well.'

'Have a glass of sherry.' Brackley put aside the rug and got to his feet. Taking his stick, he went across the room to the decanter and glasses, which stood on a silver tray on a small table by the window.

100

'I promise that the food today will be better than what I gave you at the Lords.' He poured two glasses of sherry. 'Grace is hunting, but you will see her before you have to leave.'

Bentall heard the door of the library open behind him. He half-turned, but saw only the door closing again. Someone had looked into the room and then withdrawn. Brackley had glanced up as he was pouring the wine, but said nothing. They drank their sherry.

'Let's go in to luncheon,' and leaning on his stick, Brackley led the way to the dining-room. The luncheon was served by the butler, who stood behind the host by the sideboard throughout the meal. What he had come to say, Bentall realised, would have to wait until they were alone again in the library. Brackley ate very little and they talked about the business of the party's National Union, the possibility of an election in the summer.

'In my opinion, the PM would do better to delay until next year and run the whole course of the Parliament. "You need the time," I told him the other day. But they pay little attention to the old ones nowadays.'

When they had finished their meal and before they rose from the table, Brackley said to the butler, 'We'll have coffee in the library, Painter.'

'Very well, my lord. Will the Admiral . . .' Brackley interrupted him before he could complete his enquiry.

'No. I don't wish to be disturbed.'

Over the coffee Roger Bentall explained to George Brackley that Tomas Tarnovic had instructed lawyers and intended to defend the claim by pleading Justification.

'What does that mean?'

'It means that the defence to your claim for damages will be that what Tarnovic has written about you was true. I know that is all nonsense, but the effect of it is that there's now no point in applying to the Court for an injunction to stop him from repeating the libel. Once a defendant has given notice that the defence will be a defence of Justification, the defence of truth, then the Court will never grant

101

an injunction. The issue has to be left to be decided by the jury at the trial.'

Brackley looked steadily at Bentall. 'You mean that now I shall have to give evidence and be cross-examined?'

'If it comes to a trial, yes.'

'When I first consulted you, I understood from you that there was no risk of any trial and that you would silence the man before it ever came to that.'

Bentall confessed that he had hoped to do this and that this defence of Justification was a very surprising development, which none could have anticipated.

'Why not? Was it not your duty to anticipate such an eventuality?'

'Everyone believed the fellow was a crank acting from a sense of imaginary grievance.'

'And he now appears to be a man with a purpose.'

'I still believe that he's a crank and, of course, he can have no chance in succeeding, for the burden of proof rests upon him to prove the truth of his story and not on you proving the truth of yours.'

'I should hope not. His story is a pack of lies. No, it is the fact of a trial which concerns me. I'm not a fit man. Grace does not know, and you must keep this to yourself, but the strain of a trial would be very damaging to my health. Indeed, such an ordeal could prove dangerous.'

'I'm sorry to hear that it is so serious. I did not know.'

'Now you do. I must tell you frankly, Bentall, that I am disappointed. I understood from you that there would never be a trial. That was the consideration which led me to agree to your advice that I should issue a writ. I would never have let you commence this action if I'd thought it would lead to a public trial.'

'But your reputation had been gravely impugned and people were starting to talk.'

'That was gossip, which I and my family would have treated with contempt.'

'If you'd done nothing, Lord Brackley, the Press would have followed it up. I'm quite sure of that.'

Brackley shook his head and the lawyer went on: 'But, in any event, I remain convinced that despite what they are now saying, the case will never come to a trial.'

'As convinced as you were when you gave your earlier advice?'

Bentall went on hurriedly: 'When the other side discover that they are unable to find any supporting evidence of the rubbish that Tarnovic wrote, they will settle out of Court.'

So the discussion continued. It was an uncomfortable afternoon for Roger Bentall and his resentment against Tarnovic and his lawyers grew as the meeting went on. At four o'clock tea was brought to them by the butler, and Grace Brackley, home from her day in the hunting field, joined them.

'We had two good runs but no kill,' she said.

At 4.45 Roger Bentall left in the Rolls for the station. Before Grace went up to change, she said, 'I don't like that man, George.'

When she had left the library, George Brackley was joined by his house guest.

'I didn't expect you to look into the room before luncheon, James. I warned you that I was having the lawyer.'

'I thought that you'd gone into the dining-room. He didn't see me.'

They both sat, one on either side of the fire.

'What did he want?'

'He came to tell me that, contrary to everything he had said earlier, Tomas Tarnovic intends to defend the action. There will now be a trial and I shall have to give evidence.'

'So now it is really beginning.'

'Yes. Originally the lawyer was emphatic that he would silence the fellow without a public trial. Now he says that if I had done nothing, the Press would have taken it up.'

'Would they have dared?'

'They might have started hinting, but it would have died away. What influenced me was that some in the party had got to hear of it and they expected me to act.'

'Do you think there could be anyone behind Tarnovic?'

103

'The lawyer thinks it possible.' George Brackley pulled the rug over his knees. 'We'll find out before it's over. If I survive.'

'Of course you will, George. You're a great survivor. You always have been.'

Brackley sighed. 'It is all so long ago. So very long ago,' he said wearily.

The two old men looked at each other. Brackley closed his eyes. Soon he was dozing, leaving Admiral Layton to his own memories, while George Brackley dreamt the dream of war, which now so insistently haunted him.

TEN

Leslie Turner pushed through the outer swing-door of the Garrick Club. He was feeling exceedingly pleased with himself.

'Your guest is waiting, Sir Leslie,' the hall-porter sang out as Turner passed.

'Thank you,' he replied and mounted the stone steps to the inner door to the hall. He was a short man with a rubicund face, thinning grey hair and a sharp, pointed nose. Standing at the foot of the staircase reading the early edition of the *Evening Standard*, he saw the vast, barrel-like figure of his guest.

'Jumbo,' he said. 'I'm sorry to have kept you. The jury was out for longer than I expected.'

'I've been reading the stop press. You must be very happy. Have you been celebrating at the Wig and Pen Club?'

'No, I came straight here from chambers. Come on up to the bar.'

They mounted the wide staircase, Leslie Turner slowing to keep pace with the labouring Jumbo Lancaster.

'I expected the jury to find for my client, but not give her that enormous sum of damages. Juries certainly have it in for you newspaper fellows.'

'The amount was obscene. But you know what I think about juries and libel damages. You're killing the Press.'

'Not me. I usually appear for the newspapers. But this was a bad libel. The paper was very, very stupid to rely on that unsatisfactory fellow who had written the story. As the case went on it became more and more plain that he'd invented most of it.'

'Maybe. But the damages were outrageous. Three hundred thousand for calling that creature a tart! Well, not quite a tart, but I suppose that's what his piece meant.'

'Exactly. That's what the words meant – a tart. And that's why the jury gave her the damages.'

'She probably is.'

'That's the trouble with you newspaper people. You base too many of your stories on "probably"! When you do and then can't prove the truth of what you publish, you're in trouble and you have to pay. Have a glass of champagne?'

'A bottle,' said Jumbo.

'One glass at a time. Sit over there.' Leslie pointed to one of the club-fenders. Jumbo gingerly lowered his bulk on to it and remained poised uncomfortably on the edge, fearing that at any moment it might collapse beneath him. Leslie Turner went to the bar. As he waited for the barman to pour the wine, he saw that Simon Harrington was standing beside him. Simon turned.

'That was a wicked result, Leslie.'

Nettled, Leslie said, 'The damages were more than I expected.'

'And far more than you deserved. They should have given your woman a fiver – at the most.'

Leslie Turner did not reply. The two used to get on well enough when Simon used to be briefed as Leslie's Junior Counsel. Leslie acknowledged Simon's ability, although he thought Simon altogether too sure of himself. Simon acknowledged Leslie's success with juries, but thought him pompous. When recently Simon had become a QC and the two had begun to be regular opponents, Leslie had liked Simon less, not because Simon was being talked about as a threat to his own dominance as the leading QC at the libel Bar, but because of Simon's ill temper.

So when Simon made this remark, Leslie made no reply and picked up the two glasses of wine and went over to Jumbo.

'Wasn't that Simon Harrington who was talking to you?'

106

'It was.'

'They say he's going places.'

'I expect he is,' said Leslie shortly and raised his glass to drink.

Jumbo said, 'Here's to your next success. But I hope that'll be when you are defending a newspaper, not screwing one.'

'I will drink to that. Newspapers pay better.'

'You hadn't much to say to Harrington. Don't you like him?'

'I do, but over the past two years he's become too aggressive, both in and out of Court.'

'Was he like that before the accident?'

'No, to be fair he wasn't. Have another glass of champagne?'

'Of course.'

Later they went down to the dining-room and sat at a small table beneath one of the windows facing the long table in the centre of the room. On the other side against the inner wall, Leslie Turner could see Simon Harrington, also at a table for two. His guest, Leslie noted with surprise, was the Master of Leslie's college at Cambridge, St Michael's.

'Do you think the Government will win the election?' Jumbo asked.

For a short time several years ago Leslie Turner had been Solicitor General in an earlier administration. Then he had lost his seat and gone back to the Bar and had not tried to return to the House. He was now, as Jumbo well knew, wholly out of politics and Jumbo had not sought this luncheon to canvass Leslie Turner's political opinions; Jumbo wanted something else. But he would come to that a little later. First he would flatter his host by deferring to Turner's experience.

Turner considered Jumbo's question. Then he replied gravely, 'More likely than not.'

'You might have been Lord Chancellor by now if you'd stayed in politics.'

107

Leslie Turner smiled, gratified. 'I don't think so. I was never close enough to the party chieftains.'

'Like George Brackley?'

'Yes. Like George Brackley. I was happy to get back to the Bar.'

Now was the time to come to the matter in which Jumbo was interested. 'Tell me,' he said. 'I have been hearing a story about old George Brackley. Am I right in thinking that you were in government with him?'

'You are. He was Secretary for Defence when I was Solicitor.'

'There's talk about his issuing a writ over an accusation about his conduct as a soldier in World War Two.'

Turner said nothing, crumbling the bread on his sideplate. Then he said, 'Well, it's on public record that the writ has been issued and served. Anyone can see it if they wish. So yes, George has issued a writ.'

'Whoever against and whatever for?'

'A crank who has been writing and circulating unpleasant rubbish about George when he was serving in the Balkans fifty years ago.'

'Fifty years ago! Why on earth has old George bothered to sue?'

'Well, the abuse was very widely circulated – to MPs, ministers, ex-ministers.'

'But that often happens to people in politics. Why didn't he just ignore it?'

'It was so offensive that he was advised that the writer ought to be silenced.'

'By you?'

'No, by his solicitors. That was before I came into it.'

'And will the writer be silenced?'

'I am sure he will.'

'So in the end it'll come to nothing?'

'That's what we hope and expect. But for the moment the crank is sticking to his guns, insisting that the nonsense he wrote about George is true. But that will change. He'll pack it in before the case ever comes to trial. If he doesn't, the damages will be enormous. They'll make what my young woman got this morning look like pocket-money.'

'If the crank doesn't chuck in his hand and does take the case to trial, then old George Brackley will have to give evidence. How'll he like that?'

Turner looked sharply at Jumbo. 'You mean because he's been ill?'

Jumbo had not meant that. 'No, I mean that George is still quite an influence in the party and an election is coming up this year or next. It won't be very pleasant if he has to stand up in Court while some nasty member of your fraternity tries to prove he's a liar – and a fraud.'

Leslie Turner shook his head. 'I hope it won't come to that. If it does, George is such a splendid fellow that the jury will have no difficulty. It's all a farrago of nonsense.'

But there will be an election next year, mused Jumbo, and if there's a libel case that, too, will be next year. To have old George embarrassed will not do my friends any harm. Mud sticks, as Jumbo who in his time had thrown plenty, knew only too well.

But he said no more. So the case was still alive. He had learnt what he wanted and he changed the subject.

Across the room, Simon was lunching with Malcolm Poynter. The Master of St Michael's was a man in his early sixties, a first cousin of Simon's father, who had died when Simon was a boy. Malcolm had supervised his cousin's education and got Simon his first start at the Bar. He had white hair and a slight, rather lopsided face, which gave him the appearance of being continuously amused – and for much of the time, he was. He spoke from the corner of his mouth, slowly, as though he was picking his words with care – which he also often was.

'Why are you so interested in that seedy pre-War generation at Cambridge?' asked Poynter.

109

'A friend of mine needs to do some research.'

'For a book?'

'No. Straightforward enquiries.'

'Are any enquiries ever straightforward? God knows but there have been enough into those people. I can't think that there's room for more. What they then believed in so passionately and worked for so treacherously has been rejected as bogus even by their own spy-masters. If there are any who do know more, they must now be very old men.'

'I know. But is there anyone alive who was up in those days whom you know?'

'Sixty years ago? Not many.'

'Any?'

'The only one I can think of is Gervase Gregson, one of our old Fellows. But he is now a recluse and very odd. He is not, and never was, what you might call a very engaging person.'

'Where is he now?'

'He lives in Grantchester in a secluded old house with a housekeeper who is almost as weird as he is. He never appears in the town or in the College and he doesn't welcome visitors. As Master, I feel that I have to keep in touch with him. From time to time he sends me messages, invitations to tea sent by postcard to the Master's Lodge because he won't have a telephone. I'm the only one from the University whom he still contacts.'

'What does he talk about when you visit?'

'The old days. It's always the same, stories about former dons and undergraduates and the golden days in the summers of his youth – mostly spent, as far as I can gather, on punts on the Cam playing jazz on a portable clockwork gramophone.'

'Any girls?'

'Certainly not.'

'That fits.'

Poynter looked at Simon, his mouth slipping even further to the side. 'You sound interested.'

'I am. I'd like to talk to Gregson. Could you arrange it?'

'What do you want from him?'

'I want to identify the friends, if you like the circle of a particular man. It concerns some very important litigation in which I'm involved. My client is old and has no money and he's up against some very powerful people. He has written an extraordinary story about a well-known man who is now suing him.'

'So it is a libel case?'

'Yes. The other side has money and power and influence; our client is poor, unknown and a foreigner. All the cards are stacked against him. There could be a Cambridge factor – some connection with pre-War Cambridge.'

'And you think Gervase Gregson might know something which could help you?'

'From what you've told me it sounds as if he might.'

'Gregson is not a very pleasant fellow, but I wouldn't wish to involve an old man unless you promise that it is essential.'

'I promise you it is. I want to discover something about a man's background. I'm not looking for a witness – only for clues. Gregson might be able to show that what our client is saying has a basis of truth.'

Poynter turned the glass in his hand. Finally he said, 'I can make no promises, but I'll see if I can arrange it. As I told you, Gervase Gregson won't usually meet strangers, but I'll try him out. You may have to come to Cambridge at short notice.'

'Of course.'

When Simon went to the desk to pay his bill for lunch, Leslie Turner came up behind him.

'I was rather short when you spoke to me when we were getting drinks at the bar, Simon,' he said pleasantly. 'I was still pretty bewildered by that enormous award of damages which we got this morning.'

'So you should be,' said Simon. 'It was infamous. I'm glad I wasn't responsible for it. You're getting the law a bad name, Leslie.'

111

He walked out of the dining-room and followed Malcolm Poynter into the hall.

Bloody young man, thought Turner.

That evening Alexandra picked up Felix from the studio and drove him to the club in Kensington. He led her through the empty hall to the bar, where the solitary barman was reading a newspaper. He looked up when Felix said, 'Good evening, Starjevic. I'm meeting the Chairman, Mr Misic.'

'I'll go and tell him you're here.' Starjevic disappeared.

Alexandra looked round the sad, empty room while Felix went behind the bar. 'Would you like a drink? Plum brandy, the house special?'

She shook her head and sat at one of the small tables. Felix poured himself a glass and came over to join her. They sat waiting in silence. The barman returned. He saw the glass in front of Felix. 'Have you paid?'

'No,' said Felix. 'Isn't it on the house?'

'Not in here,' said the barman. 'It will be when you're with the Chairman. He always has plenty in there. At the club's expense.'

Felix put a ten-pound note on the table. 'Keep the change.'

The man looked at Felix. 'He's expecting you. Down the passage. It's the room facing you.'

'Casting bread upon the water,' said Felix as they walked down the corridor.

Milan Misic rose from behind his desk. At the sight of Alexandra a delighted smile broke over his face and she noticed his gold teeth.

'Please come in and be seated.'

He came round his desk moving more swiftly and gracefully than she had expected from so heavy a man. He drew up a chair for her.

'Felix said he was bringing a friend to talk about the club. He did not tell me that he was bringing so beautiful a friend.'

112

Alexandra caught again the flash of gold. Milan Misic went back to his chair behind his desk.

'I've come to ask about Tomas Tarnovic,' she said.

A curtain seemed to drop over Milan Misic's face. The smile vanished; a wary look came into the dark eyes.

'He is, I believe, a member of your club?'

'Yes,' he said slowly. 'Tomas Tarnovic is a member.'

'I understand he comes here regularly, each Saturday night?'

Misic's eyes never left Alexandra's face, but he was no longer looking at her with admiration. He passed his tongue swiftly over his lips. 'Oh, yes. He's one of the few who still use the premises.'

'I'm a lawyer, a solicitor, and I act for Tomas Tarnovic, who has become involved in litigation. I need to learn a little about his past history — '

Misic interrupted her, shifting his ungainly body in his chair. 'A lawyer?'

'Yes. Mr Tarnovic's lawyer, and I want some information.'

Misic interrupted her again. 'Information?'

'Just about you and him and your families during or just after World War Two.'

'That is all before my time, madame,' Misic said uneasily. 'You should ask Tomas Tarnovic. He is the person to answer. I cannot help you.'

'I'm sure you can, even if it's only to tell me anything you might have been told about him. I understand that before World War Two, he was quite a prominent figure in Belgrade.'

'He may have been. I do not know. I do not know him well. Tomas Tarnovic has not been long in this country, which is now my home. He's only known to the old ones who come to the club.'

Felix interrupted him. 'Milan, stop pretending. Your father served with Tomas in the old days before the war, when Tomas was at the palace in Belgrade. You and your family know all about him.'

113

Misic looked angrily at Felix. 'I know nothing of the kind. My father may have known him —'

'Of course your father knew him, as did mine. At the start of the War, your father was Tomas's adjutant in Belgrade. All your family knew Tomas.'

Misic struck the table with the flat of his hand. 'That may have been so. But Tarnovic is not a friend of mine. He's a trouble-maker, as I told the others.'

Alexandra said quickly, 'What others?' There was a silence. Alexandra repeated, 'What others? And what did you tell the others?'

Misic pulled out a handkerchief and mopped his face. 'The others who came here asking about Tomas.'

'When was this?'

'Three days ago, the day before yesterday, I cannot remember.'

'What did they want?'

'What you want. Information about Tomas. Questions, nothing but questions about that old man. Madame, I do not like this. I do not know what it's all about and I don't wish to be mixed up in it. I am a guest in this country. I am not a citizen. They warned me —'

'Warned you?' said Felix. 'Who warned you and what against?'

'What do you think? As I said, I'm a guest in this country.'

Alexandra said, 'You mean that they threatened you? To hurt you, to harm you?'

'They talked about permits to live here and residence in this country and they warned me that very powerful people were interested in the Tarnovic matter. Listen, madame, I'm sorry, but I can't help you. I know nothing. I know nothing.'

He stood up. Alexandra remained seated looking up at him. 'Mr Misic,' she said quietly, 'I promise that no one will do you any harm and no one will take away your permission to reside in this country as a result of your talking to me.'

'You tell me that, but the others did not. They hinted at what could happen. I have a family.'

114

'Nothing can happen to you or your family. Those other people were lying. They were trying to frighten you. All I'm asking for is information. There can be no harm in giving me that.'

Misic turned away and walked to the wall behind his desk. Then he turned again and came back, leaning over the desk, his arms stretched out with his hands forming two huge fists.

'I have nothing to tell you. I have nothing to say and I wish you to leave my office.'

'Mr Misic,' Alexandra began again. 'Mr Misic, I assure you that nothing can happen to you. All that I want to know is if you can help me by telling me about Tomas's past.'

Misic struck the desk, this time with his fist. 'No, no, no! I have nothing to say to you. I know nothing about this matter. I know nothing about Tomas Tarnovic. I refuse to get involved in this quarrel. Please, madame, leave my office. I have nothing more to say to you.'

Alexandra stared back at him. Slowly she rose to her feet.

Felix said, 'Your father would be ashamed of you, Milan.'

Misic turned on him. 'My father! My father is dead. He does not need permits. I want nothing to do with this Tarnovic business. Please leave.'

Alexandra said, 'I'm sorry. I came for some information and all that you have done is shout at me.'

'I am sorry, madame. I am truly sorry.'

'So you should be,' said Felix. 'You are contemptible.'

When they left, Misic sat again at his desk, his head between his hands.

In the corridor they met the barman. 'More shouting,' he said. 'Just like the other night.'

'Was that when the others came to talk to Milan?'

'Yes.'

'Starjevic,' Felix asked, 'what were the others like? Can you describe them?'

'There were two of them. One was tall and thin, with a scrubby moustache and,' Starjevic pointed at his throat, 'a prominent Adam's apple. The other was heavily built, black curly hair.'

Felix gave him another ten-pound note. 'Let me know if they come back. And tell me anything you may hear.'

When they were outside, Felix said, 'They have scared Misic all right.'

Alexandra began to run to the car. 'We must get to the printer – and quickly,' she said.

In Lees Road in Lambeth, the woman with the white hair pulled back tight across her head opened the door to them.

'I telephoned,' said Felix.

The woman stood aside and they entered the hall. 'Follow me,' she said and led them down the dark corridor. She opened a side door and stood as they went before her into a small parlour. 'Please be seated.' As they sat beside each other on a small sofa, she closed the door behind them and sat herself in a chair facing them, her hands folded in her lap.

'I hoped to see Kosta or Alexei,' began Felix.

'My son, Kosta,' said the woman, 'is out. My husband Alexei is dying.'

'I'm so sorry,' said Alexandra. 'I did not know.'

The woman turned her grey eyes from Felix and looked at Alexandra. 'Why should you?'

'I heard that he was ill, but I didn't know that it was so serious,' said Felix.

Alexandra said, 'We'll not keep you long. I'm sorry to have disturbed you at such a time.'

'I know why you are here. You have come about Tomas Tarnovic. Kosta told me that you would. Tomas Tarnovic is in trouble, as my husband warned him that he would be.'

'Yes,' said Alexandra. 'We have come about Tomas and he is in trouble.'

'It is not only Tomas Tarnovic who is in trouble because of his foolishness. It is also my son.'

'Your son?'

116

'Tomas Tarnovic persuaded my son Kosta to print for him the pamphlets which Tomas wrote. Now they have warned my son that he is in danger of being taken to Court and of losing everything.'

'They? Who are they?'

'The people who came here to see him.'

'Two men?'

'Yes.'

'When was this?'

'Yesterday. They warned him that unless he apologises and promises to have nothing more to do with Tomas Tarnovic, they will see that a claim is brought against him as the printer of Tomas Tarnovic's libels. They said that they could strip my son of everything that he possesses.'

The woman's grey eyes never left Alexandra's face. 'This house belongs to my son. My husband is dying. My son is our sole support. He does not wish to talk with you or with anybody about Tomas Tarnovic.' She rose to her feet. 'If you have any sense, madame,' she said to Alexandra, 'you will not trouble yourself over Tomas Tarnovic. He is not worth it. Wherever he goes, he brings trouble. As he always has; as he always does.'

She went to the door and opened it. She stood with her hand on the doorknob, looking at them. Alexandra rose. 'I'm sorry.'

She and Felix walked to the front door. Alexandra waited for the woman to open it. 'If ever — ' Alexandra began.

'No,' said the woman. 'Never.'

ELEVEN

They drove in silence, crossing the river at Chelsea Bridge.

'You can't blame her,' said Felix at last.

'No. But I must telephone Simon Harrington and tell him what is happening.'

'Is he the barrister?' asked Felix.

'Yes.'

She stopped to telephone from the Royal Court Hotel in Sloane Square. While Felix waited in the car, Alexandra spoke to Harrington's chambers and the girl clerk said that Mr Harrington had left, but he might be at his flat. The clerk gave her the number. When she had dialled, she heard the ringing and waited. At last Simon answered. 'Who is it?' he said brusquely.

'Alexandra Layton. Can I come to see you about Tomas Tarnovic? It's important.'

'Of course.' The voice had softened. 'Where are you?'

'In Sloane Square.' He gave her his address. She said, 'I have Felix with me.' There was a pause.

'Bring him with you.'

She had difficulty in finding a place to park and it was some time before they walked up the stairs from the street to the smart outer door of the house in Onslow Square. Over the entry-phone Simon told them to come to the flat on the first floor. He was waiting for them, dressed in an open-necked blue-striped shirt and fawn canvas trousers. On his bare feet were a pair of leather slippers. He looks younger, she thought.

'I'm sorry to bother you at home, but I thought you should know what is happening. This is Felix.'

Simon looked at Felix and then put out his hand. He turned away, calling over his shoulder, 'Close the door behind you, Felix.'

He took Alexandra's coat and laid it on a chair before leading them across the hall and into the drawing-room. 'Will you have a drink? Whisky, vodka, wine?'

'Vodka,' said Felix. 'On the rocks.'

'And you?'

'A glass of wine.'

Simon left to get the drinks. Alexandra looked around the room, at the tables piled with books and legal briefs bound by their pink tape. Some loose papers were scattered on the floor around an armchair where he had been working. She walked over to the piano in the corner of the room and looked at the photograph in its silver frame. Felix was studying the pictures on the walls. 'Interesting,' he said. 'Very interesting.'

When Simon handed her the glass of wine, Alexandra said, 'We had great difficulty parking. Is it always so bad here at this time of the evening?'

'My guests tell me so. I haven't a car. Do sit down.' He sat in his armchair, bending down and gathering together the papers scattered around his feet. He had not taken a drink for himself.

Alexandra and Felix told him what had been said by Misic and Mrs Djuric, Simon listening in silence. When they had finished he said, 'They are taking us very seriously.' Then, to Felix: 'You are our only link with the community. Will you make further enquiries for us?'

'If you wish. And if it will help to get the old fool out of trouble.'

'From what you've just told me, it looks as if the other side have got to the people first. But we must keep trying.'

Felix told them more about the club and the Orthodox Church in Kensington. When he had finished his drink, he looked at Alexandra, then at Simon. 'I must go,' he said standing up.

Alexandra rose. Simon said to her, 'Can you stay a little?

I want to show you the defence which has been drafted by Perry Fanshaw.' Then to Felix: 'This is technical, legal business,' and he got up and went to the door. He watched as Felix kissed Alexandra on both cheeks.

'Will you be coming to the studio tomorrow?' Felix asked.

'I'll telephone. I may have too much work.'

Simon led Felix across the hall. 'Thank you for your help. We're up against it, as you can see. The other side could get ugly if they think we are uncovering anything. How can I get hold of you?'

'Alexandra knows.' Felix walked down the corridor to the staircase.

In the drawing-room Simon handed Alexandra the document Perry had drafted. 'See what you think of it.' He took her glass and returned with it filled. 'If you approve, you must serve it on Baker and Turnbull without fail on Monday.' He turned to leave the room again. 'I won't be a moment.'

Alexandra read through the formal plea of the Defendant Tomas Tarnovic, in answer to Lord Brackley's claim, that what he had written about Lord Brackley was true. When she had finished, she laid it down in her lap. Now they were all committed.

Simon reappeared. He had put on a jacket and walking shoes and socks and had her coat over his arm. 'Will you come and dine? We ought to talk more about these developments.'

They walked to an Italian restaurant in the Brompton Road, a pretty place, decked with hanging baskets of flowers; a substantial tree appeared to be growing from the centre of the room. When they were shown to a table and Simon set about the business of summoning the waiter and ordering, she noticed that he was far less self-assured than he had been when she had dined with him at his club. This, she could see, was not his home ground. Amused, she watched his ineffectual signalling to the waiter.

'Do you come here often?'

120

'No. I don't go out much.'

'Where do you usually eat?'

'In my club. Or at home.'

'Are you a good cook?'

'I am certainly not. Where do you live?' he asked.

'Quite near to you. I have a flat, not as large as yours, in Drayton Gardens.'

'And a family home in the country?'

'My father lives in Wiltshire. I see him mainly when he comes to London. He is a retired admiral.'

'And your mother?'

'She died when I was a child. My father remarried.'

The waiter brought their food and when they had begun to eat, Simon said, 'After what you told me this evening about the threats to Misic at the club and the reaction of the printer's mother, I'm anxious about you.'

'Why?'

'If what Tomas has written is the truth, certain people might be prepared to go to considerable lengths to prevent him from proving it. Before we ever get to Court we could have a pretty rough fight on our hands.'

'But what could they do?'

'You've had some experience this evening. They will try and build a wall of silence to keep us from the truth, using threats or bribes. Witnesses, if we ever find any, might take long and expensive vacations in far away places. They could be employing some pretty ugly people.'

'Are you still so sure that what Tomas says is the truth?'

'I'm becoming more certain because of what seems to be happening. But please, I don't want you involved in going round asking questions. Promise me that you will let Felix do the leg-work in searching for witnesses.' She was pleased that he should be concerned. 'You concentrate on the war records. There must be plenty at the Public Record Office at Kew about the British decision to support the Communist Tito and to ditch Tomas's friend, General Mihailović. We must make a thorough search through the signals which

121

passed between London and Cairo during the period when Brackley was in the Middle East.'

'It will be an enormous task.'

'Perry Fanshaw can help. He's very willing. He knows there is no money in it, but it'll be good for him to be in an important libel action.' He turned to get the attention of a waiter. At last he managed to order coffee.

What can he do with himself besides playing the piano if he goes out so rarely, she thought. 'You work too hard.'

'It's all I have to do.' He spoke very quietly, almost to himself. She felt the loneliness, almost the desolation about the private him – which the public him tried to disguise beneath the air of authority.

For a moment she thought he was going to say more, but he called for the bill. They walked back to her car. She took out her car key and turned to thank him.

'No,' he said. 'I'll come in the car with you to see you safely home and then walk back. The exercise will do me good.'

She unlocked the car. 'It is not necessary,' she said.

He did not say a word during the short drive. At her front door, when he saw that her key was in the lock, he held out his hand. 'Good-night. Let me know if you get anything from the records at Kew and leave the Serbs to Felix.'

She took his hand and then leaned forward and kissed him lightly on the cheek. 'I will. Thank you for dinner.' She smiled at the surprise on his face. He was still standing there as she closed the door.

In her flat, she flung off her coat and then went into the bedroom and sat at her dressing-table. She loosened her hair, which fell to her shoulders, rested her hand on her chin and stared at herself in the glass, thinking of him. This is absurd, she thought. I am falling in love with a man I hardly know. Then she got up and began to undress.

As she opened the cupboard to hang up her dress, she saw that the hangers were all neatly aligned with no gap between them. She had been in a hurry when she had changed before she had left to fetch Felix and she had slid the hangers aside until she had found the dress which she was now holding in her hand. She stood for a moment, wondering if she was mistaken.

She opened one of the drawers at the side of the hanging cupboard. They held her underclothes and appeared to be as she had left them. She went back to the dressing-table and studied the brushes and jars and the few pieces of jewellery. Nothing had been disturbed. She was imagining and she hung the dress in the wardrobe and put on a dressing gown.

She went to her desk where she had laid the file which contained Tomas's statement before she had gone out earlier in the evening. She had brought it from the office and had planned to work on it when she had got home, but it was now too late. She would put it in her briefcase to take with her in the morning. As she picked it up, a loose page fell to the floor and she opened the file to replace it. The file seemed disarranged, as if someone had leafed through it. She felt a moment of panic and began to look around the room. There was only the bedroom, the sitting-room, the kitchen and the bathroom. Slowly she walked to the small kitchen and switched on the light. There was no one and she went back through the bedroom into the bathroom. They too were empty. She ran to the front door, making sure that it was double-locked and bolted. Then she looked at each of the windows; there was no sign that any had been forced. Had Simon's words about the case getting ugly made her imagine that someone had been in the flat?

She walked around the rooms, trying to remember if everything was as she had left it. In any case, how could anyone have got in? There was no sign of any forcible entry. If anyone had, it could only have been by using a key and the only other key was held by the cleaning-lady, Mrs Lake, who lived across the river in Battersea and who came when Alexandra was at the office on Monday and Thursday. Mrs

123

Lake had not been today, Friday, and she would not come again until Monday.

Alexandra decided to telephone Simon. It would be comforting to hear his voice. But then as she stood with the receiver in her hand, she thought that he might think her silly, so she replaced it and walked into the kitchen to turn on the electric kettle to make a hot drink. I'm overtired, she thought. She sat waiting for the kettle to boil and thought about Simon. She would have liked to have heard his voice. That was the authoritative part of him, the part he presented to the world. And the inner person? That, she thought, was different – lonely and vulnerable.

She took her mug of jasmine tea into the bedroom. It was absurd to have become so interested in a man with whom she had only spent two evenings. And who was the woman in the photographs? She must ask around. Someone surely would know about him.

She undressed and got into bed. As she lay in the dark waiting for sleep, the feeling that someone had been in her room returned, but she soon drove it from her mind by thinking of Simon. Even if he were married, she did not care. Then she slept.

But she had been right. Someone had been into her flat that evening, as they had on two other occasions: as now they could whenever she was out, whenever they wanted. For on the Monday of that week, Mrs Lake had been hoovering when she had heard the bell of the front door leading to the street.

There were four flats in the house and in each a buzzer which opened the main front door. Alexandra's was on the second floor; there was no caretaker and the basement housed only the boiler which provided central heating for the common front hall and the staircase.

Mrs Lake picked up the entry-phone receiver, which hung on the wall just inside the front door. 'Yes? Who is it?'

'Is that apartment number two?' It was a man's voice, a comfortable, reassuring voice.

'It is.'

'Miss Layton's apartment?'

'Yes.'

Outside the front door the man put his handkerchief discreetly in front of his mouth. 'Can you hear me all right?'

'Not very well.'

'Yes, that's the trouble. My name is Trench and I'm from the landlords, Brompton Developments of Pelham Crescent. There've been complaints about the working of the entry-phone and the automatic door. Would you mind testing it with me?'

'All right.'

'Will you replace the receiver and I'll call again. I have to test the intercom.'

Mrs Lake replaced the receiver and waited. The buzzer rang again but jerkily and when the man spoke his voice was faint.

'Something's wrong, but I don't think it's serious. Perhaps a minor electrical fault. Would you mind pressing your buzzer and letting me in? I'd better check your entry-phone.'

Mrs Lake did so and opening the front door of the flat, stood on the landing waiting for Mr Trench. When he appeared up the stairs, she saw a large, comfortable-looking man with dark curly hair, neatly dressed in a suit. He was accompanied by a tall man with sandy-coloured hair, a scrubby moustache and a prominent Adam's apple. He wore dark-blue overalls.

'Thank you for helping. Any fault affects the whole system and is a great nuisance for the tenants. This is my card.'

He handed Mrs Lake a business card. She took it, but she was not wearing her glasses and could read nothing. If she had, she would have seen that it was neatly printed with the name Mr E. Trench of Brompton Developments. She handed it back to him. He looked very respectable.

125

'Can my electrician take a quick look at your entry-phone?'

Mrs Lake led them into the flat and the electrician went over to where the receiver was hanging on the wall.

'While he's doing that, may I check your keys to make sure that they aren't bent or damaged, as that could be causing the trouble.'

Mrs Lake took her keys, which she had left on the small table in the hall, and handed them to the man in the suit, who walked to the window to examine them. Mrs Lake watched him. Then the electrician called to her, 'Come over here, love, and hold the receiver while I unscrew the plate.' Mrs Lake joined him.

At the window the burly man, with his back to her, took the impression of both sides of the two keys on the pads in the small flat box which he had in his pocket. 'The keys are all right.' He walked back into the hall and put Mrs Lake's keys back on the table.

'I've found the trouble,' said the electrician. 'There was a loose connection.' He screwed up the plate. 'It should be all right now. Thank you, love,' he said taking the receiver from Mrs Lake and replacing it.

'Are you sure?' asked the man in the suit.

'Quite sure. But we'd better test it on our way out.'

'I'm sorry to have troubled you,' said Mr Trench, 'but it's a nuisance when these gadgets don't work properly. I will buzz you from down below to check that it is now all right.'

They went out, shutting the door behind them. They could only have been in the flat for two minutes. A moment later the front-door bell rang.

'Is that all right now?' The handkerchief of the man in the suit was back in his pocket and Mrs Lake could hear him perfectly. That had been on the Monday.

On their visit the next day they were longer than on their first. They had watched Alexandra drive away and using the keys they had made from the impressions, they entered the empty flat. They put a device in the telephone junction-box,

126

which served both extensions in the sitting-room and beside the bed. They placed another device behind the top edge of the high wardrobe in which Alexandra hung her dresses. Then they went down to the basement. In a corner behind some scraps of wood and two bricks they placed the small tape recorder. From then on anything said on the telephone or in the room would be recorded on tape.

They had returned for a third visit on the Friday, in the evening after Alexandra had gone out with Felix to interview Milan Misic and the printer. They removed the tape from the recorder in the basement and replaced it with a fresh one, but the positioning of the microphone on the top of the wardrobe had not been giving a clear recording. They moved the device from the top of the wardrobe and opened the door thinking to put it inside. In doing so they had moved the hangers, but they had finally settled for a position under the rim of a small table, fixing the device with adhesive.

The man in the suit, Ned Waring, saw the file with Tomas's statement on the desk. He photographed it with his miniature camera, sheet by sheet. Then they left and drove away.

'We are earning our oats all right,' said Waring.

They parted in Ruislip and Les Price went home to Annie.

TWELVE

In Roger Bentall's office at Baker and Turnbull in Clifford Street, Bagot Gray was sitting on the sofa on the far side of the room. He was a tall man, in his late forties wearing a light-grey suit, almost tropical in weight and style, with a blue tie and, at the end of his long legs, matching blue socks above highly polished black brogue shoes. He was smoking a Montecristo cigar. Everything about him was and looked expensive.

When Gray had worked with Bentall previously, he had been impressed by Roger Bentall's energy and shrewdness, but he had not liked him. So when he was informed that Mr Bentall of Baker and Turnbull wished to discuss with him the matter of Lord Brackley's action for damages for libel, Gray had hesitated. It was the business of Bagot Gray, as it was the business of Jumbo Lancaster, to know about such matters as the Brackley Affair – which was what it was now being called in Westminster and the City – and since he knew Grace Brackley, he called her and told her of the approach from Bentall.

'Please do what he asks. I'd be much happier if you were involved,' she entreated him over the telephone. 'I don't like that man and I'd be much comforted if I thought that you might be keeping an eye on him.'

As a result, Gray was sitting in Bentall's office – eyeing Roger Bentall.

'What I want is an investigation into the background and activities of Tomas Tarnovic during every one of the past fifty years.'

'That's a tall order,' said Gray. 'And it won't be cheap.'

128

'Lord Brackley and his wife are rich enough. He and I, you know, do much work together on matters connected with the party.' Gray knew this.

Bentall rose from his chair and walked over to the window. With one hand on the curtain, he leaned against the wall and looked down at Clifford Street.

'There are those who would not be unhappy should his reputation come under fire. I should also tell you, in confidence, that this case is important to me not only in respect of Lord Brackley's reputation, but also of mine.' As Gray said nothing Bentall went on: 'When this matter first arose, I gave Lord Brackley very explicit advice. I told him to sue, to issue a writ immediately. I was convinced that this man was a crank and could be easily silenced. If I had not given that advice, Lord Brackley might have ignored the whole affair.'

Bentall returned to his desk. 'Now the man has found himself lawyers and says that he'll prove that what he wrote was true.'

Gray blew a circle of smoke above his head.

'Lord Brackley is old and unwell. If this is allowed to go on, he will have to go to Court, give evidence and be cross-examined.'

'Why should you be concerned?' said Gray at last. 'Lord Brackley will be awarded enormous damages. Do you really need to go to the trouble and expense of hiring my people?'

Bentall shuffled some of the papers on his desk. 'As I've indicated, expense is the least of my worries. No, I am responsible for advising Lord Brackley to issue the writ and I assured him that the case would never come to Court. Now there has arisen this recent development – Tarnovic getting himself lawyers and claiming that what he wrote about Lord Brackley is true.'

'You did not expect that?'

'I did not. But I intend to make sure that this case will never come to a trial.'

'How will you do that?'

'By seeing that his lawyers clearly understand that Tarnovic has no chance of succeeding.'

'Who are his lawyers?'

'An insignificant firm of solicitors; but they have instructed Simon Harrington as their leading Counsel.'

'I know him well.'

'Harrington is formidable, a new silk and ambitious. A sensational libel trial featuring an ex-Cabinet Minister would suit him at this stage of his career. But he's clever and when he sees that there is no evidence to corroborate Tarnovic and that the case is hopeless, he will not make a fool of himself in Court. He'll force his client to withdraw.'

'Why will an investigation into the life of the Defendant help?'

'Because I suspect that there's something odd about the man and that there may be somebody behind him. There are people who would want to damage Brackley – and the party.'

'You really think that is possible?'

'I do. That's why I want to discover all about Tomas Tarnovic, where he has come from and what he has been doing in every one of the past fifty years.' Bentall looked at his watch. 'We must go. It takes time to get to the Temple in the afternoon. I told Leslie Turner that I was bringing you. He is a pernickety fellow, but he is the best.'

He picked up the telephone. 'Is the car ready? And make a note that I have an appointment at the Hyde Park Hotel tomorrow at lunchtime. I shall be about an hour in the Temple.' To Gray he said, 'The car is waiting.'

In his chambers in Brick Court in the Temple, Sir Leslie Turner studied the document which Roger Bentall had just handed to him. It was the formal defence of Tomas Tarnovic in the case of *Brackley* v. *Tarnovic* signed by the junior barrister who had drafted it. While he was reading, Bagot Gray looked round the musty, shabby room – at the heavy bookshelves, the few dreary prints on the walls and the old, unpolished furniture. The man must be earning hundreds of thousands of pounds, he thought, and yet is content to work in these Dickensian surroundings.

'Sir Leslie,' he said, taking his cigar-case from his pocket, 'would you mind if I smoked?'

Leslie Turner looked up from his reading and peered at Gray over his half-moon glasses. He had no idea why Bentall had insisted on bringing this man, but his clerk had told him that Bentall would explain. 'I would rather that you did not,' he said and resumed reading. Bagot Gray put away his cigar-case.

'I note that this pleading is signed by –' Turner examined again the document, 'by someone called Peregrine Fanshaw. I have never heard of him.'

'Neither had I,' said Bentall.

Leslie Turner pressed a bell beside his desk. His clerk came into the room. 'Robinson, look up in the *Law List* and find out in whose chambers a Mr –' he looked again at the pleading, 'a Mr Peregrine Fanshaw practises.'

'Very well, Sir Leslie.' The clerk withdrew.

I could tell him, thought Bentall. But I won't. Let him find out for himself.

'And the solicitors, I see, are Arrun and Co. A small firm, I believe.'

'Yes,' said Bentall. 'John Arrun as a young man was articled to Henry Baker, who before he died was the Senior Partner in Baker and Turnbull.'

'I remember Sir Henry well. He was an excellent solicitor.'

'Of the old school,' said Bentall. 'John Arrun later started his own firm, Arrun and Co. Personally,' he went on, 'personally, I'm surprised that any firm of responsible solicitors should get mixed up in such a disgraceful action.'

Leslie Turner removed his glasses from his nose and smiled at Bentall. 'Come, Mr Bentall. This is a professional matter and everyone has the right to representation. Even if it's only by the modest firm of Messrs Arrun and Co. and –' he replaced his glasses and for the third time he looked at the signature on the pleading, 'and by the young, as I presume that he is, the young Mr Peregrine Fanshaw.'

The clerk re-entered the room. 'Mr Fanshaw is in Mr Simon Harrington's chambers. I have ascertained that in Lord Brackley's case Mr Harrington will be leading Mr Fanshaw for the Defendant.'

'Oh,' said Turner, laying the document abruptly on his desk.

Bagot was amused. He doesn't fancy that, he thought.

'So, Simon Harrington will be leading for the Defendant. Very well.'

'I should explain, Sir Leslie,' said Bentall, 'why I have brought Mr Gray with me. Doubtless you will have heard of him and his organisation?'

Turner inclined his head towards Bagot. He had never heard of Gray or of his organisation, but he had no intention of disclosing it.

'Mr Gray and I are more accustomed to working together in commercial or financial enquiries, such as in a take-over bid.'

Turner nodded gravely. He did not see how this could be very relevant in the case of *Brackley* v. *Tarnovic*, but he said nothing.

'Mr Gray's organisation is expert in discovering the background and standing of corporations and individuals.'

Leslie Turner cottoned on. 'And you want him to look into Tomas Tarnovic?'

'Precisely. I thought that you should be informed that we had instructed Mr Gray, and I wanted you to meet him.'

Leslie Turner bowed across his desk. Bagot nodded. 'To identify Tarnovic's missing years,' mused Leslie. 'Do you think that you could do this, Mr Gray?'

'Given time, Sir Leslie.'

'There should be time enough. The case cannot come to trial for months.'

'I've also asked Mr Gray to discover whether there is anyone behind the sudden appearance of Tomas Tarnovic,' said Bentall.

132

Turner swung his head to look at Bentall. 'Anyone behind him?'

'With your experience of politics, Sir Leslie, doesn't it seem odd that a man should suddenly appear fifty years after the event and start to blackguard the reputation of a leading member of the Government party and an ex-Cabinet Minister shortly before an election?'

'You mean that someone may have instigated Tarnovic's story in order to obtain some political advantage?'

'Yes.'

Turner pondered this. He said mildly, 'I suppose it is a possibility, but surely highly improbable. And this also is what you want Mr Gray to investigate?'

'Yes. Another alternative is that this is no more than a blackmailing action from start to finish.'

'A blackmailing action, Mr Bentall?'

Bentall was leaning forward. Bagot Gray noted the intense expression on his face. He is obsessed, Gray thought.

'We know that Tarnovic has no money and I believe that if Lord Brackley had been prepared to offer the man money, Lord Brackley would've heard no more of him.'

'That is pure speculation, Mr Bentall. In my opinion, we should concentrate on the issues. They are clear enough – either the man Tarnovic has invented his story; or Lord Brackley has invented his – and the latter possibility is quite beyond belief. So our duty is to authorise Mr Gray to investigate Tarnovic so that we know as much as possible about him. Nothing more.'

Bentall sat back in his chair.

'The burden will be on Tarnovic to prove what he has alleged and I agree that it will be helpful if we can show the reason why Tarnovic has resorted to his lies. In any event, I will want to know for my cross-examination where he has been and what he has been doing over all these years. But that is as far as we should go.'

*

133

As Bentall's Daimler drove Roger Bentall and Bagot Gray out of the Temple and on to the Embankment, Bentall said, 'He has very little imagination.'

Bagot did not reply.

'Can I drop you anywhere? I'm going back to my office.'

Bagot Gray got out in Albemarle Street and stood watching as the car turned out of his sight. Bentall picked up the car telephone and dialled the private number of Les Price in Ruislip.

The next day, the Daimler dropped Roger Bentall at the Hyde Park Hotel. Retaining his overcoat, he entered the Polo Bar and saw there was no one there he knew. Then he left the hotel and walked across the Park to the Serpentine. He sat on a bench and after waiting uncomfortably in the cold east wind, he was joined by Price.

Price handed him an envelope. 'These are the transcripts.'

Bentall placed the envelope in his pocket and, without a word, retraced his steps across the Park to the hotel.

At about the same time, Alexandra took a taxi from her office in Fetter Lane to the Naval and Military Club in Piccadilly. Her father was standing waiting for her in the hall.

'I'm so glad you could come. I didn't expect to be in London, but I had to see Miller at the bank.'

She slipped her arm through his. 'Is he boring you about your overdraft?'

'As usual. These aren't easy times for retired old people with too much land and too little money.'

'I suppose the place is heavily in hock.'

'It will be before you get it, and those grandchildren you promised me.'

'You will have them, I promise you.'

'But when?' he grumbled. 'When? That's the question.'

'Soon.'

They passed into the dining-room and sat and ordered

their food. She watched him affectionately as he studied the menu, the full head of silver hair above the clear blue eyes in the weather-beaten face.

'I can't stay very long. I only want an omelette.'

He handed the waiter the menus and gave their order. 'Always in such a rush. Do you really enjoy your hectic life and that dreary work in the lawyer's office?'

'Yes, of course I do.' Alexandra laid her hand on his. As she did so, she saw how mottled it was with the brown marks of old age. 'You shouldn't have married so late. I am the child of your middle age.'

'And none the worse for that. You modern girls are all so different nowadays.'

'And none the worse for that,' she mimicked.

'When will you be down again?'

'I'm not sure. There's a lot of work in the office at present.'

They began to eat. After a time he said, 'When you were last home and we went for our walk, you asked me about my old chief at the Ministry of Defence, George Brackley, remember?'

'Yes, I do.'

'Is he in some case that you are working on?'

'Yes.'

'I can't imagine Brackley allowing himself to get involved in litigation. I thought he was too wily an old bird to get mixed up with lawyers.'

'Sometimes it can't be helped.'

'Are you on his side in this matter?'

'No, I am not.'

'I'm sorry.'

'Someone has to be on the other side. That's the system.'

'It's a damn silly system. But if you have to be on one side or the other, you ought to be on the right side.'

'Perhaps his is not the right side.'

'Of course it is. He's a splendid chap.'

'Splendid chaps aren't always what they seem.' This time she saw his look and put out her hand again. 'I know that

135

you admired him when you worked for him at the Ministry. So perhaps we shouldn't talk about it.'

'No. I don't mind. It's just that I'm surprised. But as you say, people are not always what they seem.'

'That is what the case is all about. Does that upset you?'

'I'm just an old fool, but I'm not usually wrong about people. You seem very certain.'

'I am.'

'Because you're paid to be as a lawyer? Or because you really believe it?'

The question stung her. 'Because I really believe it. It's certainly not just because I'm a lawyer – and, in fact, I'm not being paid. My client has no money.'

'My clever daughter working on a case for nothing! Your grandfather would be ashamed of you.'

'It's not so unusual when the client is poor and you believe in his case and other people do as well.'

'What other people?'

'Our Counsel, the barrister I am working with. He's great and he agrees with me about the case. He's as certain as I am. He wasn't at first, but he met my client and then he agreed with me.'

He noticed the colour in her cheeks. He said quietly, 'Tell me about this barrister, this man who agrees with you. Do you like him?'

'I like him – a lot. But I wouldn't tell anyone else. Only you.'

He was silent for a moment. 'Is he handsome?'

'I think so. He's very lonely, at least I think he is. Oh, I don't know.'

'Are you in love with him?'

'A little. But perhaps it's just because we are working together. It's very exciting, Daddy. It's my first big case.' She looked at her watch. 'It's late. I shall have to fly. I have to go to Kew.'

'Whatever for?'

'To look up some records.' She looked at him and saw

that he looked sad. 'I'll see you again soon. You know that I love to see you.'

'And I you.'

'I'm sorry that I'm not on the side of your old boss. It really is a great chance for me.'

'You certainly sound very excited about it.'

'I am. I really am.'

'I was glad to hear about your barrister. Jessica wanted you to marry a merchant banker.'

'Daddy!' she said. 'That's going too far. I expect he's married.'

'Married? Don't you even know?'

'I don't. But I'll find out – soon.'

'Don't leave it too late. That would be a mistake.'

'I won't.'

She got to her feet. He remained seated and she went behind the back of his chair and bent forward and kissed the side of his cheek. His head was lowered and he did not move.

'It was lovely seeing you,' she said. He remained looking down at the remnants of their meal. 'I hope you didn't mind all that shop. But I'm so thrilled to be in such an important case.'

Her hand was still on his shoulder. He did not look round but raised his, the hand that was mottled with age, and put it on hers. Almost in a whisper he said, 'Goodbye, Alexandra.'

After she was gone, he remained where he was. When the waiter came he angrily signalled him away. Then he rose and walked wearily out of the dining-room across the hall to telephone to Brandsby in Yorkshire.

THIRTEEN

In the library at Brandsby, George Brackley was sitting in his chair before the fire waiting for Grace to return from her day's hunting. He was always anxious when she was out and glad when she was back. There were too many accidents in the hunting-field. Of the people in wheelchairs in the House of Lords, so many were the result of accidents while hunting. He wished Grace would give it up, but he knew that she loved it.

They had been married now for thirty years and they were very happy. He had met her in the States, in George-town, at a party to which he had been taken at one of the tall brick houses, which had reminded him of the house of his parents in Kensington where he had spent his childhood. At the time he had been a junior minister at the Defence Ministry and had been sent to Washington to take part in the negotiations between the British and American Governments which had followed the abandonment of the Skybolt missile.

George Brackley was a contemporary of the new young British Ambassador, who was the friend of the young President whom Brackley had also known when the President had been a young man in London before the War. That was one of the reasons why George Brackley had been included in the British team. On the day of the party the work had been completed – a reasonable compromise achieved. In the afternoon Brackley had been to the White House and the President had remembered him. It was his first visit to Washington and he had decided to stay over the weekend before returning to London.

The room where the party was being held was crowded, crammed with politicians, diplomats, journalists – a regular Georgetown party. In those days, the drinks had been martinis or Old-Fashioneds, lethal drinks, and he had been nursing his carefully in a corner of the room while talking to the senior Senator for Illinois. He had looked up and seen pushing through the crowd towards them a tall, long-legged girl with short dark hair and violet eyes.

'Hullo, Uncle Harry,' she had said and kissed the Senator's cheek. But as she did so, her eyes had met his over the head of her uncle.

'Grace,' the Senator had said. 'What brings you to Washington?'

'I came with my mother. We had a royal command to dine at the White House. I was dreading it, but it turned out to be great fun. They've certainly made some changes. It's not so stuffy as it was.'

She was looking at George. She could not be more than twenty, he thought.

'How long are you here for?' the Senator enquired.

'Only for a few days. We're going back to Bryn Mawr on Monday. I'm Grace Donner,' she said to George, holding out her hand.

'George Brackley, from England.'

They had extricated themselves from the scrum inside the house and made their way into the garden. She must be twenty-five years younger than me, he thought as he followed her, his eyes on her long legs. In the garden he told her that he had never before been in Washington and she had asked if he had any time to see something of the country. 'You ought to see Mount Vernon. Our house outside Philadelphia on the Main Line is modelled on it.'

'I've a couple of days free now. I would love that,' he had said. 'I'd also like to see the sites of the battlefields – Bull Run, Manassas.'

The Ambassador had come up to them. 'This is Grace Donner,' George had said.

'I know your mother. She's been to the Embassy several

times. We're going back to the house with a few friends to have supper in the garden, quite informal. We'd be delighted if you would care to come,' he said to Grace.

'I'll come,' she had said.

The next day, George and Grace had driven to Mount Vernon and joined the line of sightseers. As he had followed her in the queue through the dining-room, George had looked up at the portrait of his namesake. What was the warning that Washington had given to his stepdaughter over 'involuntary passion'? How when the torch was put to it 'that which is within you must burst into flame'. You are quite right, Mr President, George had thought. As they left, he had bought Grace an ice-cream cone and she licked it while they drove away on the road to Virginia. Later they had eaten hamburgers and wandered around the Civil War battlefields.

'Let's drive on,' she had said. 'I have the key to my cousins' lodge in the Blue Ridge Mountains. Are you in a hurry to be back?'

'No. I would like that.'

They had bought eggs and rashers of lean bacon at a country store, watched impassively by two old men smoking corn-on-the-cob pipes. He had tried to buy wine, but there was none so he settled for Bourbon.

The dirt track led off the road and wound through the woods to the single-storey wooden house, which faced west with a view through a clearing in the trees to the hills beyond. She had unlocked the house and they had taken two chairs and sat in the garden, facing the hills. It was very warm. He went to telephone the Embassy and was glad to hear that the Ambassador was out. George left a message. He would be staying with friends and be back tomorrow.

Then he had cooked the eggs and she the bacon, drying off the fat so that it was crisp. He wanted mustard, but she had given him marmalade. They drank the whiskey and sat again in the garden. By now it was dark. He leaned over and kissed her.

'Let's dance,' she had said and put on the radio.

140

As they danced, he kissed her again, unable to keep his lips from her skin, holding her to him and then taking her head between his two hands while his tongue explored her mouth. She broke away from him and threw off her clothes and knelt and unbuttoned his. She pulled him on to the sofa and when he had mounted her, she had dug her nails into his naked shoulders and whimpered and then shouted so that the woods beyond the garden must have heard her. They had gone to the bedroom and throughout the night turned and twisted, sometimes one then the other on top or beneath until, as dawn broke over the hills, they fell asleep.

They had been married that autumn in the Episcopalian Church in Bryn Mawr. Few of his friends had managed to come. The Minister at the Embassy, Leo Blakesley, who had been in Cairo during the War when George Brackley had been training for his time in the mountains twenty years earlier, was his best man. They had solemnly opened the dancing at the reception in the marquee in Grace's mother's vast house and got away as soon as they could to New York. The next day, they boarded the *Queen Elizabeth* for the voyage to Southampton, five sybaritic days before the start of their life in London.

It had been a good marriage. Thirty years later he loved her as much as ever.

He was dozing when Grace got home. She came into the library and kissed him. He woke and smiled at her. She had removed her riding boots but was still in her hunting clothes.

'Had a good day?'

'Wonderful. A great run early on, right across the fields above Lower Bingley farm, round the spinney and on to Stokeley.'

'Over all those stone walls? I don't like that.'

'You old silly! They're easier and much lower than the fences.'

'I worry about you when you're out hunting.'

'I know. But I love it and today was the last in the season. So no more worries.'

'Until next year. I suppose you're starving.'

'Well, I'm hungry. They're bringing tea in here. Do you mind?'

'Of course I don't.' The butler wheeled in a trolley. 'In the old days everyone had eggs after a day's hunting.'

'Not me. Just tea and scones.' She handed him a cup. 'And you've been dozing in front of the fire?'

'Yes. I was thinking of the old days, of you and me and when we were first together.'

She smiled. 'And that sent you to sleep.'

'We've been very happy.'

'We have, and we're going to be very happy for a long time yet,' she said briskly. 'You are looking much better than you did last week.'

'I'm feeling much better.' He paused. Then he said, 'I must go to London tomorrow.'

'Why, George?' she exclaimed. 'The last time you came back with that wretched cold.'

'That was in the snow, in the Land Rover. This time I will take the Rolls. That'll be more comfortable.'

'I think you are mad. You are only just recovering from your cold. Tell them to come here.'

'I can't, not this time.'

She did not reply at first. Then she said, 'I suppose it's about the wretched law case.'

'Yes, it is.'

'You know how I dislike that lawyer of yours. I don't trust him.'

'I know.'

'He should never have pushed you into starting it.'

'I had no alternative.'

'For Heaven's sake, why not? You should have ignored it. A crackpot foreigner telling lies about you and sending his stupid pamphlets to your friends —'

'And to my enemies.'

'Your enemies! Who are your enemies? Just a pack of old

142

men who are jealous of what you achieved in your career. Now that you're retired, what harm can they do you?'

'They can harm my reputation. Many in the party still look to me. And the Press know about the pamphlets.'

'The Press! They've too much sense to repeat the man's lies. They wouldn't dare.'

'They would not dare to print anything now, but if I had done nothing, they might have started hinting and speculating why I'd let the story pass. I don't want to go to my grave with those lies left unanswered.'

'But a trial at your age when you haven't been well—'

'All I have had has been a cold!'

'I'm not talking about that. You know what I'm talking about – the trouble you've had with your heart.'

'You have been speaking to Telfer.'

'Of course. I telephoned Harley Street. I love you, George, and I don't want to lose you. Now you have got to go through all the beastliness of this stupid law case. The only ones who will get anything out of it will be the media and those damned lawyers.'

'Bentall has briefed Leslie Turner as my Counsel. It is him I am going to see. Do you remember him? He was Solicitor General in our Government.'

She shook her head. 'He couldn't have made much impression.'

'They say he's the leading man for this kind of case.'

'He may be, but I blame that nasty little man, Bentall, for getting you into it.'

'He's said to be a very good solicitor.'

'Well, he's a very unpleasant man.'

She got up and came over to him and knelt, taking his hand in hers. 'Oh, George,' she said. 'I have such a horrid feeling about this. It can't be too late to stop it. Please stop it. Please. For my sake.'

He put his free hand to her cheek and caressed it. 'It's too complicated, Grace. It has gone too far. I can't stop it now, not without disgrace. I could not face that and you would not want me to.'

143

FOURTEEN

Simon telephoned from chambers. 'We ought to have a Council of War,' he began briskly. 'Are you free on Saturday evening?'

'Yes, I am.'

'Can you come to Onslow Square at seven o'clock?' Perry Fanshaw, he said, would be there and he asked her to bring Felix. So it was to be a business meeting. She had hoped that it might be something more – and it was. 'Would you care to stay on after we've all talked – and have dinner with me?'

She heard the hesitation in his voice, so different from his brisk tone when he was setting up the meeting. 'I would love to,' she said.

Alexandra spent Saturday enjoying herself. She did no work and lay in late, telephoning for appointments with the hairdresser and, a new departure for her, with Helen, the aromatherapist recommended by her friend, Zinnia Laughton. Then she passed half an hour on the telephone gossiping with Zinnia.

'You sound very cheerful,' said her friend.

'I am.'

'Why?'

'Lots of exciting work.'

'That sounds hideously boring. Nothing else?'

'Perhaps.'

'I thought so. I suppose he's married. They always are.'

'I don't know if he is married.'

'You don't know! How long have you known him?'

'A few months. I've only been out with him twice. But I'm going out with him again tonight.'

'And you don't know if he's married? What on earth has come over you, Alexandra?'

'He has a photograph of a woman in his office.'

'Of his mother.'

'Of course it's not his mother, nor his sister.'

'Alexandra, you are wild! Of course he's married. He probably has six children. For Heaven's sake don't get involved.'

'I am involved.'

'Don't be a goose, Alexandra. Get uninvolved.'

'I can't. I like it.'

Thereafter, she lazed about the flat deciding what she would wear that evening. She went to her wardrobe and lingered, taking her time. She was determined not to wear black – she wore that in the office. The conference at Onslow Square might be work, but the dinner afterwards she was determined would not. Eventually, she chose a red tunic with a boat neck and a scolloped edge, which she would wear over a white shirt. The tunic had long sleeves with three buttons which fastened on a point at the wrist. She chose a white piqué skirt and red shoes. Satisfied, she went off to her appointment with the aromatherapist; the hair appointment was in the early afternoon. When Helen was twisting and pressing the soles of her feet, Alexandra said, 'I suppose I ought to do my toe-nails.'

Helen smiled. 'A special occasion?'

'Could be.'

At lunchtime, Felix telephoned.

'I got your message. I couldn't call back until I got rid of my painters. They were all very tiresome this morning. They kept arguing with me.'

He agreed to come to the meeting at Onslow Square. She asked if he had heard from Tomas.

'Not recently. On my way to His Learned Lordship this evening, I'll call in on him. I'm busy this afternoon.'

'Doing what?'

145

'Sleuthing.'

'Where are you sleuthing?'

'I have an informant whom I'm going to see. It could be interesting.'

'You're making me feel guilty. I'm spending a thoroughly lazy day.' She was lying on her bed, eating an apple.

'Good for you. See you tonight.'

When she came back from having her hair done, she flew to the answer-phone and saw with relief that there had been no calls. For a moment she had feared that the meeting, and so the evening, might have been cancelled. She went to her cupboard and idly flicked through the dresses. Was she wrong to have rejected black which always set off the whiteness of her skin and the blondeness of her hair? She decided to stay with what she had chosen. Tonight was an occasion for colour. If it wasn't, then she would make it one.

She went to her bedroom and lay on the bed watching television, flicking from channel to channel. Of course, the girl must be his wife. But where was she? Was he separated from her?

At four o'clock she was walking to the bathroom to run her bath, when she thought that she should telephone her father and thank him for lunch.

Jessica answered. 'Your father's not here. He has been very busy lately and away quite a lot. He was in London earlier in the week.'

'I know. We had lunch together. He said he'd come to London to see the bank manager. But today is Saturday and the banks are shut. So the Admiral has gone missing.'

'Really, Alexandra! Your father is not missing. He came back from London a few days ago. You sound very mischievous.'

'I am feeling mischievous.'

'He was in London only for one evening. Tonight he has to go to some function with the Lord Lieutenant. He will be back for dinner at 8.30 if you want to speak with him then.'

'No, I have to go out. Give him my love and thank him

146

for lunch.' She ran her bath and lay in it, the radio on the chair beside her.

On Sunday morning the record of those telephone conversations with Simon, Felix, Zinnia and Jessica were all listened to by Roger Bentall as he sat in his car, outside his villa in Highgate.

She was greeted at the door of Simon's flat by a stout young man in his late twenties with a ruddy complexion and straw-coloured hair.

'I'm Perry Fanshaw. I'm the brains in Simon's chambers.' He held out his hand. 'He got me to draft the Tarnovic defence, but officially I'm instructed by you.'

She smiled as he took her coat and ushered her into the hall.

'I saw you when you came to King's Bench Walk some weeks ago. But your hair is different tonight. It looks wonderful. Do come in.' He opened the door of the drawing-room. 'Your friend Felix is here. I'm to give you a drink.'

She kissed Felix who was standing by the fireplace. 'It's a Boucher,' he said and turned back to study the painting.

'Where is Simon?'

'The great man has gone to change,' said Perry. 'He was playing the piano and like all geniuses, he didn't notice the time. He won't be long. What would you like?'

Perry brought them drinks and Simon followed him into the room in a rush. He was wearing a light-coloured grey suit with a bright-blue tie. More becoming, she thought, than his lawyer's subfusc.

'I'm sorry not to be ready when you came.' He advanced towards Alexandra and for a second she thought he might be going to kiss her, but he turned away awkwardly. Perhaps he would have, she thought, if the others had not been there.

The conference began. He had said nothing about how she looked.

147

'I shall have to go soon,' said Felix. 'So may I start?' He reported that Tomas was still not well. Old bruises and old skin, Tomas had said, take time to mend and his leg, his war wound, was troubling him.

'That fall a month or two ago knocked him up more than we thought. But the main sufferer has been his dog whose only promenade recently has been on the patch of grass outside the flat. I'll take him for a good run tomorrow. I have to report that his master, or our master if that is his right description, is supremely indifferent to what is being done on his behalf. Not that he is ungracious about what we are doing – especially not about Alexandra who, would you believe it, is his great favourite.'

'I would believe it,' said Perry.

'It's just that the old fellow seems to consider it all a waste of time and that he has only to speak and Lord Brackley will be exposed.'

'It's only what I expected,' said Simon. 'At least now we have got his statement, which Alexandra took from him. It's a terrible story.'

'He certainly suffered,' said Felix.

Simon turned to Alexandra. 'Each week brings us closer to trial. Soon you and I will have to pay him another visit.'

Felix went on: 'The other side have been very active. They seem to have approached everyone in the community.'

'Who are they?'

'The same two men. The tall one with sandy hair and a large Adam's apple. The other, the burly man with dark crinkly hair. He comes regularly to the club and drinks with Milan Misic. The barman at the club thinks his name is Ned.'

'What have they been saying?'

'Warning everyone against helping Tomas, telling everyone that Tomas has lost his wits and has become senile and that the authorities are taking note of everyone who is helping him.'

'Bastards,' said Perry.

'So no one is prepared to say anything to me and no one will talk with Tomas. The printer, Kosta, won't even see me.'

'Then they've been pretty effective?'

'Yes. The only one who will talk is the barman at the club, Starjevic. Remember him?' Felix asked Alexandra. She nodded. 'He'll be losing his job when the club closes and he hates the Chairman, Milan Misic. I saw him again this afternoon, not at the club but at a pub in Earls Court. He has given me a lead to a man called Velkjo Ostrojic, who lives near Kendal in Cumbria. This is his address.' Felix held out a piece of paper and Alexandra took it from him. 'Starjevic believes that Velkjo at one time may have served under Tomas in the army, so he may be able to help. The barman also thinks that Velkjo Ostrojic may be living here illegally and if so, no one in London may know of him.'

Simon looked at Alexandra. 'He must be seen, and quickly.'

'He is not in the country at present and he won't be back for a week or so.'

'Where is he now?'

'In France. Starjevic does not know where.' Then he added, 'There is one other thing that Starjevic told me. It may be nonsense, but you ought to know about it. One evening, when he had to go into the office to bring them some more drink, he overheard part of a conversation between Misic and the man called Ned. From what he heard, Starjevic thinks that they seem to know everything about what Tomas's legal team are up to. Especially you,' he said to Alexandra.

'Me?'

'Yes.'

'Are they shadowing her?' asked Simon quickly.

'Starjevic believes they may have got her bugged, because the man said something about the Home Office and a warrant. Is that possible?'

'At the office?' said Perry incredulously.

'I don't know, but from what Starjevic overheard, he

thought it was at her home. As I said, it could be nonsense.'

They all looked at each other. Then Alexandra said quietly, 'When I got back to my flat the other night, I had a strange feeling someone had been there while I had been out.'

For a moment no one spoke. Then Felix said, 'Well, judging from what I have learned about the behaviour of those two gentlemen, somebody probably had.' He got to his feet. 'I have to go as a kind and very discriminating lady is taking the impoverished artist out to dinner.' He grinned at Alexandra. 'I must go or I shall miss my date.'

Simon went with him to the front door. 'Thank you. Keep in touch.' Felix nodded and ran down the stairs.

Back in the drawing-room, Simon said to Alexandra, 'You had better not use your telephone this weekend unless you have to. And if you do, watch what you say. I shall get it checked on Monday by someone who can get your flat "swept" – professionally.'

'This case,' said Perry, 'grows curi'oser and curi'oser. Now we are into the dirty tricks department.'

'As Felix said, it may be nonsense, but we must take no chances until we have an electronic check done. Have you a chain on your front door?'

'Yes, I have.'

'You must put it on whenever you are in the flat. We'd better get the lock changed on Monday.'

We, thought Alexandra, the proprietary we. It was rather comforting.

'Have you anything to report, Perry?'

'Very little. I have been looking through the SOE files at Kew, particularly the Cairo files and the operational logs of the British liaison officers in the Balkans in 1943, to see if we can get anything on Brackley's mission, which began in November 1943. There was no record of any signal during the time when he and Hopkinson were with Tomas, but I found some reports from Brackley to Cairo.'

'In what month?'

'December '43.'

'That would've been after he had joined the Partisans. By then he'd've been using the WT of the other British liaison officers who were with Tito.'

'The sum total of my research is that so far, I have found nothing much which could help.'

'You must keep at it, Perry. I'm sure there's a clue there somewhere.'

'So far I haven't found it.'

No one said anything until Simon asked, 'Anything more, Perry?'

'No.' Perry took the hint. 'Then I'll be off now. I shall go back to Kew on Monday.' He went over to Alexandra and took her hand. 'I have never said this to an instructing solicitor before but I think you look ravishing.'

'Go away, Perry,' growled Simon.

Alexandra laughed. 'Thank you. At least someone has noticed that I'm dressed not for a conference but because I've been asked out to dinner.'

When Perry had gone Simon said awkwardly, 'I was going to say how wonderful you looked, but I didn't want to in front of the others.'

'I don't mind that you didn't.'

He poured her another glass of wine. 'Are you hungry?'

'Not in the least. Perry said you were playing the piano when he arrived. What were you playing?'

'Schubert.'

'Play some more.'

She sat watching him play and then got up and came and leaned over the piano. When he had finished, she said, 'You play very well.'

He smiled and began to play again. 'Chopin,' he said.

She waited until the piece was over and he was sitting looking up at her. She picked up the photograph in its silver frame. 'Who is she?'

He shut the lid on the keyboard with a snap. 'My wife.'

She put the photograph back on the piano and turned away.

'She is dead. I killed her.'

151

She swung round. 'You what?'

He was still seated at the piano. 'Two years ago I was driving her to London from the country. It was in the morning and it was quite clear when we started out. I was driving too fast and suddenly we came into a bank of mist. There were no fog warnings. I braked, but there was a pile-up ahead and I ran into the back of it.'

She had her hand to her throat. 'How terrible,' she whispered.

He raised and again closed the lid of the keyboard. 'She was holding the unfastened belt with her finger crooked in it. I told her to fasten it and she told me to mind my own business. Then the accident happened. She was flung forward into the windshield and was killed – instantaneously.'

Alexandra was standing very still, looking at him as he sat, his hands now in his lap. 'And you? What happened to you?'

'Almost untouched. A bang on the head and a broken wrist.'

She came over to him and stood behind him, resting her hand for a moment on his shoulder. 'It was not your fault.'

He got up and walked away from the piano. 'That's why I don't drive now.' He turned and faced her. 'When I heard that I had killed her I was glad.'

Alexandra whispered, 'Glad?'

'When she died we were quarrelling. We were always quarrelling. She hated me. She told me that very soon after we were married and I had grown to hate her. Now she has her revenge, because I cannot forget that morning when I killed her.' He went and sat on the sofa. 'I keep the photograph to remind me of what I felt when I heard she was dead.'

'Why did she marry you if she hated you?'

'She told me not long after we had married. She said she'd only got married because everyone did. When we married I thought I loved her, but that did not last. She hated my work, she hated my life. We hardly touched each other after we were married.'

He walked across the room and stood leaning against the chimney-piece. 'Can you understand that? To be glad at someone else's death and a death which you've caused yourself. I could not forget how I felt when they told me that she was dead and I knew that I was free of her. That weekend she had told me she wanted a divorce. She had been to a lawyer and she said she would take every penny I had. I told her I did not care. I only wanted to be free of her. And a few hours later, I was. Because I had killed her.'

'You must not say that,' she repeated.

'It's the truth. That was two years ago and during those years I have lived with my guilt at the flood of relief I felt when they told me she was dead. Then a few months ago, it went.'

Alexandra was sitting on the sofa and he walked towards her and stood looking down on her. 'It was when you walked into my room in King's Bench Walk and came into my life.' He put out his hand to her. She took it and he held it tightly as he said, 'I am in love with you, Alexandra, and I have been from that very first moment when you came into my room and started to tell me about old Tomas.'

He let go her hand and walked away and stood with his back to her. 'I didn't mean to tell you. I hadn't planned to say this in case you wouldn't see me again. And I could not bear that. Because I love you, Alexandra. I love you – so very much.' She got up and he turned and looked at her as she came towards him. Then she was in his arms and he was kissing her. 'I love you,' he kept saying. 'I love you.'

'And I love you,' she said.

They sat for a long time on the sofa while he kissed her lips, her eyes, her forehead.

'Let's make love,' she said.

He picked her up and carried her from the room down the corridor to the bedroom. As he opened the door with her in his arms, he looked down at her face. 'It's only been my room,' he said. 'No one else has lived here.'

He laid her on the bed and lay beside her, his fingers lightly touching her face and her hair. He started un-buttoning the sleeves of her tunic. She sat up and pulled it over her head, then the shirt and then she undid the catch on her skirt while his hands were caressing the skin of her shoulders, her arms, the sides of her body. When she was naked, he marvelled at the whiteness and the softness of her skin, his fingers stroking her side, down her thigh, down her flanks. He slipped out of his own clothes and began to kiss her breasts, taking her nipples between his lips. His tongue played over them, nudging them until they grew hard. Then he left them and covered the rest of her body with light, gentle kisses until his mouth was back on hers and his passion became stronger and more violent as he lay on her.

She strained to meet him, her knees now gripping his sides and she began to cry, softly at first, then louder, pull-ing his head ever harder down on hers, her tongue now deep in his mouth until, with a final cry, the passion flooded from her.

She lay for a time beside him, her fingers playing with the dark lock of hair or running along the lines of his forehead, staring into his dark-brown eyes, while one of his hands was on her breast and the other lay on her thigh.

He got up and went from the room and came back with some wine. 'Are you hungry?' he asked. She shook her head. 'Nothing?' She shook her head again and they sat drinking the wine. Then they made love again, this time more fiercely, all gentleness lost in their desire for each other.

It was very late when she fell asleep, but he stayed awake, watching her until she opened her eyes.

'I must go,' she said.

'Can't you stay?'

'No. I want to be alone now – for a time. I will come to you tomorrow.'

'In the evening. I have to go to Cambridge.' He fetched her one of his sweaters with a high collar. 'It will be cold,' he said and she put it over her tunic.

He walked with her to the car and got in beside her as she drove to Drayton Gardens, parking once more round the corner in Roland Way. In her flat he marched around, looking, inspecting. 'Just in case,' he said and gave her a final, gentle kiss. 'When I've gone, put the chain on the lock and remember about your telephone. I'll call in the evening as soon as I'm back. Then come to me at Onslow Square.'

He watched from the corner and waited until he saw the light go out in her bedroom window. There was no one about in the early Sunday morning. It was beginning to rain as he turned and walked home.

FIFTEEN

On the following morning as Simon was boarding the train from King's Cross to Cambridge, the burly man with thick, dark hair, whom the barman at the club, Starjevic, believed was called Ned, climbed out of his car in the yard of a busy public house on Hampstead Heath. He went into the bar and ordered vodka on the rocks. He would keep the lawyer waiting. Let him sweat a little, Ned thought.

After he had finished his drink, he strolled leisurely back into the car park where Roger Bentall was seated in his white Mercedes, reading a Sunday newspaper. Ned Waring tapped on the passenger window, which Bentall lowered.

''Morning,' he said.

'You are late. Get in.'

Waring climbed into the passenger seat. 'Sorry to have kept you, but we've been busy. You've given us a lot to do.'

'Where are the tapes?'

Waring handed over the envelope. Bentall took them from the envelope and placed them among the row of music tapes in the rack. That's neat, Waring thought; that's a neat place to hide them.

'Tell Price to bring me today's tapes to the Park tomorrow at lunchtime. He knows where.'

Bentall then asked him whether everyone who knew Tarnovic had been seen and warned.

'All we know of,' said Waring. 'The only one who now sees Tarnovic is the painter, Felix Ilic. He is acting as a runner for the Tarnovic lawyers. Yesterday lunchtime we followed Ilic to a pub in Earls Court. He met Starjevic, the barman at the club. The barman gave him the name of a

156

man in Cumbria called Ostrojic who might be useful for Tarnovic.'

Bentall took a pad from his pocket and made a note of the name.

'He lives in Cumbria and Starjevic believes that he might be living here illegally. The man had just left the country for a trip to France.'

Bentall nodded. 'I will deal with that.'

'There's something more that you should know and this is not good news.'

Bentall looked at him sharply. 'What do you mean?'

'Starjevic told Ilic that he believed that Tarnovic's lawyers had been bugged.'

'What! How does he know?'

'I don't know.'

But Waring knew very well. On the Friday evening he had gone to the club and drunk too much of Misic's plum brandy. To impress Misic he had been boasting how power-ful he and his friends were and that the Government was behind them. They even knew, he had said, everything that Tarnovic's lady lawyer was doing and saying. 'All perfectly legal, of course,' he had added with a wink. 'A warrant, you know. From the Home Office.' It was then that he had noticed that the barman had come into the office bringing another bottle.

Bentall swung round in his seat, his eyes flashing behind the heavy lenses of his horn-rimmed glasses. 'How could they have found out?'

'It's probably just a hunch of the barman, to impress Ilic, who gives him money. No one's touched the system or the recorder.'

Bentall knew at once what would have to be done. When this was reported to the lawyers, they would arrange a search. 'Get in there and get it out. All of it.'

'Take it out?'

'Yes. If they find it, they will know who put it there. Take it out. At once.'

'We're picking up a tidy bit of information.'

'Do as I say. Get in there today or tonight before they organise a sweep.'

There was a pause. Waring said, 'It's risky work. If you want it out today, it'll cost you another grand.'

Bentall turned his head and stared at him. Malevolent-looking bastard, Waring thought. But he smiled at Bentall and repeated, 'Very risky work indeed.'

Bentall turned away, his hands in their kid gloves gripping the steering-wheel. 'I said, get it out. Today.'

'Another grand,' Waring said softly.

Bentall nodded. 'Very well.'

'When can we have it?'

'When you have removed the system. Telephone me as soon as you have. And tell Price to bring me what tapes there are tomorrow. Then you can have your money. Now get out of my car.'

From noon on that Sunday morning, while Simon was at Cambridge and Alexandra lazing inside, Waring and Price kept watch over Drayton Gardens, sitting in the car in the rain and waiting for the chance to earn another grand.

Shortly before lunch, Simon arrived at the Master's Lodge at St Michael's in Cambridge.

Earlier in the week, Malcolm Poynter had telephoned King's Bench Walk with news of Gervase Gregson. 'I've had a card from Gervase. He has invited me for tea on Sunday. Are you free?'

'Certainly.'

'I shall send him a note telling him I'll be with him on Sunday afternoon and I'll be bringing my cousin, who would like to meet him. If he puts me off because of that, I will telephone. Otherwise I'll expect you for lunch on Sunday.'

Over lunch Malcolm Poynter told him that he had heard nothing from Gervase. 'But you never know. When we get to the house he might easily turn us away.'

'It's worth a try.'

At half-past three they drove into the village of Grant-chester. They passed the church and the vicarage and turned up an unkempt drive, the gravel green with weeds. It led to a square stone house with the paint peeling off the windows. A gutter had come loose and hung drunkenly from the left front of the façade.

Malcolm rang the bell. They could hear it pealing in the distance, but nothing happened.

'This may mean that he's not at home because I've brought a stranger.'

Simon looked round the side of the house at the tangled and overgrown garden. What had once been a lawn was inches deep with weeds and thistles. He could hear Malcolm ring again.

'Someone is coming.' They stood listening to the noise of the slow withdrawal of bolts, top and bottom; the un-hitching of a chain and eventually, the turn of the heavy lock. The face of an old woman with long grey hair on her head and whispers of hair on her upper lip and chin peered around the door.

'Good afternoon, Mary,' said Malcolm cheerily. When she saw who it was, she opened the door wider. As Malcolm went to step inside he said, 'This is Mr Harrington, my cousin.'

The old woman looked at Simon. 'The Professor said nothing about him.'

'I told the Professor that I was bringing Mr Harrington. I'm sure he won't mind.' And he went into the hall. Simon followed.

'Gervase,' Malcolm called out. 'Gervase. We are here.'

The old woman began bolting and locking the door behind them and Malcolm walked to the bottom of a broad staircase, which swept up from the hall and divided into two arcs under a tall window in the half-landing above. 'Gervase,' Malcolm called again. 'Gervase.'

Behind him Simon could hear the old woman shuffling away. Then, on the landing where the stairs divided, he saw silhouetted against the light from the window the tall figure

159

of an old man with a large head crowned by long, snow-white hair. He was dressed in a crimson padded dressing gown, open at the neck, his bare feet in red Morocco slippers.

'I hope that we haven't disturbed you, Gervase. Were you resting? Had you forgotten that we were coming?'

The figure remained stock-still on the landing. Then he pointed at Simon. 'Who is he and what is he doing here?'

'He's my cousin, Simon Harrington. I wrote that he would be with me.'

'Why have you brought him?'

'He has been lunching with me at the Lodge. He wanted to meet you. I wrote about him in my postcard.'

Gervase Gregson began slowly to descend the stairs, his gaze fixed on the stranger. 'I do not receive strangers.'

'You should have warned me if you didn't wish me to bring him.'

'You should have known.'

By now Gervase was on the bottom step, staring intently at Simon.

'Perhaps you'd like me to leave?' Simon said.

Gervase stepped from the bottom step and came within a yard of him, inspecting him from head to toe. 'He reminds me of someone I once knew,' Gervase said. 'He can stay.' Then he turned and walked to the side of the hall. He said to Malcolm, 'Come, Master. Follow me.'

Simon exchanged glances with Malcolm, who gave a shrug and they followed the old man down a passage which led from the hall and into a library – a dark, square room, the walls lined with bookcases, the floor littered with books, a coal fire smoking in the grate. Gervase lowered himself slowly into a shabby winged armchair on one side of the fireplace. Dirty white stuffing protruded from splits in the leather. He switched on a reading-light on the table beside him. Malcolm sat in the armchair opposite.

'As you are here,' Gervase said to Simon, 'sit.' And he began to hum to himself under his breath, as he settled his crimson robe around him.

160

Simon took a straight-backed chair and placed it between the two of them, facing the meagre fire, which now and again emitted puffs of smoke. To his left and behind Gervase's armchair was one of the two large windows which lit the room. Through it he could see the unkempt garden in the pale March sunshine.

Malcolm was about to speak when Gervase said, 'Was your cousin at the College?'

'No, he was at —'

Gervase interrupted. 'Let me guess.' He turned his great head towards Simon. 'He was at King's. He looks as though he was at King's. I had many friends in that college. Indeed, all my closest friends were at King's, in particular Jamie Mathewes, who became the Dean. He is dead now.'

'I know,' said Malcolm.

'Jamie Mathewes was the stage producer.' He turned his head to Simon. 'Are you an actor?'

Before Simon could reply, Malcolm said, 'Simon was at Trinity. And not so long ago. Or what does not seem long ago to us old fellows. All of only twenty years.'

'You are still only a boy,' said Gervase sternly to Malcolm. Then he put his hand to his mouth and tittered. 'But that's a naughty remark to make to the Master of my College.'

The flutter of his hand when he made the gesture and the high-pitched titter contrasted vividly with his previous commanding tone. It was as if for a moment a mask had slipped. Then it was back in place. 'Tea,' he said. 'Tea for the Master of St Michael's.'

The old woman had come into the room bearing a heavy silver tray on which stood a silver teapot and jug and a plate of dry water biscuits. Simon got to his feet to help her.

'Sit,' ordered Gervase. 'She likes to do it herself.' And, indeed, when Simon approached her, the old woman had turned away from him. He watched as she lowered her burden on to a pile of books standing on the table beside Gervase.

161

'Well done, Mary,' Gervase said and the old woman smiled and bobbed and shuffled from the room. Gervase poured the tea. Simon saw that there were only two cups. 'Pray take the cup to the Master, young man. And the biscuits. He is probably hungry. The food in College is abominable.' He poured himself a cup and began to sip from it and looked at Simon, who had returned to his seat between them. 'You don't take tea? I suppose that is another of the fashions of the young.'

'He has no cup,' said Malcolm.

'Ah.' Gervase emptied the sugar from the sugar-bowl on to the tray and filled it with tea. 'Now he has.'

Simon cradled the bowl in his hands. In the pause which followed Malcolm said, 'My cousin is very interested in Cambridge in the years just before the War.'

Gervase peered suspiciously at Simon. 'He is not, I trust, writing a book?'

'No. I'm not a writer.'

'There are too many books. You look like an actor.'

'Nor am I an actor.'

Malcolm intervened. 'I told my cousin that the only person who remembers the old days in the College and who knows everything about the Cambridge of sixty years ago is Professor Gregson. So he asked to meet you.'

'I'm the only one alive.'

Gervase had his eyes on Simon, who said, 'I am very honoured to have the chance of meeting you. I've heard much about you.'

'You are very young. What did you wish to ask me?'

'I wondered, Professor, if you ever knew someone called George Brackley, who was up at Trinity in the 1930s?'

Gervase turned to Malcolm. 'What did your young friend say, Master?'

You know what I said, thought Simon, you know very well.

Malcolm replied, 'He asked if you knew George Brackley when he was an undergraduate at Trinity. He is now Lord Brackley.'

'Why does he want to know?' Gervase turned his old, hooded blue eyes back to Simon.

'A friend has asked me to enquire and Malcolm suggested that you might have known Brackley.'

There was a pause while Gervase cracked a water biscuit and nibbled at it. 'You said George Brackley. I remember a *Boy* Brackley at Trinity.' He emphasised the word Boy.

'That may be him. Did you know him well?'

'Of course I knew Boy Brackley,' Gervase replied crossly. 'Why ever should you think that I did not?'

'I am sorry. I never said that you did not.'

'Why on earth should you suggest that I did not know Boy Brackley?'

'Forgive me. You have misunderstood me.'

'No, I have done nothing of the kind. I knew everyone, everyone of any interest. Of course, I knew Boy very well. Why does the Master call him Lord Brackley?'

'That is what he has become.'

'Whatever for?' He spoke as sternly as before. Then he paused and once again tittered – as he had when he had rebuked himself for having made what he had called a naughty remark to the Master. 'I know why. Yes, I know why. It was the stage of course, the stage. Like handsome Larry Olivier. Larry was not at Cambridge, though.'

'No, it was not the stage –'

'It must have been. Boy was one of those whom Jamie used to call his chorus, the stars of the Marlowe and the Footlights. Boy was an excellent performer, quite excellent. A very talented impersonator. Jamie gave him solos to do, solo turns, you know, in the May Week Revue. Yes, Boy was one of Jamie's very best.'

He picked up three sugar lumps from the tray and dropped them into his cup. 'Jamie, of course, was my dearest, closest friend.'

'What kind of a turn or solo would he do?'

Gervase stared at Simon. The mask was back in place. 'What do you mean? Jamie was not a performer. He was the producer. You ought to know that. Jamie not only produced the Footlights May Week Revue but many pieces on the West End stage, even when he was a don at King's. He was very well known. And,' he added severely, 'Jamie Mathewes was a first-class Shakespearian scholar. I am surprised that you should think he was an actor. That is most ignorant.'

'But Boy Brackley was an actor – in those days?'

'Of course he was. I told you that he was. And a very good one, too. Jamie thought a lot of him. He said Boy would go far on the stage. But I said that he was too pretty.'

Again the titter and the hand fluttering to his mouth. He is very horrid, thought Simon as Gregson went on: 'And the Master says that he is now Lord Brackley? Who would have thought it! He must have done very well. Personally, I never thought he would succeed. But I was wrong and Jamie, as usual, was right. Jamie was so very clever, you see.'

Malcolm stirred uncomfortably in his chair. Simon went on imperturbably. 'In Boy Brackley's time at Cambridge was there still active the group in which everyone later became so interested and which was known as The Apostles?'

Gervase lowered his cup on to its saucer with a clatter. 'The Apostles!' he said. 'That group of humbugs and impostors! Why do you talk of them? I can never understand why everyone always goes on and on about those tiresome people and the wretched Maynard Keynes. I never liked that fellow. I used to warn Jamie against getting mixed up with Maynard. He was the one person in King's whom I disliked. As for The Apostles, they were pretentious and very, very disloyal.'

'Because they were Marxists?'

'Of course not. I do not mean that at all. Why do you keep trying to put words into my mouth, young man?'

'I'm sorry. I do not intend to.'

'I am talking about friends – and disloyalty over friends.'

'E. M. Forster said that it is better to betray your country than your friends.'

'That has nothing to do with it. You really are a very obtuse young man. I am talking about stealing. Theft. Unscrupulous theft.'

'Theft of what?'

'Of friends, of course. That's what I found so unforgivable – and so brutal. They were always seeking to betray and steal and take away other people's friends.'

It was growing dark and Malcolm, anxious at the irritated note in Gervase's voice, intervened again. 'Do you mind, Professor, if I turn on this light?' Gervase waved his hand dismissively, keeping his eyes on Simon. Malcolm switched on the table-lamp beside him.

Simon went on quietly, 'Did Jamie agree with you about stealing friends?'

'Certainly, after I had told him that is what these people liked to do. Then he was most distressed. After that, he kept clear of those unpleasant people.'

'And Boy Brackley?'

'It was nothing to do with Boy. Why do you keep going on about him? I'm talking about my friend, Jamie. Boy Brackley had his own friends.'

'Who were his particular friends?'

'How can I remember? I find it difficult to remember now. Sometimes a few faces, a few names swim back into my memory.' He put his cup back on the silver tray. Then he said gently, 'But I like to think about them. The poet Maeterlinck, you know, said that the dead live again when their friends talk about them and I like to talk about them to anyone who is interested. And you, young man, appear to be interested, for you're asking enough questions. You are a very questioning young man.' He smiled at Simon and Malcolm, relieved, saw that Gervase was enjoying himself. He was probably admiring Simon's unruly lock of hair.

'I am very interested and I hope that I'm not asking too many questions. But it may be important for my friend and myself.'

'It can't be. It can't be important now. It is all so long

165

ago. Anyway, I didn't know Boy's crowd very well, except for a few of them.'

'Boy Brackley was at Trinity. Did he know Anthony Blunt when Blunt was a don at the College?'

This, thought Malcolm, is what Simon had come to discover.

Gervase did not reply and Simon repeated the question. 'I heard you. There's no need to press me and I'm not deaf. I was thinking about poor Anthony. He is dead, you know.'

'I know.'

'Poor Anthony. He was a very attractive person. I liked Anthony. They stripped him in the end.' Again the titter. Before it had been accompanied by the hand lifted to his mouth, but this time the hand swept back the long white hair. 'Of his knighthood.' He tittered again.

'Anthony Blunt's friends, Burgess and Maclean, escaped,' said Simon.

'And a very good thing, too. I was glad for them, although I never fancied Guy. He was so grubby.'

'Why do you say that it was a good thing that they escaped?'

'Because there was no point in their remaining. It would have been most painful for them – and most embarrassing for their friends. Do you know that after they had gone, a man came to see me to ask me questions, to interrogate me. Think of that! Me! He interrogated me!'

'Was the man called William Skardon?'

'You are quite right. That was his name. William Skardon. However did you know?' Gervase turned to Malcolm. 'Your young friend, Master, seems to know everyone.'

Malcolm smiled. But was Simon getting what he wanted?

'Mr Skardon, you know, was not very bright. He got nothing out of Anthony, until Anthony decided to tell, all those years later. He was a clever one, Anthony was,' he said admiringly.

'What did Mr Skardon ask you about?'

'About Kim and Guy and Donald. I liked Mr Skardon. He was rather sweet and he had a most distasteful task,

166

prying into the private lives of those silly boys. But you know, he appeared to believe that they had done great harm. I could never see why. It was all a great deal of fuss about very little.'

'Was George Brackley interested in politics?'

'I have no idea. If you are talking about Boy Brackley, he was an actor.'

'Was Boy Brackley ever an Apostle?'

'Boy, an Apostle? Oh, I don't think he was bright enough for Maynard and all those fellows. Anthony liked Boy though. I heard him once say that Boy had much potential.'

'Anthony Blunt said that?'

'Yes, when Anthony was a don at Trinity. He used to have parties and Guy used to come from London. Guy Burgess, you have heard of him? Guy used to come from the BBC, I think. Dirty fellow, always drinking. But amusing, very amusing. But, as I told you, Boy was really one of Jamie's group.'

The old man paused. Simon stayed silent and then Gervase went on almost dreamily: 'Jamie used to bring them when we went on the river and Jamie would recite poetry and feed them on Pimms. Do you young people drink Pimms nowadays?'

'Sometimes.'

'It is very intoxicating. That's what Jamie liked to do with his group when they weren't rehearsing. He liked to bring them on the river and get them slightly intoxicated. He said it loosened them up.'

Another titter. Malcolm squirmed in his chair and leaned forward and poked the fire with the tongs.

'I have often told the Master about those parties on the river,' said Gervase.

'You have,' said Malcolm. 'Many times.'

'Jamie would bring his gramophone. It was called a portable gramophone, the size of a typewriter, but in a red leather case. Jamie was very proud of it and it was very handy for the river, but you had to keep winding it up, which was tiresome. He used to bring the records, but they

167

broke very easily if you dropped them. I remember one afternoon when Boy Brackley sat on one and broke it. It was, I think, Jamie's favourite, Constant Lambert's "Rio Grande". There was a terrible to-do.'

He smiled and ran his hand through his white hair. He was looking now into the fire which, thanks to Malcolm's poking, had begun to burn more brightly. 'Or was the "Rio Grande" later? I can't remember. But Jamie loved music.' He was talking now almost to himself. 'It was a happy time. It was never the same again. I like to talk about it.' He turned back to look at Simon. 'Especially to those who are interested. And you certainly seem to be interested.'

'I am. What did Anthony Blunt mean when he said that Boy Brackley had much potential? Potential for what?'

'How do I know? It was that group, you know. They were always involved in something. They only included me because I was Jamie's friend.'

'By then Guy Burgess and Maclean must have left Cambridge?'

'I expect so. Anthony called himself a talent-spotter, always on the look-out to recruit disciples.'

'What was the creed to which Anthony wanted to recruit disciples?'

'Your friend, the nice man who came to see me after those silly boys, Guy and Donald, had gone, he asked me that. He seemed to think it was all political, but I don't think so. With Anthony it was also about life and art. I was very fond of Anthony, you see.'

'Did Boy Brackley become a disciple?'

'I expect so. There were quite a few of them; they all became Anthony's disciples sitting at the master's feet. Not your kind of Master.' He bowed to Malcolm. 'Boy was a very impressionable young man. And so were all his friends.'

'The other actors?'

'Not only the actors. Boy had other friends besides the actors. He used to bring them to Jamie's. They came down from London. Some were not even at the University. One was an artist, an amusing, wild young fellow, very political, called Sam. Another was a most unlikely young man who had just joined, of all things, the Navy. Boy once or twice brought him to tea at Jamie's rooms.'

'This friend was in the Navy?'

'Yes, wasn't that odd? A young sailor. He'd been at Dartmouth with Guy.'

'With Guy? Guy Burgess would surely have been much older.'

'Would he? Yes, come to think of it he would have been. Perhaps this boy had not been there with Guy, but there was something between them about Dartmouth. Or was it Eton? Guy was also at Eton, you know.'

'You said this friend of Boy's was a sailor. An officer?'

'I suppose so. He'd just finished at the Naval College. That was the link with Guy.'

'What did they say about Dartmouth?'

'Just nonsense. I found it very irritating. Guy was always making jokes. One was about something called, I think, Divisions. I remember Guy and this boy singing it out together.'

'Singing?'

'Well, chanting, you know.'

'Chanting what?'

'"Fall out the Jews and the Roman Catholics." They used to say it at each other whenever they met, as a kind of greeting. They said it was the order given at the start of the Church Parade at Dartmouth and Guy and Boy's friend made a joke of it. You see Boy's friend had been a Catholic and Guy was, of course, a Fascist.'

'I thought that Guy was a Marxist.'

'That was later when everyone began making such a fuss about them all. But perhaps I'm wrong, perhaps Guy only pretended to be a Fascist. He loved to shock. He was not an agreeable fellow. But amusing, very amusing.'

'And Boy took this friend to visit your friend Jamie?'

'Yes, of course he did, with the others who came from London. And Jamie used to take them to Trinity to see

169

Anthony. Anthony was always so pleased to see Boy's friends, especially the sailor.'

'Who was this friend? The sailor you spoke about?'

'I remember him because of his name. You see, he had the same name as my friend. We used to make quite a joke of it. For there was my Jamie – Jamie Mathewes. And there was Boy's Jamie – Jamie Layton, the sailor.'

There was a sudden silence. Malcolm waited for Simon to continue. He looked across at Simon, but he could only see the outline of his face in the dimness of the room lit solely by the lamps on the two tables. He could see that Simon was now sitting very still – whereas while he had been asking questions, he had been leaning forward to catch the old man's words. Now he sat bolt upright. No one spoke. Malcolm looked from one to the other. Under the light of the lamp on the table beside Gervase, he could see that the old man was lost in reverie, smiling to himself.

At last Simon broke the silence, speaking very quietly. 'You spoke of Boy Brackley's friend, Jamie Layton. How do you spell that name?' And Simon spelt out the letters – LAYTON.

'How would I know! How could I possibly know! I just remember the two Jamies in my Jamie's rooms in King's. My Jamie and the other one, the sailor who was brought by Boy.'

Gervase rested his head on his hand. 'They're all dead now. Only I am alive. And I only just.' He sighed. Then he said, 'I have enjoyed our talk, conjuring up the ghosts of my youth. It's not often anyone is so interested. I am glad, Master, that you brought your young cousin. Now if you will forgive me, I am a little tired.'

Malcolm got to his feet. 'Of course, Professor. We must go. I hope we haven't kept you too long. I greatly enjoyed listening to you talk about the old days.'

Simon rose. Gervase was still seated in his armchair. He looked up at Simon, peering at him through the fingers of his hand on which his great head still rested.

'I wonder why, young man, I wonder why you were so

170

interested.' Then slowly and with an effort he clambered to his feet and cupping his hands round his mouth he bellowed, 'Mary. Mary.' Then he lowered his hands. 'What's the use. She won't hear. I will have to let you out.'

He walked to the door of the room and then stood aside deferentially allowing the Master to precede him, but pointedly following Malcolm ahead of Simon. In the hall he struggled with the bolts and lock. Simon helped him. Malcolm noticed how white and strained Simon looked.

When the door was opened, Malcolm said to Gervase, 'Thank you for our tea. Remember, you must let me know if the College can do anything for you.'

Gervase bowed. Simon put out his hand without a word. Gervase took it and held it, the hooded, rheumy blue eyes searching Simon's face.

'You remind me of Jamie, my Jamie. That was why I have had you here and why I talked with you. What is your name?'

'Simon.'

Gervase still had Simon's hand in his. As he loosed it, he said, 'Of one thing I am quite certain.'

'Of what are you so certain?'

'That you are up to something, my fine young fellow.' And he shut the door.

As he drove Simon to the station, Malcolm asked, 'You got what you wanted?'

'More, far more than I bargained for.'

They did not speak again until they arrived at the railway station, when Simon abruptly thanked Malcolm and disappeared.

Simon sat in a cold and empty carriage on his way back to London, staring at his reflection in the dark window. It had begun to rain heavily and he watched the slashes of rain and the raindrops as they ran in courses down the glass, while he agonised over what he would now have to say to Alexandra.

171

It was Tomas's case, which his Counsel would have to present in Court – that Brackley had been mixed up with the Communists and had sabotaged the Cetniks to promote the cause of Tito's Communist Partisans. At the trial, it would be his job to destroy Brackley in cross-examination. Now that might involve destroying Alexandra's father.

He would have to tell her this when he saw her – just when all that he wanted to talk about was their love and what her coming into his life had meant to him.

He got to his feet and leaned against the window of the carriage, watching the lights flash past as the train rumbled south towards London. Then he flung himself down again on the seat. He had no alternative. Alexandra must be told – and at once.

When the train drew into King's Cross, he telephoned her to say that he was back. As they had planned, she swiftly replaced the receiver and, excited and happy, set out to come to him.

He was waiting for her at the top of the stairs and she ran to him and he took her in his arms, kissing her tenderly. With one arm still around her he led her through his front door and into the drawing-room, sitting beside her on the sofa, taking her head in his hands and kissing her again and again. After a moment she broke away, her blue-green eyes peering into his.

'What is the matter, Simon?' she asked. 'I know that something is wrong. What is it?'

So he told her all that he knew.

After watching all day, Waring and Price had seen Alexandra come out of the front door, walk to her car and drive away.

While Price kept watch, Waring entered the flat. He removed the device from the telephone junction box and the second device from beneath the desk. He collected the tape recorder from the basement.

172

'Pity,' he said in the car. 'Just when it was getting inter-esting.'

'We could put it back when they've done their sweep and the heat is off.'

'No, the lawyer will be scared now. Still, it's earned us another grand.'

'Provided the bastard pays.'

'Oh, he'll pay all right. He can't afford not to. Stop at a pub and I'll telephone him that all's clear.'

Over their drinks in the pub Waring said, 'I fancy that you and I might have a word with that barman. I think we owe him one.'

SIXTEEN

Early on Monday morning Roger Bentall took a call in his office from Bagot Gray.

'You know that Simon Harrington is a friend of mine.'

'Yes.'

'I had a call from him very early this morning asking me to arrange for my people to do a "sweep" in a flat in Drayton Gardens. It's the home, he said, of the solicitor who is instructing him in a libel case, *Brackley* v. *Tarnovic*. Simon said the case had become very political and sensitive. Someone, he said, is up to dirty tricks – and he suspected that a bug might have been planted.'

'Yes.'

'I told him I'd call him back later this morning.'

'You have been retained by me, Bagot, in the case of *Brackley* v. *Tarnovic*.'

'I have. But if I refuse, it will be obvious that I've been retained by you for Brackley. You may not wish Harrington to know that.'

'I do not. The preparations for trial and the gathering of information are confidential.'

'The only way to avoid the disclosure is for me to do what he asks. But before I do – ' Gray paused and then repeated, 'before I do I must have your word of honour that, as far as you are concerned, there is no device in those premises.'

'Of course you may have my word,' said Bentall solemnly. 'I swear to you that, as far as I am concerned, there is no device on those premises.'

'Very well. I'll tell Simon Harrington that I shall arrange for the sweep to be done this morning.'

Later on that Monday, Gray's technician, Letchfield, reported to him.

'We did the sweep. Mr Harrington was present on behalf of the owner, who is out of London. It's all clean.'

'You are quite certain?'

'I am.'

'Very well. Thank you.' But Letchfield remained. 'What is it?'

Letchfield held up his right hand, picking with his thumb at the nail of his first finger. 'Under a table in the sitting-room I thought, mind you I only thought, that I felt a certain tackiness – the kind that could be left by Cellophane tape which is sticky on both sides. That's often used, you know.'

Gray nodded and Letchfield went on: 'It felt slightly tacky, but mind you there could be many legitimate reasons for finding that. So I said nothing.'

Gray looked at him. After a pause he asked, 'You can't be sure?'

'No. No one could be. All I can say is that it was slightly tacky. But I thought that you might like to know.' He turned to leave. At the door he stopped. 'One other thing. There was no dust – so if there had been anything there, it would have not been long gone.' Then he left.

Bagot Gray remained seated at his desk. In front of him lay a buff folder, which contained what his people had so far discovered about what Sir Leslie Turner had called 'Tarnovic's missing years'. The trail had led them across Europe and China and now to the west coast of the United States. He got up and locked the file in the safe. As he did so, he thought about Bentall. At the conference in the Temple with Leslie Turner, he had thought that the man was becoming obsessed over the case. Now had come Simon Harrington's request. But Bentall had given his

175

word and nothing had been found and the place was clean.

Nevertheless, what Letchfield had said remained at the back of Gray's mind.

Even before Simon had telephoned Bagot Gray and asked him to do a sweep of the flat at Drayton Gardens, Alexandra was in her car driving west.

Her face was pale and drawn, her hair pulled severely back and fastened at the nape of her neck. She wore no make-up and she had pulled one of Simon's sweaters over the dress that she had worn when she had left Drayton Gardens so happily on the previous evening to join him in Onslow Square.

They had spent most of the previous night talking, he telling her what Gregson had said; and then with his arm around her comforting her as she told him angrily of the lunch with her father, of how they had spoken about the Brackley case and how her father had never told her about his long friendship with George Brackley.

'He tried to use me to get information for Brackley,' she stormed.

Simon tried to calm her, but she said that she had to see her father. She had to face him with what he had done.

'He only asked to see me because he wanted to pump me. I shall never, never forgive him.'

'Why not let it rest,' said Simon, 'at least for the moment? Wait until you're calmer and have had more time to think.'

'No,' she said. 'No. Don't you see what he did? He tried to use me, his own daughter, in order to help that man, his friend. I must see him. I want him to know that I know about him and Brackley.'

She said that she would go in the morning and nothing he could say would dissuade her.

'Then you must get some rest. You must stay here.' He led her into the bedroom. 'I can sleep in the other room.'

She stretched out her arms to him. 'I want you to be with me.'

176

After they had made love, he lay awake watching her tossing and turning in her sleep. Just before dawn he slept, and awoke two hours later. He went to the kitchen and made coffee and toast and sat beside her on the bed as she drank and ate. She was on the road soon after seven o'clock and an hour and a half later, she swept up the long drive to her father's home. It was not her home and now it never would be.

As the car drew up, she saw her father's face looking out of the double window of the dining-room to the right of the front door. By the time she was out of the car, he was standing at the open door. She stopped and stared at him.

'Who is it?' she heard Jessica call out from inside the house.

'It is Alexandra,' her father said. He stood aside and Alexandra without a word swept past him and past Jessica, who was standing at the entrance of the dining-room, her napkin in her hand. Alexandra went straight to the library, where she stood waiting for her father.

'Alexandra!' she heard Jessica exclaim. 'Whatever is she doing here at this time of the morning?'

'She has come to see me,' her father repeated. 'Don't disturb us.'

He came into the library, shutting the door behind him. 'You look tired,' he said. 'Would you like anything to eat or drink?'

She shook her head.

'Then at least sit down,' and he sat in his usual armchair. But Alexandra remained standing on the far side of the table in the centre of the room, looking down at his trim figure in a tweed jacket and light corduroy trousers, with his tanned, handsome face and bright silver hair.

'You've come about George Brackley.' It was a statement, not a question.

'About Brackley and you,' she corrected him. 'When I first asked you about him, all you said was that you'd served under him when he was at the Ministry of Defence.'

'That was true.'

177

'But not the whole truth.'

'At the time I saw no need to say more. It didn't seem important at the time. You didn't tell me then that you were involved as a lawyer acting against him.'

'I was not – then. But I told you when we were at your club. I told you and you asked questions. You asked questions because you wanted to find out what we knew, what we were doing. You were spying on me.'

'I was not spying on you, Alexandra.'

'You were. You only asked me to meet you because you wanted to find out how much we knew.'

He rose from his chair and walked across the room to the window. 'That is not true. I always want to see you. What is true is that I did need to find out whether you were involved professionally in his case. It was important that I should know. But that was all.'

'Important for whom? For you, or for George Brackley?'

'For me, of course.' He waved his hand towards the chair opposite him. 'Alexandra, why won't you sit and let us talk about this sensibly?'

'I don't want to sit, but I certainly want to talk about it. When we met for lunch, you were trying to use me to find out what we were doing about Brackley's case.'

'I was doing nothing of the kind. I needed to know whether you had definitely become the solicitor for the other side because I had just been staying with Brackley in Yorkshire and he had told me that the case was going to be defended.'

'You didn't tell me that you had been staying with him and I know why you didn't tell me. If you had, you knew very well you wouldn't have got what you'd been sent to find out.'

'That is not true, Alexandra.' He had risen from his chair and was standing with his back to the window. With the light behind him she could not clearly see his face. She watched as he walked back to his chair and sat bolt upright.

'I only learnt last night,' she said, 'of your so very intimate friendship with Brackley. Then I understood why you had suddenly asked me to see you. It was because you had been instructed to pump me, to find out all you could about the case.'

'I had received instructions from no one.'

'You were using me. You were going to betray anything I said—'

He interrupted her. 'Alexandra, listen to me. When you came down that Sunday some months ago, you asked me casually about George Brackley and I told you what I thought of him, that I liked him, that I admired him.'

'You didn't say then that he was one of your oldest, your closest friends.'

'No, I did not. But at the time you only said that you had seen his name in some legal papers and then we spoke of other things. I didn't think it necessary.'

'Not necessary! And it wasn't necessary when we talked at lunch at your club!'

'No. George Brackley had just informed me that there was now going to be a trial and I needed to know if you were definitely the lawyer in the case.'

'Brackley got you to see me.'

'He did nothing of the kind.'

'You were going to betray me.'

'That is untrue.' He rose again from his chair and went back to the window. Over his shoulder she could see Jessica on the lawn with the dogs. 'I am sorry that you should even think it.' He turned to face her. 'I repeat. I had been in Yorkshire staying with George Brackley. He asked me to come to consult me as an old friend with regard to what he should do about the libel case.'

'And then you immediately got me to see you so that you could find out what we were doing, so you could report to him.'

'I did not.' He had raised his voice. For a time neither spoke. He went back to his chair. Then he went on more quietly. 'After we had lunch together, I telephoned George Brackley and told him that you were one of Tarnovic's lawyers and that I could not discuss the case until it was over. At the lunch I had to find out if you were officially involved. After you'd said that you were, you told me that you were in love.'

'What has that to do with it?'

'We began to talk of the barrister with whom you had fallen in love.'

'Are you saying that my telling you that I was in love stopped you from telling me about Brackley?'

'There was no more to say about Brackley. I was very happy to hear your news.'

'My news! You want me to believe that you were so happy to hear my news that you forgot all about confessing that George Brackley, whom I was acting against, was your greatest, closest, your dearest friend!' She leaned across the table which separated her from where he was sitting. 'Oh, for God's sake, I am not a fool. You deliberately arranged that lunch because he asked you to. You were using me to find out as much as possible so that you could tell everything I knew to your – your lover.'

James Layton rose from his chair and stood on the other side of the table between them, his blue eyes flashing with anger, his face flushed under the tan. He leaned forward and slapped her face. She stared at him. Then she put both hands to her face and sank into a chair. She began to weep, her head bowed in her hands.

'You,' she said. 'You, of all people.'

He began to walk around the table towards her.

'Leave me alone, leave me alone. Don't come near me.'

He stopped. 'What do you mean, Alexandra, by what you have just said?'

She was rocking to and fro. 'Don't lie to me, don't lie to me any more. We know all about you. We know about Cambridge and your visits and your friends. You were Jamie Layton, his Jamie Layton.'

'What are you saying, Alexandra?'

'You were Brackley's Jamie Layton.'

He came and bent over her as she sat, his arms on each

180

of the arms of her chair, his head close to her hands which she still held to her face.

'I was not his Jamie Layton, as you call it. I was never his Jamie Layton.' Then he straightened, still looking down at her as she rocked back and forth. He turned and walked to the window, staring out at the garden. Jessica and the dogs had disappeared.

'I am sorry that I struck you. I have never done anything like that in my life, but you said a terrible thing. George Brackley is my friend. I admire him, I trust him and I would help him if I could. We have known each other since we were children. But what you accused us of is abominable.'

'What's the use?' she whispered. 'What's the use of talking any more? You have ruined everything for me. Everything.' She got to her feet and looked at him, her hand to her cheek where he had struck her.

He stood motionless and silent as she went out into the hall and through the front door to her car and drove away.

On the road she stopped to telephone. Simon was with Arrun and she left a message that she was going home and would not be coming to the office.

She had not been in Drayton Gardens half an hour before Simon telephoned. She'd seen her father, she told him. What happened between them would make no difference. She would carry on as Tomas's solicitor.

'But Alexandra, your father may be drawn into the case. You know what I shall have to do when I cross-examine Brackley and he may involve your father.'

'I know. But I don't care. I'm for Tomas.' She said that would see him tomorrow.

Simon returned to his conference and Arrun. He did not tell Arrun about Alexandra's father, but spoke about the activities of the other side and of the people who were threatening Tomas's friends. He told him what Felix had said about Alexandra's flat, that he had arranged to have it swept and that nothing had been found.

'It sounds,' said Arrun wryly, 'as if everyone's getting a little excited. But is the old man adamant about going on even though you have not come up with anything to support him?'

'As far as I know he is. But I'll ask his friend Felix to go round and have another word with him. Nearer to the trial, I shall try myself.'

That afternoon Felix went to Fulham. Tomas opened the door and the dog, Tito, bounded up to him. Tomas was wearing his camouflage flak jacket and his black beret. He had his stick in his hand.

'So you're better?'

'Yes. You have just caught us. We were going for a walk.'

'Where to?'

'To the park, any park.'

'Get in my car,' said Felix. He drove them to Hyde Park and they left the car in the parking place north of the Serpentine. They walked under the bridge into Kensington Gardens, around the end of the lake and past the statue of Peter Pan. Tomas took bread from his pocket and threw pieces to the ducks. Tito sat on the edge of the tarmac bank watching and wagging his tail. He was obviously used to this ceremony.

When they moved on, Tomas said, 'We are being followed.'

'I know. Since I got involved in your escapade I'm followed everywhere.'

'What could they want from you?'

'To discover whom I'm seeing. But I don't see many. None will talk to me. You have no friends left.'

'Why? What does it matter to them?'

'You know very well. They're all frightened because you have started your own private war and they want no part of it.'

'It will not affect them. It is my business.'

'But your enemies are very powerful and your old friends think that they may suffer if they side with you.'

They walked on towards the Speke Monument. Felix said, 'The lawyers say that you need people to support your story, but they've found none who can or will. Without them it is your word alone and you will not be believed.'

'The lawyers are trying to help and I like them, especially the girl with her lovely hair. She has the same name as someone I knew many, many years ago. The man was very rough with me at first. He was testing me. But there is nothing that the lawyers can do.'

'Why won't you give it up, Tomas? You know you're not going to win. You're only making trouble for everyone.'

'Have you read that man's book?'

'No.'

'Well, he wrote some very strong things about us. In reply, I have written about him. Why should I be the one to say sorry? If he is an English hero, I am a Cetnik hero – or I used to be,' he added.

'Were you?' said Felix.

Tomas looked at him sharply. 'Of course I was.' They had reached the Round Pond. 'When I first came to London, there were many toy boats here, sailing-boats and little ships controlled by wireless. Now there are hardly any. I used to enjoy watching them.' Tomas sat on a bench facing the Pond. Felix looked around and saw the man a hundred yards behind them walking over the grass.

Felix joined Tomas on the bench. 'You're a very stubborn old man.'

'I am proud,' said Tomas. 'So is Brackley, but he is frightened of me. Why else should they follow you and threaten my friends? Brackley knows the truth. You can tell whoever sent you that I shall never apologise to that man.'

At the club that evening, Starjevic closed the bar at 10.30. He had served only three members all evening. Milan Misic, the Chairman, had not been in. Indeed, Starjevic had not

183

seen him since the previous Friday evening when Misic had called him to bring in some more brandy to his office and Starjevic had overheard the burly man with the black hair called Ned boasting about the Government helping them against Tarnovic, and the Home Office warrant.

This Monday evening, like every evening nowadays, he spent most of it reading the paper between serving the few drinks which the few customers ordered. He knew that soon the club would have to close and he was already looking for another job. That bastard Misic would not help him; Misic would probably not even give him a reference – or if he did it would be a mean, reluctant one. Nor would any of the others who now used the place. The decent ones never came now. The old Colonel, Tomas Tarnovic, his regular Saturday customer, was in trouble. He wouldn't be coming back now.

The barman lowered and locked the grille over the bar and he slipped out of the staff entrance into the mews beside the club to make his way home to Ealing. It was a dark night and the mews was unlit, but it was a short cut which would take him to Gloucester Road Underground station. He was walking fast along the cobbled surface of the mews when the first figure came at him from behind out of the shadows by the entrance to a garage. He felt the blow to the back of his neck and fell forward with a muffled cry. A second figure appeared from behind one of the parked cars, threw a cloth over his head, pulled him to his feet and forced him back against the garage door. The second blow was to the pit of his stomach, followed by another and then a third. He slipped to the ground, the cloth still around his face. Then they started kicking him, first his belly, then his head and he could feel the blood sticky on the cloth around his face. He heard one of them say, 'That'll teach you to keep your mouth shut. Next time it'll be worse.'

He felt them turn him and take his wallet from his pocket and heard their footsteps as they ran to the end of the mews and away. Someone had heard the noise and a light came on in the room above the garage. Soon he was in the hall of one of the small mews houses; the ambulance was sent for and he was taken to the Casualty Department at St Stephen's Hospital in Fulham.

His nose and two ribs were broken, a tooth knocked out of his mouth. His whole body was badly bruised. He was detained overnight and the police took a report from him. It was another case of a 'mugging', they said.

But Starjevic knew different and he did not go back to the club. A few days later he caught the train and went to his cousins in Glasgow, where he disappeared into the anonymity of the city.

A week later Velkjo Ostrojic, who Starjevic had told Felix had served with Tomas in the army and had unwisely taken a trip to Paris to see his dying sister, was stopped by Immigration officers at Dover. One of them consulted a register and the other pointed to a note which had been recently added to the list. They spoke together out of Ostrojic's hearing as they studied his passport and checked it against the list to which the note had been added. Then they came back to him.

He had no right to reside in the United Kingdom, they said. Whitehall had discovered that he had been living illegally in Cumbria. He would not be allowed to enter the country. He could, of course, appeal, they said, but then it would come out that he had made false statements when he had first come to the United Kingdom. That was perjury, they said, and that meant prison. But if he were to turn round and go, nothing more would be said. It would be better for him if he went without fuss.

They escorted him on board the next boat to Calais.

During the months that followed, Perry Fanshaw worked away at the wartime records in Kew, but no person came forward to support Tomas. None could be found who had fought in the mountains when George Brackley had

185

descended by parachute to join the Cetniks near to the town of Orgulica in eastern Serbia in November 1943. So as the time for trial approached, Tomas Tarnovic's legal team had no witness, no document – nothing. Save Tomas's own account and Tomas's invincible certainty that when the Court heard him, Brackley would be exposed. That was all that the Defence had – that and Simon's hunch that it was in the Cambridge of the 1930s that there lay the secret to the whole story.

SEVENTEEN

Mr Justice Tetley was one of the most senior judges of the Queen's Bench Division of the High Court. He had been a judge for fifteen years, sufficient to have earned maximum pension, but as he was not yet seventy, he could serve for another five years before he reached the compulsory retirement age. That he was still what was called a puisne or plain High Court Judge, trying cases at first instance, and had not been promoted to become a Lord Justice of the Court of Appeal rankled. Once safely in the Court of Appeal, he believed that he might then have progressed to the highest pinnacle of the judicial pyramid – namely a life peerage as a Law Lord sitting on the Judicial Committee of the House of Lords. To have been a Peer of the Realm would have been, for Brian Tetley, total bliss.

But the promotion had never come. There was no place for him in the Appellate Court; younger and more junior judges were promoted over him, judges whom he considered far less qualified than himself. Nursing his grievance he thus remained a judge of the Queen's Bench Division, where he had at least been put in charge of the jury list as the judge who regularly presided over those few civil cases which were still tried by a judge sitting with a jury. Most of these were defamation actions and he enjoyed trying these, for he was a master of the intricacies of libel law, the facts were often interesting, and he enjoyed lording it, literally, over the well-known personalities who were usually involved. Moreover, were he to retire, he would not know what he would do with himself; he had no hobbies and no interests outside the law, the practice of which had been his whole life.

He lived in a substantial villa on Kingston Hill with his formidable wife Blanche, a fanatical gardener and an intense and devoted worker for good causes. Their son was a dentist with a young family, who lived in Bristol; their daughter Patricia, the brighter of their two children, had emigrated as a young woman to Australia, where she led a mysterious life as some kind of social worker in Sydney and had never married. The Judge had long suspected that she was not interested in men and he had never enquired into the circumstances of her life, nor who shared it. He was relieved that she lived so far away.

When he had been at the Bar, Brian Tetley had enjoyed an all-round practice which, as he had been a good jury advocate, included some crime and the occasional brief in a libel case. On the bench to which he had been appointed at the age of fifty-four, he had developed into a judge before whom few advocates enjoyed appearing; his caustic comments on the Bar, on witnesses, or on parties were much quoted in the Press. But he was a good lawyer and a good judge of fact. Above all, he was a monumental snob.

He had himself come from a modest background. His father had been employed on the old Great Western Railway; his mother, Penny, had been a doctor's receptionist and, she had regularly informed her husband, a cut above her railwayman spouse. At the ceremony of his call to the Bar by the Inner Temple, his mother, when they were presented to the Treasurer of the Inn, had made sure that the old railwayman was seen but very little heard.

She had been fiercely ambitious for their only child and it was much due to her coaching that Brian had won a place in the grammar school at Swindon and then a scholarship to Merton College, Oxford, where he got a first in law. To begin with, he had led a dim existence devoted to his books and earnest conversation with like-minded contemporaries, until he started to attend the debates at the Union, where he met with immediate success, for he had a handsome face and a light, agreeable voice. Once in practice at the Bar, Brian Tetley quickly made a good living and he was excessively generous to his recently-widowed mother who had made possible his rise in the world.

In his last two years at Oxford, his debating prowess in the Union and his subsequent membership of the Liberal Club had led him into a wider circle of acquaintance drawn from the larger colleges and this had brought him to the fringe of the *jeunesse dorée* at the House and New College. With them, or rather with their style, he had fallen in love and he had begun to cultivate a somewhat languid pose both in manner and in speech. He had modified this when he had been called to the Bar and had commenced his pupillage to a hard-working, no-nonsense junior on the Western circuit, but once a judge and 'Sir Brian', the languid pose was revived and developed – enhanced, he believed, by his habit of waving a cambric handkerchief in Court.

He was smiled at by many of his fellow judges, most of whom shared his grammar school and Oxbridge scholarship education but not those affectations, which had been one of the reasons why he had not advanced further up the judicial ladder. But for all his faults of personality, he remained a strong judge whose decisions were rarely reversed on appeal and whose robust sentencing in criminal cases was often tempered by surprising bouts of leniency when something touched the man beneath the elaborate façade which he had so laboriously created.

He was Simon's least favourite judge. Simon thought him a poseur who gave himself airs, and had not troubled to conceal this opinion around the Temple. But Simon was also aware of Mr Justice Tetley's ability as a lawyer and, above all, his effectiveness with a jury. For the Judge prided himself on his ability to handle juries and he undoubtedly had a way with them, making the men and women who served on them feel that while the opposing Counsel in the case were, of course, paid to say what they did, he and the jury were only there out of public duty and that between them they would do justice – and let the Devil take the lawyers! This went down well with juries and thus it was well known at the Bar that to get a verdict from a jury in a case presided over by Mr Justice Tetley was vastly more difficult if the Judge had different ideas. It was not wise, therefore, to 'lose' this judge. In other words, it was important for an advocate not to alienate him, because his would be the last word; and when he came to sum up the evidence and give directions on the law before the jury retired to consider their verdict, his was the persuasive tongue which was the last that they would hear.

A year previously, soon after he had taken silk, Simon had appeared before him in a medical negligence case, which was tried by Mr Justice Tetley sitting alone without a jury. It was heard at the time when Simon had been in his blackest period following the accident which had killed his wife and he had become involved in an ill-tempered argument with his opponent. When the Judge had intervened, Simon had turned acidly upon him. In the event, although angered by Simon's brusqueness, Mr Justice Tetley had not allowed this to prevent him giving judgement for Simon's client. But before the Judge left the bench, he had said, 'Mr Harrington, may I remind you that good temper is the advocate's best companion.' Then he had risen and left the Court.

This, then, was the judge who was in charge of the list of jury trials for the Trinity or summer term when, after many months, the case of *Brackley* v. *Tarnovic* was at last due for trial at the Law Courts in the Strand.

In late July, a week before the date fixed for the trial and more than eighteen months after Tomas Tarnovic had circulated his pamphlets, the Judge was sitting in his room in the Law Courts reading the pleadings – the Statement of Claim, which set out in full what Tomas had written about Lord Brackley and which Lord Brackley claimed had libelled him. Then the defence, which replied that all that Tomas had written about George Brackley was true. This

190

case, the Judge saw, would receive much public interest and provide him with much scope for one of his bravura judicial performances, and he reflected upon the prospect with satisfaction. If, however, the case ever came to trial; for many of the libel cases settled at the last moment and having read the pleadings, he considered that this might well be one of those. It was hard to believe that this obscure defendant was going to persist in maintaining that the well-known and respected Lord Brackley was a liar and a coward.

He rang the bell for his clerk.

'Parsons, *Brackley* v. *Tarnovic*, down for trial on the 20th. Is that a fight, or are the parties going to settle?'

'As far as I know, my lord, it's still effective, but I expect the parties are talking.'

'It could be an agreeably stimulating occasion if it ever comes to Court – which, alas, I doubt. It would make a change from the usual run of claims by entertainers against newspapers. Who are the Counsel engaged?'

'Sir Leslie is for the Plaintiff and Mr Harrington for the Defendant.'

'Ah, that young man. Then we can expect some spirited scenes. I will enjoy keeping him in order. Let me know in good time if the parties have come to an agreement or not.'

'I will, my lord.'

The Judge walked across the Strand from the Law Courts to lunch at his Inn of Court. When he entered the Hall and slipped into a seat on the High Table where the Benchers of the Inn lunched, he saw that he was opposite Leslie Turner.

'Good-morning, Leslie,' he said. 'I have just been reading the pleadings in your *cause célèbre*, which I am to try next week. Is it still a fight?'

'I'm not certain, Judge. I gather that the solicitors are talking, but I am preparing myself.'

'I hear that young Simon Harrington is against you. I hope that the young man will behave himself.'

Whatever his own experience with the prickly Simon –

who he had heard had recently grown surprisingly better tempered – Leslie was not prepared to join in any off-stage criticism of a fellow silk by a judge, particularly not this one.

'I'm sure he will, Judge. He did sometimes get overexcited, but he had personal reasons and I gather he's over that now.'

'There was certainly room for improvement. We shall have to watch him closely.' And the Judge ordered for himself a plate of cold ham and a single tomato.

Leslie Turner went into the coffee-room and as he poured his coffee, he heard Simon at his elbow say, 'Your ears must be burning, Leslie. Everyone is talking about your handling of the Tarrant appeal. They're saying that it was outstanding.'

Agreeably surprised, Leslie looked round at Simon. 'That's good of you. It was a difficult case.' To his further surprise Simon followed him with his cup to the sofa and sat beside him.

'When do you think the election will take place?' Simon enquired.

He is making amends, thought Leslie, and he was pleased. 'In the autumn.'

'Will you be involved?'

Leslie laughed. 'Not I. Those days are long over.'

'Pity,' said Simon smiling. 'I hoped I might pick up some of the briefs you couldn't do while you were away electioneering.'

'You don't need any returns from me. You're flourishing like the green bay tree. By the way, Brian Tetley had a word with me at lunch. He's to try the Brackley case and he wanted to know if it is effective.'

'Oh, God,' groaned Simon. 'I thought we'd get him. That's a head start for you. He loves a lord.'

'Watch him. You're not one of his favourites.'

'Has he any?' They both laughed.

As Leslie Turner walked from the Inn to his chambers in Brick Court, he thought about Simon Harrington. Their conversation had confirmed what he had heard – that Simon was a different fellow from the grouchy one he had been recently. But Tetley might provoke him. Then the sparks would fly. As for himself, he would keep his head down. If those two got into a fight, he would keep well out of it.

In Clifford Street later in the afternoon, Roger Bentall was on the telephone.

'Is that John Arrun?'

'It is.'

'Brackley and Tarnovic.'

'Yes. What about it?'

'I would like to speak about the case, without prejudice you understand.'

'Yes.'

'If your client were to withdraw his defence and apologise even at this late hour, I believe I could persuade my client to be reasonable.'

'Such as?'

'He would not seek damages. Each side to pay his own costs.'

'I will speak with Counsel.' Arrun rang off.

Later he went round to see Simon.

'Bentall has offered to drop the claim for damages and costs if Tarnovic will apologise and withdraw. That's a surprisingly generous offer and he ought to take it.'

'Of course he ought. But will he? No one has been able to persuade him so far.'

'You promised me that you would try to persuade him to drop his defence if we could not get anything substantial to corroborate his story. Will you try?'

'Certainly. But there is only one person who might be able to do that. Alexandra.'

'Take her with you when you talk to him? It's our duty to tell him what we all think.'

'I will try.'

When Arrun had left, Simon arranged to go to Alexandra at Drayton Gardens an hour later.

At 5.30 that evening, Henry Cranston slipped out of his seat in the Chamber of the House of Lords and walked down the red carpet of the corridor to where it joined the corridor with the green carpet of the Commons, the point in the Palace of Westminster which marked the frontier between Lords and Commons. He turned left, crossed the lobby and made for the Commons' smoking-room. Because he had been an MP before he had succeeded to the Earldom on the death of his father and now sat in Parliament in the House of Lords, he was entitled to use the Commons' smoking-room, and he had arranged to meet Walter Fairchild, the Chancellor of the Duchy of Lancaster and Chairman of the party then in government.

When Henry entered the smoking-room, Walter rose from the table where he had been sitting and after they had got their drinks from the bar, the two men crossed to a sofa at the far end of the room.

At the table next to the sofa, Crichton Smith lowered his copy of the *Sporting Times*. The two did not see him; soon they were engrossed in their conversation. Crichton raised his newspaper and eavesdropped.

'George Brackley's case comes on next week,' Henry Cranston began.

'I know. Roger Bentall phoned my office to tell us.'

'I'm to give evidence for him.'

'What can you say?'

'Nothing about the facts. I'm what they call a character witness.'

'Does George need one?'

'I shouldn't have thought so, but Bentall says it'd do no harm if I appeared. We were in Cabinet together when I was at the Foreign Office and George was at Defence. We're old friends.'

'Can't it be settled out of Court? The smears will brush off on to the party.'

'I know. Bentall tells me that he's still trying to settle.'

'Is anyone putting this fellow, Tarnovic, up to it? Is there anyone behind him?'

'I don't know. With an election in the offing, it's certainly very convenient for the other side.'

'What can I do?'

'Nothing, but I thought that you'd better know that I'm going to appear as a witness.'

'There'll be massive publicity. It's not often that an ex-Cabinet Minister is accused of cowardice in the face of the enemy. All I can do is to prepare damage limitation. The best reply to the smears would be an award of massive damages for George and a rider from the jury expressing their disgust at the defence.'

'That, I presume, is what Bentall is hoping for.'

'Tell me, what do you think of the fellow?'

'Bentall? I don't know. He's said to be very clever.'

'He's got himself into an influential position in the National Union. I'm not so sure about him.'

'I imagine that he's the best kind of lawyer to have on one's side at a time like this – pretty ruthless.'

'I heard that George hasn't been well. Is it serious?'

'Grace thinks so.'

'I hope the case doesn't affect him too much. I like George. Years ago I was his Parliamentary Private Secretary.'

'He's a great survivor. Well, I've told you that I'm to be a witness and now you won't be surprised when you see my name in print. I couldn't refuse to appear.'

'Of course you couldn't. You'll add tone to the sordid proceedings.'

'I'm not so sure. Earls are no longer very fashionable.'

They finished their drinks and the two left the smoking-room.

After a time, Crichton Smith looked at his watch. Then he put down his paper and followed them out, making for the Strangers' Bar and his appointment with Jumbo Lancaster.

At the flat in Pelham Lane in Fulham, the visitors were greeted as usual by Tito. Alexandra kissed Tomas on the cheek.

'I liked that,' he said. 'Come in.' He gestured to the chairs. 'Have you come to tell me that Brackley has given up?'

'No, Tomas. Not that. But it would be good if he had.'

'Is that so? I want my day in Court.'

The door to the small garden was open. It was still light and it was warm. The dog left them and went and lay on the grass.

'Tito does not like the heat. But I do. It suits my old bones.'

'How have you been?' asked Alexandra.

'Well enough, but not well enough to go to Felix to paint. I seem to have lost the urge.'

'The case begins next week,' said Simon.

Tomas turned to look at him. 'And about time, too.'

'We have very little evidence and as I told you when we first met, the burden is upon you to prove that what you wrote is true. You now have to make a final and irrevocable decision. Brackley has offered to drop his claim for damages and costs if you will withdraw and apologise. That is pretty generous. It is your last chance.'

There was silence in the room. In the distance they could hear the rumble of the traffic in the Fulham Road.

'So?'

'So we want your instructions. As your advisers we must recommend that you consider the offer very seriously.'

'You mean, accept?'

'Yes.'

'That is the advice of you all?' Tomas looked at Alexandra and she nodded. He rose and, leaning on his stick, went over to the wall. He picked up the photograph of General

Draža Mihailović, the leader of the Cetniks whom Marshal Tito had executed at the end of the War. Tomas held it in his hands looking at it as if it were an icon. He said softly, his back to them, 'I cannot withdraw. I told you at the very beginning.'

'I remember very well what you said. That was before we had begun our search for evidence, but we've not come up with any corroboration of your story.'

'Those who might have helped have been frightened off.' He was still holding the photograph in his hands.

'That may be so, but the result is that it is improbable that you will succeed in defeating Brackley's claim. If you do not, you face ruin.'

'We shall hear from my friends once the case begins. When they read about it, they will come forward.'

'That is possible.'

'It is certain.' Tomas replaced the photograph and picked up another, the picture of the Cetniks in their ragged uniforms. 'What do you say, Alexandra?' he enquired.

'She agrees —'

Tomas interrupted him. 'Let her speak for herself.'

Alexandra turned in her chair and faced him. 'What Simon has said is true, Tomas.'

'You are risking everything —' Simon began.

Tomas held up his hand. 'Please,' he said. 'I understand that. You have done your duty and I am grateful.' He walked back to the table. He was looking at Alexandra. 'Do they ever call you Sacha? It is the diminutive, you know, of Alexandra.'

She shook her head. Suddenly he lifted his stick and brought it down with a crack upon the table. 'I will never apologise to that man! Never! Never! Never!' He struck the table again. 'He betrayed General Mihailović! He betrayed Yugoslavia! He is a villain and a traitor!'

The dog, disturbed from his dozing in the garden by the noise, came into the room and nuzzled Tomas's hand.

Simon got to his feet. 'Then we go on,' he said.

'You need not,' said Tomas. 'I can go on alone.'

'No,' said Simon. 'It would be too difficult for you to act for yourself. But I had to warn you for one last time. I have been your Counsel from the first and I shall remain so until the last.'

Tomas looked from one to the other, to Simon standing across the table and to Alexandra in her chair looking up at Simon. 'I can see that some good has come from my obstinacy. You are lovers,' he said.

Alexandra smiled. 'Yes. We are lovers.'

'Remain so,' said Tomas, 'from the first to the last.' And he too smiled, the winning smile that had so captivated her when first she had talked with him as they stood painting in Felix's studio.

EIGHTEEN

Everyone stood as Mr Justice Tetley in short bob wig and dark-blue robe with a red sash swept into Court. He nodded perfunctorily to Counsel who faced him, and then turned, bowed and smiled at the jury in the jury-box on his right and took his seat. All in the Court then sat. In the well of the Court, below the Judge and the jury, Lord and Lady Brackley, with Roger Bentall beside them, sat in the front row behind a table facing the Judge. Lord Brackley was dressed in a dark suit and his regimental tie. With his fine profile and abundant white hair, he looked exceedingly distinguished, but his face was pale and there were dark patches beneath his eyes. Beside him, Grace in a grey-and-white-patterned silk dress looked equally pale and tense; all she was thinking about was the strain on her husband's heart.

Directly behind them, one step up in the front row of Counsels' benches, sat their two Queen's Counsel, Sir Leslie Turner QC and James Fenton QC. In the bench behind them sat William Robson, a leading Junior at the libel bar, who was accompanied by his pupil, Janet Wells, who had been given a noting brief. James Fenton QC had been added to the Brackley team because he was the leading academic lawyer specialising in defamation law and the co-author of the latest edition of *Gatley on Libel and Slander*, the textbook regarded as the bible for all those who practised in the law of libel. Bentall had thought that the presence of Fenton, who had no experience of practice in Court but who was the acknowledged expert in this branch of the law, would impress the Judge. In all, Roger Bentall had briefed four Counsel. It was a formidable team.

'The best that money could buy,' Perry Fanshaw had said to Simon as they had waited for the Judge; 'the flower, the most expensive flower of the libel bar.'

Simon had only growled; at the start of any case he was edgy and until he came into Court, he usually paced the corridors speaking with no one.

In the same front row in the well of the Court and behind his own table, separated from Roger Bentall by only a few feet, sat John Arrun and beside him Alexandra, dressed in her office uniform of dark suit and white shirt, with her blonde hair fastened at the nape of her neck by a velvet bow.

Next to her sat Tomas. Above faded blue jeans, he had on a black alpaca coat of old-fashioned cut, buttoned high in the front over his one white shirt, freshly ironed although a little frayed at the cuffs, and a black tie. He sat with his head held high, looking supremely unconcerned and curling his moustache. Before taking his place, he had stared at his surroundings with curiosity, which, however, was soon satisfied, for within a few minutes of the start of the case, he had his eyes closed. Behind him and alone sat his single Queen's Counsel, Simon; and behind him, Perry Fanshaw. The Tarnovic team consisted of two Counsel only.

The seven men and five women of the jury were all in their places in the jury-box. Simon examined them carefully. The men varied in age from about the late fifties to one in his mid-twenties and were all in jacket and tie save for the youngest, who wore a flowered open shirt. The best-dressed was an elderly, dark-skinned man. Of the women, three were young, perhaps between the late twenties to mid-thirties, and two middle-aged, who were sitting together. The day was warm and the women were in light dresses.

Looking at them, Simon calculated that the lot which had led to the selection of this jury must have fallen upon the higher-priced area of perhaps Clapham or Battersea. For a case of this kind that was fortunate, for they looked like people who might watch the news each evening on TV

200

and, with a bit of luck, might know something about the history of the last fifty years. But nothing could be taken for granted with a jury.

The Court was crowded; briefless barristers in their wigs and gowns, solicitors and their clerks taking time off from their other business in the Courts were standing alongside the benches, which had filled to overflowing as soon as the usher had unlocked the doors. Henry Cranston was sitting with a young partner from Baker and Turnbull behind the Brackley team; Felix Ilic behind Perry Fanshaw. From time to time, still more spectators pushed through the swing-doors and stood at the back of those who had come earlier, craning to get sight of the parties in the well of the Court and the Leading Counsel in the front row. Above in the public gallery, many had been turned away. The lucky ones who had got seats in the front leaned over the balustrade and peered down at the Court below. Jumbo Lancaster, by arrangement with his paper's Law Courts reporter, had squeezed his bulk into the Press bench opposite the jury and directly beneath the witness-box – to the irritation of the regular Court reporters who, however, had not dared to complain.

When he had taken his seat on the bench, Mr Justice Tetley surveyed the crowded scene in front of him with satisfaction. This was just the kind of occasion which he savoured. He motioned to the Associate sitting directly below him, a large Black man in a very white wig. '*Brackley* versus *Tarnovic*,' the Associate intoned. The jury, requested to stand, were all sworn together. The Associate resumed his seat. Leslie Turner rose to start his opening statement, but Mr Justice Tetley forestalled him.

'Sir Leslie, Mr Harrington,' he said. Simon stood. The two Leading Counsel were now facing the Judge. 'Before we begin I shall, as is my practice, have a word with the jury about the daily programme of the trial and what I call the housekeeping.' He smiled at the jury and put his cambric handkerchief to his lips and the two Counsel resumed their seats.

'Good morning, ladies and gentlemen. May I welcome you to my Court – and thank you for attending here at the Royal Courts of Justice to help in the administration of justice, which is such an important part of the citizen's civic duty. Your attendance to assist in the administration of justice is greatly appreciated, for I am sure that this has imposed upon each of you considerable inconvenience. So I extend to you my thanks.'

All the jurors knew that if they had not attended they were liable to a hefty fine, but it was none the less agreeable to hear this tribute to their sense of responsibility.

He is buttering them up as usual, thought Simon, so that they will be more likely to be persuaded by him when he sums up the evidence. There would be little chance of 'winning' the Judge. He would have to take the risk of deliberately 'losing' him – and early.

Mr Justice Tetley smiled again at the jurors, looking directly at a middle-aged woman in the front row. Helen Hunter smiled back. 'Our programme will be as follows. The Court will sit each day from 10.30 in the morning until one o'clock, when we shall break for lunch. I am sure that the Jury Bailiff has told you that there does exist a cafeteria in this building – but I can't guarantee the quality of what they serve, so I beg you not to blame me should you find it not altogether to your taste.'

Helen smiled again. He was a very nice old gentleman, she thought.

'We shall resume at two o'clock and rise for the day at 4.30. This should give those of you who have business which requires attention at least a little time to attend to it. I fear that is the best I can do to assist you. I must also apologise for the unfortunate fact that the jury-box where you are sitting in this, alas, old-fashioned courtroom is rather cramped and not very comfortable. In the old days, citizens must have had shorter legs than we have today. Be that as it may, I can only express my regrets and plead not guilty for making your seats so uncomfortable. The construction of the Court is not my doing.'

He is intolerable, thought Perry Fanshaw. How much more of this do we have to endure!

'But I have instructed the Court staff to provide notebooks and pencils for those of you who may choose to make notes as the evidence proceeds. Tomorrow being Friday, we shall adjourn as usual at 4.30 and reassemble at 10.30 on Monday. If there is anything at all which you may need during the course of the trial, please, I beg you, ask the Associate sitting beneath me or that gentlemen there — ' He pointed with the hand holding the cambric handkerchief at the usher, who on cue, for he was used to this performance, rose from his seat and bowed. 'They will report your wishes or enquiries to me and if it lies in my power to accommodate you, rest assured that I shall oblige. One further matter. Learned Counsel sitting over there — ' here he gave a dismissive wave of the cambric handkerchief towards Counsels' benches, 'will shortly be telling you and me what the case is all about, of which I, like you, am at present quite ignorant.'

Liar, thought Simon. You have read the pleadings – or if you haven't, you should have.

'We are all, I know, eager to hear what they have to tell us so that we can be informed on what we have to adjudicate. That is, on what you ladies and gentlemen have to adjudicate, for although I am called the judge in a trial with a jury, I am only here to direct you upon the law and — ' this time he smiled at Counsel, 'keep those gentlemen over there in order.'

Professor Fenton QC, the academic lawyer for whom appearing in Court was a novel experience, was the only one who smiled back. The others buried their faces in their papers; they had heard it all before.

'One last matter and then I am done. I must ask you on no account to discuss the case while it continues with anyone, either here or when you return to your home in the evenings. Talk about the case with no one, save among yourselves. Indeed, if you will allow me to advise you, it is generally wiser not even to talk among yourselves during the luncheon or overnight adjournments unless you are very certain that you cannot be overheard. You will, of course, have plenty of time for discussion when you eventually retire to consider your verdict. Well, I think that is all. And now you and I can sit back and wait to be informed.'

His final smile was answered by smiles of acknowledgement from three or four of the jury, including, once again, Helen Hunter. The young man with the open-necked shirt tried to cross his legs in the constricted space of the jury-box but failed. Pompous ass, he thought.

'Yes, Sir Leslie,' said Mr Justice Tetley with, for the time being, a final wave of the handkerchief. 'Pray begin.'

The rest of the morning was taken up with Leslie Turner's opening statement on behalf of Lord Brackley the Plaintiff, whom Turner described as one of the most distinguished of the nation's public servants, now retired, and a much decorated hero of World War Two. This was the man who had been infamously traduced – Helen Hunter was not quite sure what that meant, but it sounded bad – in two pamphlets written and circulated by the Defendant who, although apparently at one time a citizen of Yugoslavia and not a citizen of the United Kingdom, had lived in London for many years enjoying the liberties and hospitality which had long been denied to the citizens of his country of origin. After recounting the career and service of Lord Brackley and emphasising his awards for gallantry as a young man, Counsel then told the jury of Lord Brackley's wartime exploits and his arrival by parachute to join the guerrilla group in the mountains of Yugoslavia in November 1943, reciting, with some embroidery, the story told by Lord Brackley in his memoirs. This took him to the luncheon adjournment.

'Would that be a convenient moment, my lord, to adjourn?' he enquired shortly before one o'clock.

'Certainly, Sir Leslie.' The Judge turned his winning smile on to the jury. 'Now, ladies and gentlemen, we shall break for lunch and you will have your first experience of testing the cafeteria of the Royal Courts of Justice. Remember, don't blame me if you don't like it.' By now he was on his feet and everyone in the Court rose. 'We shall resume to hear the remainder of Sir Leslie's fascinating opening at two o'clock.'

Oleaginous bastard, thought Simon. When the jury had all left the Court, he said to Tomas, 'You must keep your eyes open and look as though you are attending to every word.'

'It is very difficult,' said Tomas humbly.

'It may be, but the jury will be watching you.'

'I am not sleeping. I am rehearsing my part in my mind.'

In the robing room Simon asked Turner, 'Will you have Brackley in the box this afternoon, Leslie?'

'I expect to. He'll be some considerable time in examination-in-chief. You won't be cross-examining until tomorrow.'

In the afternoon, Leslie Turner turned to the libels, 'the words complained of', and having supplied the jury with copies, he took them carefully through Tomas's two pamphlets, comparing Tomas's version with that in Lord Brackley's book and categorising the pamphlets as 'the most wicked libels which could ever have been made about anybody, let alone about a man of the distinction of Lord Brackley'. He concluded his opening by giving to the jury the classic definition of libel – 'any imputation which may tend to cause a man to be hated or despised'.

'However,' he added, 'there is no need to distinguish between hatred and contempt, although it may be more natural to say that one hates the villain and despises the coward. In this case, what this Defendant has deliberately sought to do is to brand this distinguished public servant and brave officer as both a villain and a coward.'

With one eye on the Judge, he hastily added that, of

course, all matters of law were solely the province of His Lordship, who at the relevant time would direct them on the law, and from whom the jury would take the law and not from Mr Harrington or himself. Here, Mr Justice Tetley nodded sagely and played a little with the handkerchief, while Leslie Turner, in a final and spirited conclusion, declared that when they had heard the evidence, he had no doubt that they would return, without hesitation, a verdict for the Plaintiff; and would mark the vile lies which had been so wantonly published about him by awarding Lord Brackley a very, very substantial sum of damages as a vindication of his splendid character and reputation. Leslie Turner then paused.

Helen Hunter, filled with indignation at the wicked behaviour of the foreigner Tarnovic, was there and then ready to award Lord Brackley many thousands of pounds. She turned to her neighbour, a thin, sallow woman with grey hair, to express her thought, when she heard Leslie Turner say loudly, 'Lord Brackley.'

George Brackley, his handsome face now even more pale, grasped his stick and after Grace had given his hand a squeeze, rose and made his way slowly up the steps and into the witness-box. He took the oath. In front of him across the Court, he could see the jury; on his left, almost level with him was the Judge's bench; and below him, seated next to the girl with the shining hair who must be James Layton's daughter, he saw the man who must be Tomas Tarnovic. When the Brackleys had entered the Court in the morning, and at the luncheon break, George Brackley had purposely avoided looking for or at his opponent. Now he had to see him, for he was there sitting below him and Brackley could see a man as old as himself, with a theatrical curling moustache and hair as white as his own. Could that be the man, the Cetnik Commandant with the dark hair and short pointed beard whom he had joined in those caves half a century ago? Only if he could look closely into those sad eyes, the only feature which he remembered, could he be certain.

'Lord Brackley,' he heard the voice of the Judge, 'would you care to sit while you are giving your evidence?'

'I should prefer to start by standing, my lord, but my knees are not very good and — '

'And you may sit at any time you choose. Usher, bring a chair into the witness-box so that Lord Brackley can sit whenever he wishes.'

The examination-in-chief by his own Counsel began with Leslie Turner intoning, as in a litany, the honours and decorations which Lord Brackley had gained and the public posts that he had held throughout his career. The interest of the young juror had been momentarily aroused by the sight of a figure in the witness-box, but not for long. He's very old, he thought, older even than the Judge. The young juror listened for a while and then relapsed into his own thoughts about a girl called Sandra and about the football he would see on the following Saturday.

For her part, Helen Hunter liked what she saw; she admired Lord Brackley's handsome features and she approved of his quiet, cultivated voice as he answered Turner's questions. How dare the foreigner, she kept telling herself, write such wicked things about so fine a man?

One of the middle-aged jurors, a spruce, neat man with large horn-rimmed glasses and slightly pursed lips who planned to become the foreman, was impressed by the list of military decorations that the young George Brackley had won. His own father had won a Military Cross at the Battle of El Alamein and he had the medal in its case by his father's photograph in the sitting-room of his home. But this juror had not altogether liked Brackley's politics. He had been a student at Exeter University when Brackley had come down to speak and he had stayed away. Still, he admitted, he looks a fine old fellow.

Turner now took Brackley through the early part of his life. He asked only one question about Brackley's time at Cambridge.

'When you were an undergraduate at Cambridge, did you know a fellow student called Stepan Stepanic?'

207

'I have no recollection of anyone of that name.'

Simon wrote this in his notebook and sidelined it in red.

Brackley then went on to give evidence of joining the Army at the start of the War in 1939, of being present at the fighting in the retreat to Dunkirk and the evacuation in 1940. Next he told the Court of how he had volunteered for service with SOE and his departure for service in Cairo and the Middle East.

At this point, Simon leaned forward and rested a hand on Tomas's shoulder in front of him. Tomas half-turned to look at Simon, who smiled and nodded, indicating that now the Defendant should pay particular attention. They were coming to the heart of the matter.

Simon had on the bench in front of him a copy of Brackley's memoirs, *A Time To Remember*. It was flagged and marked and Simon followed Turner's questions and Brackley's answers, comparing them with the text of the book, noting only the few variations or embroideries.

Turner now slowed down the exchange of question and answer as he came to Brackley's descent by parachute into the mountains in November 1943, his reception by the Cetnik guerrillas, the chaos of the march to the head-quarters, the ineffectiveness of the command and the first abortive operation to destroy the railway line. When Brackley began to speak of the battle during which the Cetniks had been annihilated by the German Mountain Division, the courtroom became still and hushed. In a practised, quiet voice, he told of the dramatic ambush, the opening up of the German Spandau machine guns firing into the column, the Verey lights soaring up into the night sky, the mortar bombs falling among the screaming Cetniks.

When the witness described this, he paused for a moment and the courtroom waited, expectant. The silence was broken by a snort and the loud rap of the ferrule of a stick on the floor. Mr Justice Tetley looked up and across the well of the Court at Tomas. The cambric handkerchief was waved ominously.

'Mr Harrington,' he said sharply, 'kindly tell your client

to behave. I will not have demonstrations during a witness's evidence – nor indeed at any time in my Court. See that he is kept under control.'

Simon half-rose and bowed. He placed his hand again on Tomas's shoulder. What a rude man, thought Helen Hunter looking at Tomas. Typical of a foreigner.

Brackley's evidence continued, quiet, convincing, reasonable. He had come to the end of his account of his time in the mountains at about twenty past four and Leslie Turner began to turn to the circulation of the pamphlets, the libels.

'Lord Brackley, you are looking tired – understandably if I may say so.' The Judge smiled at the witness. Then he looked at the jury. 'And I expect the jury are, too. It is their first day of their unaccustomed duties cramped in their uncomfortable box. So now let us adjourn and resume at 10.30 tomorrow morning.' He rose, bowed to the jury, nodded pleasantly to Lord Brackley, ignored Counsel and left the Court.

As the Court was clearing, Simon said, 'You must behave, Tomas.'

'It is very difficult,' said the old man. 'It is very difficult to listen to the lies.'

'I know. But you will have your turn. Now go home and rest.'

Felix led Tomas from the Court. Outside, a mass of photographers made Tomas pose at the entrance to the Law Courts. This he did willingly. The television cameras tried to take him as he crossed the Strand. He was asked to cross again and he happily complied.

Simon and Alexandra walked back to King's Bench Walk.

'Brackley is doing very well,' said Alexandra.

'I knew that he would.'

'Tomorrow you will start to cross-examine?'

'Yes. Much depends upon tomorrow – and upon me.'

She slipped her hand into his.

NINETEEN

It was half-past eleven on the morning of the next day, Friday, when Turner finally sat down, his examination-in-chief concluded. Simon rose to cross-examine. As he did so, Alexandra saw Grace turn and look over her right shoulder towards him. For a moment her eyes met Alexandra's; then Grace turned away to look at her husband as he stood in the witness-box waiting, prepared for what was to come.

'Lord Brackley, did you personally give any instructions to thugs to frighten off Colonel Tarnovic's friends from giving evidence for him?'

The question surprised the witness. The Judge raised his head to look at Simon.

'What do you mean?' said Brackley. 'I don't understand.'

'I will repeat the question. Did you personally give instructions to thugs to frighten off Colonel Tarnovic's friends from —'

The Judge intervened. 'Mr Harrington, what are you suggesting to Lord Brackley?'

'I am suggesting nothing. I am asking the witness a question.'

'You are asking Lord Brackley whether he has employed thugs to deter persons from giving evidence. That would be a criminal offence.'

'I am aware of that. I wish to know if this witness is responsible.'

Bentall, sitting next to Grace, gripped his hands under the table. Bagot Gray, who had not been present on the first day of the trial, was sitting next to Henry Cranston in the benches behind Counsel. He had laid a buff folder on the bench in front of him, his hands folded upon it.

'You are making a very serious accusation,' said the Judge.

'I am accusing no one. I'm seeking an answer to a question. The jury will later hear of the activities of certain people who in the past months have approached members of Colonel Tarnovic's community and warned them against giving evidence for him. I wish to know if the witness knew of this.'

'You are suggesting that someone has been committing criminal offences. Have you evidence of this?'

'I have.' Simon turned to Brackley in the witness-box. 'Well, Lord Brackley?

'The witness is not obliged to answer that question,' said the Judge.

'But I wish to, my lord,' said Brackley. 'I have no knowledge of any such behaviour.'

'Were you aware,' asked Simon, 'that persons said to be acting for you had been going round talking to acquaintances of Colonel Tarnovic?'

'No. I left the preparation of my case entirely to my solicitor.'

'Who is?'

'Mr Bentall, of Baker and Turnbull.'

Simon pointed to Roger Bentall sitting beside Grace. 'This gentleman here?' Bentall swung round angrily.

'Are you now accusing Lord Brackley's solicitor of committing criminal offences?' said the Judge. 'Have a care, Mr Harrington, have a care.'

'I repeat, my lord, I am not accusing anyone – at present. The jury will hear later of what has been going on during the preparation of this case.'

Simon was standing very straight, staring at the Judge. This, thought the young juror, is more like it. Helen Hunter looked bewildered.

Simon turned again to the witness. 'If there has been such behaviour — '

211

'If,' said Mr Justice Tetley ostentatiously writing in his notebook.

'Yes if,' repeated Simon, 'if there has been any such behaviour, are you saying that you know nothing about it?'

'Nothing whatsoever.'

'If there has been — '

'If,' said the Judge.

'If, if, if,' repeated Simon loudly.

Careful, Simon, careful, thought John Arrun. It's very early to get into a quarrel.

'If there has been any such conduct, you would regret it?'

'Of course. It would be wholly wrong and totally unnecessary.'

'Wrong yes, but why unnecessary?'

'Because I have told the truth. No witness who told the truth could say otherwise.'

'Is that because you believe that no witness remains alive who could tell another story?'

'No,' said Brackley confidently. 'If your client is to be believed, one witness is alive. He is your client. In his pamphlets he tells another story. But it is not the truth.'

Leave it, Simon, John Arrun said to himself and leave it Simon did. Brackley, thought Arrun, was going to prove a formidable witness. But by that preparatory exchange, Simon had prepared the ground.

Bagot Gray in his seat at the back of the Court looked thoughtful. Between the wigs of the barristers sitting in front of him, he could just see the back of Roger Bentall's head as he sat bolt upright in the front row. Bagot Gray knew what Simon had been after.

Simon continued. 'You would agree, would you not, that there can be no reconciliation between your version of what happened in the mountains in 1943 and that of Colonel Tarnovic as described in his pamphlets?'

'Mr Harrington, why do you keep calling the Defendant Colonel Tarnovic?' asked the Judge before Brackley could reply. 'What right has the Defendant to that title?'

'Tetley is overdoing it,' Leslie Turner whispered to James Fenton seated at his side. 'We don't need his help.'

'The same right as Lord Brackley has to his,' answered Simon. 'I call the Plaintiff Lord Brackley because he is a Peer of this Realm and I call the Defendant Colonel Tarnovic because that is the rank he held in the Royal Yugoslavian Army when he was engaged in fighting the Nazis.'

Mr Justice Tetley waved his handkerchief dismissively. 'Go on,' he said. But Simon did not at first go on. He stood very still, looking at the Judge. The courtroom was very quiet. The pause seemed interminable. Counsel and Judge stared at each other. The Judge was the first to drop his gaze. 'Yes, Mr Harrington,' he said more mildly.

Simon turned back to the witness. 'I will repeat my question, *Lord* Brackley.' He emphasised the Lord. 'Do you agree that there can be no reconciliation between your version and that of Colonel Tarnovic?'

'I agree that no reconciliation between the two versions is possible.'

'So that one or the other must be lying?'

'Yes, and it is certainly not I.'

'Very well. Now I want to take you back to the beginning, to your youth. Who was Jamie Mathewes?'

'Jamie Mathewes? Jamie? I only know one Jamie and he's my oldest friend, Sir James Layton, the Admiral.' Brackley was looking directly at Alexandra.

'I asked you,' said Simon sharply, 'who was Jamie Mathewes?'

'I have, at present, no recollection of anyone of that name.'

'As earlier in reply to Sir Leslie, you had no recollection of the name Stepan Stepanic?'

'Where are we now, Mr Harrington?' said the Judge wearily, raising the handkerchief to his lips. 'Are we still among those thugs of whom you were asking when you began?'

Simon did not look at him. 'No,' he said shortly. 'We are not.'

213

He has given up altogether on the Judge, thought Arrun, but he's taking a risk. Helen Hunter looked at Simon and thought: he is a very sharp young man. The juror in the horn-rimmed glasses pursed his lips further. The young juror in the open shirt was amused. He enjoyed hearing the younger man talk back to the pompous old man on the bench.

'I am referring to the time when you were an undergraduate at Cambridge University, Lord Brackley. Have you no recollection of Jamie Mathewes at Cambridge University?'

'Now that you've mentioned Cambridge, I do remember. Jamie Mathewes was a contemporary of mine at the University.'

'At King's College, was he not?'

'I believe so. It is over fifty years ago.'

'Before Mr Harrington was born,' said the Judge jovially.

'And when even Your Lordship was young,' said Simon smiling sweetly. The Judge looked at him, hard. Two of the spectator barristers smiled at each other as Simon went on: 'Jamie Mathewes was much involved in the university dramatic activities, was he not?'

'I seem to remember that he was.'

'Did he not produce the annual revues which were staged by one of the University's dramatic clubs, the Footlights?'

'Yes, he did.'

'And in which, at that time, you played a principal part?'

'Yes.'

'So you were a friend of Jamie Mathewes?'

'I was.'

'You said that he was a contemporary, but, in fact, he was older than you?'

'Yes. Now I remember, he was.'

'You were an undergraduate, a student and he was a don, a Fellow of King's College?'

'He was.'

'So your friendship with this older man, with this don, came about through your mutual interest in the stage, the

214

Footlights Club with which you were both involved?'

'Yes.'

The Judge sighed, loud enough for the jury to hear him, and again put his handkerchief to his lips. What possible relevance could this have, he seemed to be indicating.

'What other dons or Fellows were you then acquainted with?'

'Those who tutored us. I cannot remember now.'

'Were you not acquainted with one who subsequently attained much notoriety?'

'To whom are you referring?'

'Were you not a friend of a Fellow of Trinity?'

Brackley was silent for a moment. 'You mean Anthony Blunt?'

'Yes, Anthony Blunt. For what has Anthony Blunt become notorious?'

'Surely, Mr Harrington, everyone in the world knows that,' said the Judge.

'I wish to God he would keep quiet,' hissed Leslie Turner to Fenton, who whispered back, 'Why? He seems to be on our side.'

'If he goes on like this, he will irritate some of the jury and lose them. That's Harrington's plan.'

Professor Fenton shook his head. He was an academic lawyer; he was not used to the tactics of a trial.

Simon ostentatiously ignored the Judge's interruption. 'Well, Lord Brackley? What was Anthony Blunt notorious for?'

'He confessed to having spied for the Russians.'

'He was, was he not, a Communist agent and a traitor even at that time when you knew him as a don at Cambridge?'

'So I now understand.'

'How did you get to know Anthony Blunt? Not, I fancy, through your interest in the stage?'

'No. Many knew him. He was a very attractive personality.'

'And a homosexual?'

215

'I believe so.'

'You used to visit him at his rooms at Trinity?'

'In company with many others, yes.'

'Did you talk politics with him?'

'I do not remember. I may have. At that time, our generation talked much about politics. It was the time of Hitler.'

'And of Stalin. Did you know that Anthony Blunt claimed to have been at Cambridge what he called a talent-spotter?'

'I had heard it – subsequently.'

'When?'

'Lately, after Blunt had confessed.'

'Do you know what Anthony Blunt meant when he called himself a talent-spotter?'

'I presume he meant that he was looking out for people with talent.'

'For what purpose? Not, I presume, for recruitment to the stage?'

'Of course not.'

'Why then should this don at Trinity College be, as you put it, looking out for people with talent?'

'He was a very scholarly man – '

Simon interrupted him. 'Which you were not.'

'No. I wasn't particularly scholarly when I was at Cambridge.'

'Then what was Anthony Blunt's interest in you. Was it – how shall I put it – personal?'

'No, it was not,' said Brackley angrily.

'Then let us consider together what other reason there might have been for Anthony Blunt welcoming you to visit his rooms. It was not – personal. It was not your interest in the stage. Was it politics that took you to Blunt's rooms?'

'I had, at that time, little interest in politics.'

'But Blunt has said that, at that time, he was a talent-spotter. I ask you again: what do you think he meant by *talent-spotting*?'

'I presume that it was to find people who might prove to have an interest in his beliefs.'

'Which were the beliefs of Marx and Stalin. Was not his

216

talent-spotting directed to those at the University whom he might convert?'

'It may have been.'

'To convert to Communism and Stalinism. Did he try to convert you?'

'He did not.'

'Why did you visit him?'

'I have told you. He had a very attractive personality.'

Grace was twisting her hands on the table in front of her. Beside her, Roger Bentall sat very still, his arms folded.

'Blunt was a don, older than you and a homosexual. What was so attractive about his personality?'

'His manner, the way he talked.'

'Was he very persuasive?'

'In a way, yes.'

'What was he persuasive about?'

'Art and art history.'

'Was that a subject in which you were interested?'

'Not particularly.'

'What did he talk about that did interest you?'

'General matters, social matters.'

'Social matters. Do you mean Communism? Did he talk about Communism?'

'Sometimes.'

'Did he persuade you to become a Communist?'

'He did not.'

'Do you think that you were one of those whom Blunt talent-spotted on behalf of the Communist party?'

'I have no idea.'

'Had you given him any idea why you should have been talent-spotted?'

'No, I had not.'

'So it just happened that for some reason, nothing – personal; nothing to do with your main interest, which was the stage, but for some reason, of which you cannot tell us, Blunt spotted you and invited you to visit? Is that right?'

Brackley did not reply.

217

Simon said, 'So, Lord Brackley, you cannot help us further?'

'No.'

'Or is it that you do not wish to help us?'

'Certainly not. I cannot.'

Simon paused and then asked, 'When you were at Cambridge, did you know Guy Burgess?'

'I met him, yes.'

'Was he another secret Communist and a traitor?'

'So I have learnt since.'

'And a homosexual?'

'So I believe.'

'And older than you?'

'Yes.'

'Had Guy Burgess left Cambridge before you went up, before you went there?'

'Yes.'

'How did you come to know Guy Burgess?'

'I met him at Anthony Blunt's rooms.'

'And he became a friend?'

'An acquaintance. He knew many people. At that time he was considered a very amusing companion.'

'Amusing,' Simon repeated. 'Amusing. So you found Anthony Blunt, the Communist talent-spotter, an attractive personality and Guy Burgess, another Communist traitor, amusing? Is that it?'

Brackley did not reply.

Simon bent and took from the papers in front of him a sheet, which he held in his hand.

'During this period in your life, did you ever have occasion to visit Hampstead?'

'Hampstead, in London?'

'Yes. Hampstead in London. Did you ever visit there at about the time when you were an undergraduate at Cambridge?'

'I expect that I did. My home was then in London. So I may have visited Hampstead.'

'I am referring to visits to a particular household in

Hampstead, where the daughter of the house was called Kitty. Does that help you to remember?'

Brackley would have liked to have sat; his heart was beating irregularly, but he knew that to sit at this stage would be unwise. He gripped the edge of the witness-box. 'Do you mean Kitty Klugman?'

'I do. Did she have a brother, James?'

'Yes.'

'In later life James Klugman wrote several books, did he not?'

'I believe that he did.'

'That was many years after you first got to know him?'

'Yes.'

'He wrote a book called *From Trotsky To Tito*. Did you ever read that book?'

'No.'

'Even though you served with Marshal Tito and knew the author?'

'I did not read that book.'

'Then did you read James Klugman's *History of the British Communist Party*?'

'No, I did not.'

'James Klugman and his sister Kitty were both Communists, were they not?'

'They were.'

'And you knew this when you first visited them in the late 1930s at their home in Hampstead?'

'I did.'

'Unlike Blunt and Burgess, they were, at that time, quite openly members and supporters of the Communists, were they not?'

'Yes.'

'And those who visited them at their home at Hampstead went there to talk politics, did they not?'

'Not necessarily. I did not.'

'James Klugman was older than you and, like Guy Burgess, had already left Cambridge before you went there. Why did you go to his house in Hampstead?'

'As far as I can remember, someone took me there.'
'Who was that?'
'I cannot now precisely remember.'
'Was it Burgess?'
'I told you, I cannot now remember.'
'Or was it that other Communist traitor, Donald Maclean, who was also a close friend of Klugman?'
'Donald Maclean was a friend of James Klugman. They had been at school together.'
'Did you meet Maclean at Klugman's Hampstead home?'
'On one occasion.'
'Anthony Blunt in his confession claimed that James Klugman had converted him to Communism. Did you know that?'
'I have heard that.'
'James Klugman was another of those who called themselves "the talent-spotters", those Communists who had been instructed by their Russian Control to spot any among the students at the universities who might be recruited into the Communist party. Did he try to recruit you?'
'No, he did not. I told you that, at that time, I was not interested in politics.'
'Your principal interest at that time was in the stage, in acting with the Footlights. Why were you a visitor to Anthony Blunt in his rooms in Trinity College and to James Klugman at his home in Hampstead, neither of whom were in the least interested in the stage, but both of whom were interested in talent-spotting for the Communist party?'
'I was taken there, like many others. I didn't then know that Guy Burgess, or Donald Maclean, or Anthony Blunt were Communists.'
'I shall return to Blunt and Burgess, but you certainly did know that James Klugman was?'
'Yes. He made no secret of it.'
'Did that concern you?'
'At that time, not in the slightest.'
'Why do you think that you were a welcome visitor at the home of James Klugman?'

'I have no idea.'

'Consider, Lord Brackley. Do you not think that it might have been because you were known to be a friend of Anthony Blunt, whom Klugman had himself recruited into the party? Was not that the reason why you were invited to join the comrades at Klugman's home in Hampstead?'

'Anthony Blunt was merely an acquaintance.'

'Was he not more than that? You were a constant guest in his rooms?'

'I used to visit him, yes.'

'Did you ever meet Kim Philby, perhaps the most important of the traitors?'

'I had met him, yes. Once or twice.'

'So is the position that, when you were at Cambridge, you knew Anthony Blunt, Guy Burgess and Donald Maclean, and had met Kim Philby, all of whom turned out to be Communist traitors?'

'I did not know that at the time.'

'And you were a visitor to the home of the Klugmans, who were open Communist supporters. You have said that you had then no political interests. But what were your political sympathies when you were at Cambridge?'

'I had none.'

'Were you a member of the Conservative, or Labour, or Liberal Associations?'

'I was not.'

'But you had the Communist friends about whom I have asked you?'

'I said that they were acquaintances.'

'They were certainly persons whom you visited frequently?'

'Yes.'

'You were mixing in Communist circles?'

'I was not aware that they were.'

'I suggest that answer is quite untrue. Neither Blunt, nor Burgess, nor Maclean in private disguised their sympathies with Communism. Is that not correct?'

221

'At that time, many people talked about politics, but, as I said, I was not interested.'

'But they, the Communists, seem to have been mighty interested in you.'

Leslie Turner jumped to his feet. 'That is not a question. That is a highly tendentious statement by Counsel.'

'You are quite correct, Sir Leslie,' replied Mr Justice Tetley, looking pleased. 'Mr Harrington, confine yourself to questions during your cross-examination.'

Simon nodded and continued. 'Shortly after your visit or visits to the Klugmans' home in Hampstead, the War broke out. In 1939, did you join the Army?'

'I did.'

'After your last visit to Klugman in Hampstead in time of peace, when did you next see James Klugman?'

'Some years later.'

'When?'

'In 1942.'

'Where?'

'In Cairo.'

'That was the year, was it not, when you came to Cairo to join SOE as a potential liaison officer, who was to be dropped by parachute to join the guerrillas then fighting the Germans and the Italians in the Balkans?'

'Yes.'

'When you arrived in Cairo, was the Communist James Klugman by then a major on the staff which was directing the operation in which you were to be engaged?'

'Yes.'

'And you knew him to be an active Communist.'

'He had been when I had known him, yes.'

'Did you meet him in Cairo?'

'Yes.'

'Often?'

'Several times.'

'On duty.'

'On duty and on leave.'

'At that stage of the War, were there not within Yugo-

222

slavia two distinct and hostile resistance movements?'

'There were. I said that yesterday.'

'So you did. James Klugman was one of the directing staff for the Balkan operations and you have told the Court that, at that time, there was much debate at Allied Headquarters in Cairo about whom the British should support by supplying arms – the Cetniks in the Royal Yugoslavian Army under General Draža Mihailović, or the Partisans under the Communist, Josip Broz, who called himself Tito. Is that right?'

'It is. But I was an operational officer. I was not concerned with the politics.'

'But Major James Klugman was. He made no secret of whom he supported, did he?'

'No.'

'He was for Tito, for the Communists?'

'Yes.'

'Because he was a Communist?'

'Because he thought they were the most effective fighting force.'

'Also because he was a Communist and wanted the Communists to prevail?'

'That was partly his reason, yes.'

'Was it known at Allied Headquarters that Major James Klugman was an active member of the Communist party?'

'I believe not.'

'But you knew?'

'Yes.'

'Did you tell anyone?'

'No, I did not.'

'Why not?'

'The Communists, the Russians, were then our allies.'

'But did you not think it proper that the Allied chiefs should know that one of their most influential advisers, urging them to support the Communists and abandon the Cetniks, was himself a dedicated Communist?'

'It was not my business.'

'Not your business!' Simon repeated. 'You were a British

officer shortly to be dispatched into Yugoslavia at a time when debate was going on about which of the two factions the Allies should support. Why was it not your business?'

'I was an operational officer. Policy was not my business.'

'But was it your interest?'

'No. It was not.'

'But it was the interest of your friend James Klugman, because he, as you well knew, was for the Communist faction?'

'Yes.'

'And you, Lord Brackley, who were you for?'

'I have told you, I was solely an operational officer.'

'Yes, but you were also an officer, who at the University had mixed in Communist circles and had on several occasions seen and talked with your friend the Communist James Klugman before you were dispatched on your mission. That is correct, is it not?'

'We shall adjourn now for luncheon,' said the Judge, gathering together his papers.

'I would like an answer to my last question before Your Lordship adjourns,' said Simon.

'So be it,' said Mr Justice Tetley tersely.

'Yes, Lord Brackley?'

'I had seen James Klugman and I knew his opinions.'

'And knowing his opinions and that he was promoting the interests of the Communist Partisans whom he wished to prevail, he sent you out to join the others, Mihailović's Royalists, or Cetniks. Is that what you are telling the Court?'

'I am.'

'Did you go to help the side which your friend Major Klugman wanted to fail – or did you go to betray them?'

Brackley's pale face flushed. 'I went to do my duty as a British liaison officer.'

'The Court will now rise,' said the Judge. 'We shall resume at two o'clock.'

While his back was turned to the Court and his clerk was drawing aside the curtain before the door which led from the bench, Simon called out, 'My lord, as Lord Brackley is still under cross-examination, should he not be warned against speaking to anyone about the case?'

Mr Justice Tetley turned. 'Lord Brackley will have heard what you have said, which is broadly correct. Two o'clock.' And he disappeared.

'That was rather fun,' said the young juror in the open shirt to Helen Hunter as they left the jury-box.

'I can't believe that all those questions were strictly proper,' she replied. 'The poor old gentleman was getting very tired.'

'Guilty conscience,' said the young man cheerfully as he made his way not to the cafeteria but to the George public house across the Strand.

'I've reserved the room at the Wig and Pen Club for sandwiches and coffee, Lord Brackley,' said Roger Bentall, steering him and Grace through the photographers at the entrance to the Law Courts.

When the three had reached the club, Brackley said shortly, 'Grace and I would prefer to be alone.' Bentall left them. In the room, Grace took him in her arms.

'It's all such a smear,' he said.

Bagot Gray walked from the Strand to the Aldwych Hotel. He had in his hand the buff folder which contained all that he and his organisation had discovered about Tomas Tarnovic. He had deliberately not shown the report to Roger Bentall, but had arranged for a private appointment with Leslie Turner after the Court rose that evening. Bagot Gray sat himself at a table with a glass of wine and went through the file yet again.

Henry Cranston's car picked him up at the Law Courts, not before the cameras had caught the former Foreign Secretary bustling out of the main entrance.

'Are you to be a witness, sir?' called out one of the reporters. Henry did not reply and was driven to the Savoy to a lunch in the Mikado Room for a group of industrialists from the North-East of England, who had asked to see some of the leaders of the party. Walter Fairchild was among the party chiefs at the lunch and as they went to their places at the table, Walter asked, 'How is the case going? What was reported in today's Press reads well.'

'That was George's case. His cross-examination has now begun. Much about George's friendship with the Blunt gang at Cambridge. It has not been ineffective.' Walter looked at him, but Henry said no more.

Simon walked back to chambers with Alexandra. Mathew had sandwiches for them. When they were alone he asked her, 'Am I overdoing it with Tetley?'

'I don't think so. He was being vile.'

'I decided that I had to "lose" him.' He took Alexandra's hand. 'Brackley is bound to bring in your father. Leslie Turner will raise it in re-examination.'

'I know. But I told you, I have nailed my colours – as the Admiral would say.'

He leaned over and kissed her lightly on the lips.

At two o'clock Brackley, without asking, sat in the chair provided for him in the witness-box and waited for Simon to begin.

'Let us recapitulate, Lord Brackley. In Yugoslavia in 1943, apart from any fighting against the German occupying forces, was there civil war between the two factions, Mihailović's Royalist Cetniks and Tito's Communist Partisans?'

'There was.'

'Before you left Cairo and parachuted into the mountains, had you made any plan with James Klugman over how you were to help or not help the unit of the Royal Yugoslavian Army to which you were being dispatched?'

'No. My role was to be that of a liaison officer.'

'With the Royalists, the Cetniks?'

'Yes.'

'Klugman knew to whom you were being dispatched?'

'Yes.'

'He had arranged it?'

226

'He was one of those who had arranged it.'

Simon said sharply, 'Major James Klugman was the offi-cer who arranged that you should be attached not to his friends the Communists but to the Royalists, the Cetniks. Is that not so?'

'Effectively, yes.'

'So he was sending you to help those whom he wanted to see fail?'

'It was the policy at that time to send British officers to Mihailović's men. Later, they were all withdrawn when it was proved that Mihailović was collaborating with the Germans.'

'Liar!' The cry came from Tomas, who was leaning for-ward, both hands on his stick. Simon cursed under his breath. The old man had given the Judge his opportunity and Mr Justice Tetley took it with both hands.

'Mr Harrington, yesterday I instructed you to keep the Defendant under control. I said specifically that I will not have interruptions from the Court. We had one yesterday from Mr — ' he emphasised the Mr, 'Mr Tarnovic and now we have this outrageous outburst this afternoon. I am sur-prised that you have not the authority to see that I am obeyed in my own Court. Well, then I shall warn him directly. Mr Tarnovic, please stand.' Tomas got slowly to his feet. 'If you make another interruption while this wit-ness, or any witness, is giving evidence, I shall commit you for contempt of Court. Do you understand?'

'No,' said Tomas, one hand on his moustache.

'No what?'

'I do not understand.'

'Understand what? That you must not interrupt?'

'No.'

'What are you talking about?'

'What you are talking about? I do not understand. What is contempt of Court? What is that? I do not have con-tempt. I have respect. I have the highest regard for British justice, I have been educated here, I have lived here — '

'Mr Tarnovic, be quiet!'

227

The young juror put his hand to his mouth to hide his smile.

'If you ever interrupt again, I shall have you sent to prison. Now sit down.' Tomas sat, curling his moustache defiantly. The Judge waved his handkerchief at Simon. 'For Heaven's sake let us get on!' He turned to the witness. 'I am sorry, Lord Brackley, pray proceed.'

'I have forgotten the question, my lord.'

'And I do not blame you. Mr Harrington repeat the question!'

'I was asking you about what instructions the Communist James Klugman gave to you before he sent you to join not Tito's Communist Partisans, whose cause he was determined would triumph, but Tito's enemies, General Mihailović's Cetniks.'

'I told you. I was sent as a liaison and explosives officer.'

'To help them fight against the German Army?'

'That is so.'

'Did you want them to succeed?'

'I wanted anyone who was fighting the Germans to succeed.'

'But it was your friend Klugman who had dispatched you to the Cetniks and he did not want them to succeed, did he?'

Brackley did not immediately reply and Simon went on. 'Klugman wanted the Cetniks to fail. Was that what you wanted?'

'I wished to do my duty.'

'To obey your orders?'

'Yes.'

'The orders given you by Klugman?'

'Yes.'

'At that time, November 1943, had not British Headquarters sent instructions to General Mihailović to execute certain operations against the Germans by attacking specific targets chosen in Cairo?'

'Yes.'

'Did not the British command give these instructions in

228

order to test General Mihailović to see whether he was committed to fighting against the Germans?'

'Yes.'

'If General Mihailović's men failed to execute those operations, was it not the intention of the Allies to switch all supplies of arms and explosives from the Royal Yugoslavian Army to Tito's Communist Partisans?'

'It was.'

'So the supporters of Tito's Partisans in Cairo, such as Klugman, wanted Mihailović's operations to fail?'

'They believed that Tito's was the more effective force. He was actually fighting the Germans.'

'And you—' Simon placed a restraining hand on the shoulder of Tomas, who was sitting directly in front of him. It was vital that the old man should not interrupt again. 'And you say that General Mihailović was not?'

'That was then my opinion.'

'But let us be clear, Lord Brackley. Major James Klugman, the Communist and the officer who dispatched you, was ideologically committed to do everything to help Tito and the Partisans?'

'That was what he wanted, I suppose.'

'He wanted the Communists to succeed and their rivals, Mihailović's Cetniks, to fail?'

'Yes.'

'For if the Cetnik operations failed, then all Allied support would be switched to Tito?'

'Yes.'

'And James Klugman chose you to join Mihailović's men, who were at that time being put to the test by British Headquarters?'

'Yes.'

'To test whether the Cetniks would carry out the specific operations against the Germans ordered by the British in Cairo?'

'Yes.'

'So failure by Mihailović's Cetniks in that test was precisely what Klugman wanted and what Klugman intended.

Was that not exactly what James Klugman told you before he sent you on your mission?'

'It may have been what he wanted – in the long run.'

'It may have been? It may have been? You knew that, did you not? You knew that perfectly well?'

'I knew that he wanted something like that.'

'And he deliberately chose you, his friend, the friend of the Communists, Anthony Blunt and Guy Burgess and Donald Maclean, to play a part in making sure that Mihailović's Cetniks failed, so that support could be switched to your Communist friends, Tito's Partisans?'

'That is not true.'

'I suggest that before you left Cairo to parachute into the mountains, you conspired with Major Klugman to play a part in the policy to abandon Mihailović?'

Brackley had struggled to his feet. 'No,' he said. 'No.'

'And when you reached Colonel Tarnovic's command that is exactly what you did?'

'No,' repeated Brackley, leaning forward over the rail of the witness-box. 'I have told the truth about what happened.'

'I suggest the truth is that in furtherance of the conspiracy of the Communist sympathisers, you deliberately sabotaged Colonel Tarnovic's raid on the railway by failing to explode the charge?'

'That is untrue.'

'I suggest that on the second operation, you hid during the battle for the bridge and failed to bring forward the explosives at the critical time to ensure that operation also failed?'

'No.' Brackley struck the ledge of the witness-box with his clenched fist.

'And that after you had made sure of these failures by Mihailović's men to meet the requirements of British Head-quarters, you ran off to your and Klugman's friends – the Communists, the Partisans?'

'No, no, no!' Brackley shouted. By now the pallor had gone from his cheeks, which had become red and suffused as he shouted at Simon. The veins of his neck stood out like livid weals.

'I suggest that when you had joined your friends the Partisans, you led them back to slaughter those you had pretended to come to help.'

'That is not true!' Brackley cried out.

'I suggest that you did all that in furtherance of the plans of James Klugman and others to make sure that the Communists triumphed.'

'I did not!'

'I suggest that you deliberately betrayed the men who believed that you had come to help them.'

Brackley thumped again the ledge of the witness-box in front of him. 'It is all lies, lies, lies!' He struck the edge of the witness-box three times as he said the words. 'I told the Court yesterday what happened. The first operation failed because they could not locate the railway line. The second because the Germans ambushed the column and they—'

Suddenly he stopped, in mid-sentence. For a moment he stared owlishly at Simon. Then he moved his head slowly and looked down to where Grace was sitting beneath him and, with a cry, slumped face forward over the edge of the witness-box. As he fell, the glass of water, which the usher had placed beside him when he had begun his evidence, fell to the ground and shattered with a crash. The Judge, the jury and the whole of the Court leaped to their feet. Grace ran from her place to the steps leading to the witness-box. The usher followed her and together they tried to pull Brackley back on to the chair, Grace cradling his head in her hands. Eventually, they got him seated, his head lolling back. Grace knelt beside him. 'Attend to him!' ordered the Judge. By now everyone in the courtroom was standing and craning to see what was happening. Only Tomas remained seated.

'*Mon Dieu*,' he said, almost to himself, '*il est mort.*'

'The Court is adjourned,' cried the Judge. A stout, red-faced nurse in uniform bustled into the courtroom, telling the people standing around the doors to make way. She went to the figure in the chair and loosened his collar and tie and waved smelling salts beneath his nostrils. His head began to move from side to side as slowly he began to revive. Simon could see the deathly pallor of his face as he looked up at Grace and tried to smile at her. A doctor pushed through the crowd and went to him, ordering people away.

The Judge had disappeared. The Associate bellowed 'The Court is adjourned until Monday at 10.30.' He went over to the doctor, who was by then holding Brackley's wrist, feeling his pulse. 'Do you want the ambulance?' the Associate asked.

Henry Cranston was beside Grace. 'I'll send for my car. Get these other people out,' he said to the Associate.

Gradually, the Court emptied. Simon led Alexandra away. Before he did so, he said to Leslie Turner, 'Let me know how he is.'

Among the last to leave was Bagot Gray, still clutching the buff folder. Grace and Leslie Turner and Roger Bentall remained with the doctor and the nurse.

'I'm all right,' Brackley murmured. 'I'm all right.'

Grace tried to hush him. After a time, the doctor said he could be moved and Grace sent Bentall to summon their doctor from Harley Street to meet them at Eaton Square. The Judge's clerk came to enquire. He gave Leslie Turner the telephone number of the Judge to call over the weekend should Lord Brackley not be fit to resume on the Monday. Henry returned. His car was at the main entrance of the Law Courts.

The usher and the nurse helped Brackley, who had an arm around each. Slowly, the little procession moved off through the corridors, down the stone stairs and along the great hall of the Law Courts, watched by the curious who had come from the other courts which were still in session. Waiting for them at the main entrance was the squad of photographers. Bentall made a way through them. 'It's all right. It's all right,' he kept saying. 'Lord Brackley has not been well. It was very hot in Court and he felt faint. He's much better now. Yes, of course, the case will continue on Monday morning. Lord Brackley is already much better and the doctor says that he'll be quite well by Monday.' But Lord Brackley did not look as though he would, thought Jumbo Lancaster, who had followed them to the entrance and now stood behind the photographers.

At Eaton Square there were more cameras; the journalists had rushed ahead in cars and were waiting for them, including a TV crew. Henry and his chauffeur helped George Brackley into the house. Bentall was dismissed.

'Is there anything that I can do? Would you like me to stay?' Henry asked Grace.

'No,' she said. 'Telfer is on his way from Harley Street. I'll telephone later.'

Henry kissed her on the cheek and left them alone.

TWENTY

As they left the Court, Simon and Alexandra met Mathew hurrying along the corridor as fast as his portly frame and short legs would permit.

'Bring my papers to me in the robing room, Mathew. I'm going straight home and I'll need them over the weekend.'

Simon swept on, his gown billowing behind him. Just before the end, he had known that his cross-examination had come alive. The student Brackley was linked to Klugman the Communist in Hampstead; and the soldier Brackley to Klugman in Cairo. And it was in Cairo that Klugman and his friends had plotted the downfall of Mihailović's Cetniks. That Brackley had shared Klugman's purposes and was a party to Klugman's plot was now at least a tenable inference. If so, then Tomas's version – that Brackley had sabotaged the operations and then betrayed the Cetniks to the Communist Partisans – became far more plausible. The defence could not now be dismissed as fanciful.

As he marched across the stone floor of the tall Gothic Hall in the Law Courts with Alexandra at his side, she said, 'Simon, I can't keep up.'

He stopped. 'I'm sorry. I need to get home to unwind. Be a darling and see if you can get a taxi while I take off my robes. I'll meet you at the main entrance.'

When he joined her, they passed together through the battery of photographers who had been waiting for Brackley. They earned their share of attention. In the taxi he took her hand. 'I need a shower.'

When he had showered, he dressed in an open shirt and white canvas trousers and they left the flat to get some air.

234

They crossed the road to the gardens of Onslow Square and sat on a bench in the late afternoon sunshine. It was very hot and thunder-clouds were building up overhead.

'You're very silent,' he said.

'I can't help feeling sorry for him, whatever he is and whatever he's done. Did you see Lady Brackley?'

'Only the back of her head and when she ran to the witness-box after he had collapsed.'

'I caught her eye when she turned to look at you as you stood to cross-examine. I think she's going through hell.'

He bent and plucked some grass and sat shredding it. 'Remember Tomas, Alexandra, and what he's fighting against – power, wealth, influence. And someone sent out thugs to frighten off those who might've supported him.'

She was looking across the garden where a four were playing tennis on the court near to the church, laughing happily. The sun had now disappeared behind black thunder-clouds. It had become very oppressive.

'Are we making him guilty by association – like in the McCarthy time in America? A lot of people must have known Blunt's circle and not known what they really were.'

She was thinking, he knew, of her father. A few drops of heavy rain fell.

'Come on,' he said. 'We must make a run for it.'

They made love while the thunder cracked overhead and the lightening lit the bedroom. *Götterdämmerung*, she thought. She felt no ecstasy as his body moved in and above hers – just the pleasure in giving him pleasure. As she lay beneath him looking up at him, she remembered him when she had turned to watch him during his cross-examination. He had looked like an avenging angel, very tall, his black hair visible at the sides beneath his grey advocate's wig, his black robe which he drew around him or threw aside as he gestured. Above all, those dark eyes which had lit up his face as the flashes of lightning now lit the room in which they were making love. He had been doing what he had to do. But she could not forget the look in Grace Brackley's eyes.

He rolled away and lay beside her, kissing her cheek and her hair until he sighed and soon was asleep. After a time, she got up, pulled on his dressing gown and stood by the window listening to the storm and watching the flashes in the dark sky. She thought of the description which Brackley had given yesterday from the witness-box – of the ambush of the Cetniks and the white Verey signals lighting the sky and the German machine guns ripping into the column.

She took her clothes and went into the bathroom, washed and dressed. The telephone rang in the bedroom and she went into him. He had woken, but he let it ring and it stopped. He stretched out his hand to her and as she took it, the telephone rang again. He leaned over and picked it up. It was Leslie Turner.

'Simon, I would like to talk. Are you free?'

'Yes. How is Brackley?'

'He is much worse. Their doctor is very worried. I have a rather odd request to make.'

'What is it?'

'I want to know if you would talk with me and with someone whom I think you know.'

'Who is that?'

'Bagot Gray. I would like to see you with him. And without solicitors.'

Simon looked at Alexandra, who was sitting on the bed beside him.

Leslie Turner went on: 'I particularly don't wish to have Bentall with us.'

'I'm here with Alexandra Layton.'

There was a pause, then Turner said, 'Admiral Layton's daughter?'

'If we're to talk, I'll want her with me.'

'One moment,' said Turner.

Simon put his hand over the mouthpiece and said to Alexandra, 'Turner wants me to talk with him and Bagot Gray. I want you there.'

Leslie came back on the line. 'Simon?'

'Yes.'

236

'That's all right. Bring Miss Layton. I'd like to keep away from the Temple, and Gray has suggested you come to his house in Wilton Crescent. He says you know it.'

'I do. This is all very mysterious, Leslie. When do you suggest that we meet? Tomorrow morning?'

'Tonight. Could you make nine o'clock?'

'Is it that urgent?'

'I would not press if it were not.'

'Very well.' He looked at his watch. 'As near to nine as I can.' He put down the receiver. 'A nine o'clock conference at 18, Wilton Crescent, the home of my friend, Bagot Gray.' He slid from the bed. 'The plot, my darling, thickens.'

A manservant let Simon into the house at Wilton Crescent. It was 9.15.

'Has Miss Layton arrived?'

'No, sir. Only Sir Leslie. He's with Mr Gray in the draw-ing-room,' and he led Simon up the stairs.

Bagot Gray, Havana cigar in hand, greeted him. 'Wel-come, Simon. Miss Layton is not with you?'

'Alexandra is coming on her own. I don't want to start without her.'

'While we wait for her, have a drink.' Bagot Gray poured champagne into a tall, thin-stemmed goblet.

Leslie was sitting on the sofa and Simon went and sat beside him. 'I hope that you don't mind waiting for Alexandra.'

'Of course we'll wait. I'm sorry to bring you out at this hour. You must be tired.'

'I am. You know, Leslie, I was quite serious when I was asking Brackley about the activities of the thugs.'

'I know you were. It's one of the reasons why Bentall is not here – and won't be in my chambers ever again.'

'So that is it. Has Bagot told you that I asked him to do a sweep of Alexandra's flat? We had reports –'

Gray interrupted. 'Sir Leslie knows all about it.' A bell

237

sounded below in the hall. 'That will be Miss Layton,' said Gray and went out of the room and stood at the top of the staircase.

'As I said on the telephone, Leslie, this is all very mysterious. But, I presume, that soon all will be revealed.'

'It will,' said Leslie as Alexandra came through the door. Simon and Leslie rose and introduced both men to her. She refused Gray's offer of a drink and sat on the sofa beside Simon; Leslie and Bagot Gray in two armchairs opposite them.

Leslie Turner began. 'As I told you, I've not asked Bentall to be with us for reasons which I've indicated to Simon. But first, I have to repeat that Lord Brackley is very gravely ill; it is certain that he will not be fit to continue to give evidence on Monday.'

'So that means —' began Simon.

Leslie held up a hand. 'I think that it'd be best if you were told everything before we come to consider what might or might not happen on Monday. They have taken him to the London Clinic and he is under intensive care. I shall know more in the morning, but the prognosis is he is unlikely to live.'

'I am sorry,' said Simon.

'Second, I should tell you that Mr Gray and his firm were engaged by Bentall to make enquiries into the background and past of the Defendant, Tomas Tarnovic. I assure you, Simon, that Mr Gray had nothing to do with the thugs about whom you were asking Lord Brackley at the start of your cross-examination.'

'I'm quite sure he hadn't.'

'Mr Gray's organisation has compiled a report on Tomas Tarnovic, a copy of which I have here.' Turner took from the table beside him a buff folder like that which Gray had in Court earlier in the day. 'I had not seen the completed report until this evening, when Mr Gray brought it to me in chambers. Bentall has not seen it. Neither, because of his illness, has Lord Brackley.'

Simon said, 'What has this to do with us? We have our

own instructions from our client. This is very irregular, Leslie.'

'I know and you shall not see the report unless you wish to —'

Simon began to get to his feet. 'I can't listen to what your people have to say about my client. It could compromise me.'

Leslie held out his hand. 'I promise you, Simon, that it will not. I would never have suggested this meeting if Lord Brackley was not so ill. Please trust me, Simon.' Simon sat back. 'I have considered the matter with great care and one of the matters I took into consideration was my confidence in the importance which I'm sure both of you,' Leslie bowed to Alexandra rather formally, 'the importance both of you,' he repeated, 'would attach not only to the interests of your client, but also to the interests of justice. I have excluded Bentall from this meeting, because from what I've learnt, I don't believe he shares our view of the duty of Counsel and of solicitors as Officers of the Court.'

Simon interrupted. 'What on earth are you talking about, Leslie?'

Leslie put the buff folder on the table beside him. 'In essence, what you're going to be told is what I would be presenting as evidence on behalf of Lord Brackley and what I would put to your client in cross-examination. You will be perfectly free to use the knowledge you gain tonight in any way you think fit: either to consult your client about what you've been told; or, if the trial continues and you so wish, to wait until the stage of the trial is reached when your client is cross-examined. All that our discussion tonight will do is give you a preview of our evidence. Accordingly, I don't think that by listening to what I and Mr Gray have to say will in any way prejudice you. But it could advance the interests of justice.'

'That is the second time you have said that.'

'I've said it deliberately.'

Simon looked at Alexandra and she stared back, as mystified as himself. Simon said, 'Very well. We shall listen and

239

we'll use anything we learn tonight in any way which we think will best help our client.'

'Of course. Mr Gray.'

'Much of what I have to say, Simon,' said Gray, 'will have been told to you by your client, but I'll go through our report, starting with the history.'

'Do as you wish,' said Simon. 'But I fancy that we already know what's in it.'

'Perhaps not quite all, for that is the purpose of our meeting.' Gray had the folder on his knee and as he spoke, he read occasionally from pages which he took from it.

'This is what we know. The father of Tomas Tarnovic was an official of the Royal Yugoslavian Court and a personal friend of King Alexander, who was assassinated with the French Minister, Barthou, in Marseilles in 1934. The son, Tomas Tarnovic, was a commissioned officer in the Household troops of the boy-King, Peter, during the regency of Peter's uncle, Paul. Later, he served as Military Attaché in London, but returned to Yugoslavia at the outbreak of War in 1939. After the fall of France and the defeat of the Luftwaffe over England in 1940, Hitler presented an ultimatum to Yugoslavia in 1941 and the Regent accepted Hitler's terms. But patriotic circles around the youthful King overthrew the Regent's government and the ultimatum was rejected. In April 1941, the German Army thereupon invaded Yugoslavia. So much for the basic history.'

'And Tomas Tarnovic was then a young Colonel of King Peter's Guard stationed in Belgrade.'

'He was. After the bombardment of the city and the defeat of the Yugoslav Army, some Royalist officers placed themselves under the leadership of General Draža Mihailović to carry on resistance in the mountains.'

'Including Tomas Tarnovic,' said Simon.

Gray looked up at him and then back to the dossier he was consulting. 'I'm now going to jump ahead to when Tomas Tarnovic became a prisoner of the Germans. When he was taken, he was in plain clothes and he gave a false

240

name. He was sent with others in cattle trucks as part of a labour force to Norway, where they were put to work on fortifications and harbour defences in conditions of unbelievable brutality and hardship. Many died, but Tarnovic survived and was later shipped to Poland in a forced labour battalion. When Poland was overrun by the advancing Soviet Army, the only consequence for Tarnovic and his companions was that they had exchanged captors, for he was sent by the Russians to further slave labour in the mines in Siberia.'

'Until he was released in 1956,' interrupted Simon.

'Yes. Those who later knew Tomas Tarnovic report that his sufferings at the hands of the Soviets, his country's nominal wartime allies, affected him even more than those he had experienced under the Germans, with whom his country had been at war. On his release from the mines, Tarnovic was in a pitiful physical and mental condition. He somehow made his way further east from Siberia and for the next five years or so we've not been able to discover exactly where he was or how he survived.'

Gray looked at Simon who nodded. Gray went on: 'According to our information, Tarnovic, at one time, was in Shanghai among what was left of the White Russian community after Mao Tse-tung and the Chinese Communists took over. In the early 1960s, he managed to make his way to Hong Kong. There he was befriended by another exiled compatriot, Milovan Leskovic, who was then employed by a shipping company and with whose father Tarnovic had once served in the Royal Guard in Belgrade.'

Alexandra shot a glance at Simon, who was sitting impassively watching Bagot Gray read from the papers in his file.

'Leskovic gave Tarnovic money to get a passage across the Pacific, where, for a time, he lived in Mexico City with another emigrant from Belgrade, Alexei Djuric. He is the father of the man in Fulham who printed Tarnovic's pamphlets.'

'I met his wife,' said Alexandra. 'She told me Alexei is dying.'

'He is, of cancer of the jaw. They had both known Tarnovic in Belgrade.' Gray looked at Simon who remained silent. 'In late 1969 Tarnovic crossed the border from Mexico into the States as an illegal immigrant. He was still very frail, but he obtained casual work usually in a bar or as some kind of "greeter" at boarding-houses used by expatriate Slavs. It was through this casual employment that his wanderings came to an end, for in 1971 one of the Slavs he met told him that his cousin, Stepan Stepanic, was living in Los Angeles.'

'The student at Cambridge,' interrupted Simon.

'Yes. Stepan Stepanic had not returned to Belgrade when war broke out in Europe. He had remained in Britain throughout the War, having bought a ground-floor flat in a small house in Fulham, number 11 Pelham Lane.'

'Where Tomas Tarnovic now lives.'

'He does. A few years after the War, Stepanic emigrated to the United States, made his way to the West Coast, and in 1964 married an American. They invested in a winery in California, which prospered for a time. Stepan Stepanic hardly recognised his cousin when they were reunited. At first, he took Tomas Tarnovic into his own home, but after a time and on the insistence of his wife, he arranged for Tarnovic to live at his expense in a nearby home for elderly people. Then, in 1981, Stepan died. In his will he left to Tarnovic some money, which provided Tarnovic with a small income, but insufficient for the expense of the Home. The winery was sold, Stepan's widow remarried and was not able or not prepared to make up the shortfall. But Stepan had also left to Tarnovic the flat in London. So, at the prompting of Stepan's widow, he came to England.'

'In 1982,' said Simon.

'Actually, the summer of 1983. We have checked the date at the Home Office.'

'You have filled in some gaps in Tomas's saga, most of which we knew, but the important period is between the German invasion of his country and his capture.'

'You're right. I shall come to that now.'

242

Alexandra turned her head towards Simon beside her on the sofa. He was crossing and uncrossing his legs, restlessly. 'Go on,' he said.

'During the years when Tarnovic lived at the Four Seasons Retirement Home in Berkeley County, Santa Barbara, he became very friendly with the proprietor, who also looked after him medically. This was a Dr Ivan Duric. There were particular reasons why Stepan Stepanic chose the Four Seasons as the home for his cousin. It was not only because Dr Duric was of Serbian extraction and had looked after Tarnovic's health, but it was also because of Dr Duric's family. The doctor himself is an American citizen and had not been in Yugoslavia during the War, although he has visited often since. But some of Dr Duric's family had. One of these relatives was a niece, Eva Janjce, who, at the end of the War, escaped into Austria and whom the doctor subsequently brought to the United States to live at his home in Santa Barbara in California. While Tomas Tarnovic was a resident at the Four Seasons, this niece saw him often.'

Gray paused from his reading and looked across the room at Simon. Then he said, 'For she had known Tomas Tarnovic in Belgrade.'

'When?' asked Simon sharply.

'From 1941 until 1943.' He paused. 'During those years Tomas Tarnovic was living in Belgrade. At no time was Tomas Tarnovic in the mountains fighting with General Mihailović's Cetniks.'

Alexandra caught her breath. There was silence in the room. Simon was staring at Gray. Then Gray said, 'Captain George Brackley parachuted into the mountains near Orgulica in November 1943. By that time, Tomas Tarnovic was a prisoner of the Germans.'

Simon leaned forward. 'How do you know that?'

Alexandra had her eyes lowered on her hands folded in her lap. She did not dare to look at Simon.

'I will tell you. In 1943, Tarnovic was living in an apartment in Belgrade with a woman who was also called

243

Alexandra,' Gray looked across the room at the girl sitting beside Simon, 'although Tarnovic always called her Sacha. Their apartment was directly above the apartment where Eva Janjce lived with her mother. From January 1942, Eva Janjce saw them both daily – until Tomas Tarnovic and Sacha were both picked up off the street in a round-up by the German occupying forces, and deported. Eva Janjce and her mother witnessed the arrest from the first-floor window of their apartment. The woman Sacha has never been heard of again.'

Gray took a document from the file. Then he said, 'I have here Eva Janjce's signed statement, which you can see if you wish. The arrests, she swears, took place in October 1943 when Lord Brackley was still in North Africa.' Gray took another document from the folder. 'I have also here Dr Duric's clinical notes of his patient, Tomas Tarnovic, which include notes of what Tarnovic told the doctor when describing to him his experiences. They include a description of his wounds sustained in 1941 and about his life in Belgrade with Sacha in 1942 and 1943.'

Simon was sitting very still, watching Gray's hands as he removed and replaced documents in the folder.

'Eva Janjce says that Tarnovic and Sacha first came to the apartment in January 1942, when Tarnovic was still recovering from severe wounds he had received in the bombing of Belgrade by the Germans in the previous April. Those wounds, Tarnovic told Eva, were the reason why he had not been able to join General Mihailović in the mountains in May 1941. Tarnovic told this to Eva Janjce in Belgrade in 1943; to Milovan Leskovic in Hong Kong in the late 1960s and to Dr Duric in the Four Seasons Home in 1978. During 1942 and 1943, Tomas Tarnovic, Eva Janjce says, had a job in the Central Post Office in Belgrade.'

Gray paused and looked across at Simon. Then he went on: 'Eva Janjce in her statement expresses her affection for Tomas Tarnovic, who suffered so terribly during the long years when he was a prisoner first of the Nazis and then of the Communists. She never believed that he ought to have

244

been allowed to come to England and to live alone. That, she says, was the idea of Stepan's widow, although she admits that Tarnovic himself decided to leave Santa Barbara, since he thought that his money might go further living in the flat Stepan had left to him in England.'

Gray took another document from the folder. 'This is the certificate of the US equivalent of a notary or Commissioner for Oaths certifying Eva Janjce swore to the truth of her statement.'

Gray held out the document to Simon, who made no movement. Gray replaced it in the folder.

'Eva Janjce and Dr Duric will arrive in London off Concorde on Sunday evening ready to give evidence to the Court.'

He took another document from the folder. 'This is the sworn statement of Milovan Leskovic of Spring Buildings, 180 Kennedy Road, The Peak, Hong Kong. He was the man who befriended Tarnovic when Tarnovic came from Shanghai in the 1960s. Milovan Leskovic's father, Ilja Leskovic, had been one of those officers who had joined General Mihailović at his headquarters at Ravna Gorna and served with the General until killed in action in 1944. Major Ilja Leskovic and Tomas Tarnovic had served together before the War in the Royal Guard. In Hong Kong, Tarnovic talked freely with Milovan Leskovic, telling Milovan of his experiences and of how he had been badly injured in the leg and in the stomach in the German air attack on Belgrade in April 1941, and of his sadness that, because of these wounds, he had been unable to join General Mihailović. Milovan Leskovic is also on his way to London from Hong Kong to give evidence.'

Alexandra saw that Gray had two photographs in his hand. He held them up. They were both of Tomas.

'The doctor and Eva Janjce and Milovan Leskovic have all been shown photographs of your client, which had been taken recently when he was walking in Pelham Lane in Fulham with his dog. The photographs were sent to California and to Hong Kong and all three have identified them

245

as photographs of the man who lived at the Four Seasons and talked with Dr Duric; the man who talked with Milovan Leskovic in Hong Kong; and the man whom Eva Janjce knew in Belgrade and who lived in the same apartment house as herself and who was taken by the Germans off the streets of Belgrade in October 1943.' Gray replaced them in the folder. 'We have confirmed from War Office records that Captain George Brackley was flown from Derna in North Africa and parachuted into the mountains on the night of November 17 1943.'

Gray placed the folder on the table beside him. 'From this, we believe that it is conclusive that Tarnovic could not have been in the mountains near to Orgulica when Lord Brackley arrived there in November 1943. The remainder of our report deals with Lord Brackley's friends when he was an undergraduate at Cambridge.' He looked again at Alexandra. 'They were many and varied and were certainly not confined to Anthony Blunt and his circle.'

Leslie got up from his chair and brought his copy of the folder to Simon. 'This is a photocopy of all the documents and statements. It's all here if you wish to see it.'

Simon took it from Leslie and held it unopened in his lap. Leslie remained standing, his back to the empty fireplace.

'That is the story of Tomas Tarnovic, which I would be presenting to the Court if I get the opportunity. I made the decision to show you the evidence Mr Gray has assembled because Lord Brackley is so seriously ill. He may die within the next forty-eight hours and if he does, his suit, which was brought to clear his name, would die with him. If that were to happen and having regard to Mr Gray's report, then a very grave injustice will have been perpetrated on the reputation of a very distinguished man. I know that neither of you would wish to be a party to that.'

For a time no one spoke. Then Simon broke the silence: 'For what possible reason could Tomas Tarnovic have invented the story he has told?'

'The doctor gives an explanation,' said Gray. 'He says that Tarnovic often spoke about the terrible wrongs that had been done to his country not only by the Germans but by the Allies. The doctor believes that Tarnovic, after his experiences, especially at the hands of the Soviet Communists, had become obsessed about the Communist take-over of his country and about Tito, who had executed his hero, Draža Mihailović. Tarnovic blamed in particular the advice of the British liaison officers in the field, who persuaded the Allied staff in Cairo to switch support from Mihailović to Tito's Partisans. These were the men, Tarnovic used to tell the doctor, who were principally responsible for the triumph of Tito.'

'Then he read Lord Brackley's book,' added Leslie, 'with Brackley's praise for Tito and accusations that the Cetniks were collaborating with the Germans. That, the doctor suggests, could have triggered off a scheme in Tarnovic's mind to make some demonstration to champion the memory of his hero, Draža Mihailović and to expose the wrong which people like Brackley had done. He obviously wanted to provoke Brackley into taking a law case so that he could have the opportunity of publicly blaming the liaison officers who, Tarnovic was convinced, had persuaded the command, and, through the command, Churchill to abandon Mihailović. Brackley gave him the opportunity. That is the theory.'

His day in Court, Alexandra thought. Tomas always said he wanted his day in Court.

Simon said, 'What of Brackley and his links to the Communists, especially Klugman?'

'We have evidence through the Ministry of Defence records that Klugman's was not the decisive voice in sending Brackley to join the Cetniks. Moreover, although Brackley did know Klugman when he was at Cambridge and some of those who turned out to be Communists, he had many other friends. We know all about Gervase Gregson with his gossip and distortions.' Leslie turned to Alexandra. 'Your father was determined to give evidence for his friend. He was not going to be deterred by Gervase Gregson.'

After a pause, Leslie went on: 'If Lord Brackley survives,

the case will not die and I'll ask the Judge to allow me to call the rest of my evidence. When Lord Brackley is well enough, he can resume his evidence. But, as I said, he may very well die within the next forty-eight hours. Then, as you know, the case will die with him and his reputation will remain wrongly traduced.'

Leslie went back to his chair. For several minutes none spoke. Then Simon got slowly to his feet. He had the buff folder in his hand.

'I understand, Leslie, why you wanted to tell us this.' They all stood. Simon said to Alexandra, 'Late as it is, I think that you and I should pay another visit this evening.'

He helped Alexandra to her feet and Gray led them out of the room and down to the front door. He watched them as they walked to the car, Simon with his arm around her. As he closed the front door, Leslie Turner met him in the hall.

'I'll be going home now. I'll let you know if I get any news of Brackley.'

'I'm sorry for them,' said Gray. 'It must have been a great shock.'

'Yes. But I'm certain that they'll do what is right.'

TWENTY-ONE

As they drove from Wilton Crescent, Simon said, 'In the morning I cross-examine the Plaintiff and in the evening the Defendant.'

Alexandra did not reply. She was thinking of when she had last seen her father – when she had insulted him and he had slapped her face. Tomas, she thought, oh, Tomas!

It was shortly after 10.30 when they turned into Pelham Lane. Ahead of them, opposite number 11, a large, black car was parked with its front and rear off-side wheels on the pavement. When Alexandra drove slowly past, the driver, who was bent over a newspaper trying to read in the dimness of the car's internal light, looked up and watched as she, too, mounted the pavement and pulled up in front of him.

'Our friend has company,' said Simon.

At the front door, he pressed the bell and kept his finger on it. Then he banged loudly with the flat of his hand. Alexandra saw the man in the car turn in his seat and watch them. They heard the dog bark and Tomas's voice from inside. 'All right, all right. I am coming.' The bolt was withdrawn, the door opened and, framed in the light, they saw Tomas.

He was dressed as he had been earlier in the day when he had been to Court. He looked excited and pleased.

'Sacha, welcome,' he said. 'Sacha – and the QC!'

'Yes,' replied Simon. 'We have come to talk, but you have a visitor.'

Seated in a chair in the sitting-room was the fat man

249

whom Simon had noticed in the Press-box in Court during the two days of the trial. So the newspapers were after Tomas. The figure did not rise, but a hand was waved in greeting as they entered.

'I'm sorry to interrupt, but we have urgent business with our client,' Simon said to the man in the chair.

'Lancaster, of the *Star*, known as Jumbo. You can guess why. I've been watching and listening to you in Court for the past two days.'

Simon nodded. 'I'm afraid that we need to have a talk, confidentially, with Tomas. It is, as I said, urgent.'

'It must be, to pay a visit at this time of the evening. Beware, Tomas, of lawyers who come in the night.' Jumbo laughed jovially. 'My visit to our friend is also on business, a preliminary arrangement about some authorship for us after the trial is finished.'

Tomas had led Alexandra to a chair and had then seated himself, one hand on his dog's head and the other proudly curling his moustache.

'What we've come to say, Tomas, is very urgent and very confidential.'

Still Jumbo showed no sign of leaving. He had a glass of plum brandy in his hand. 'Come now, Mr Harrington. I got here first and first come first served. Colonel Tarnovic has now been kind enough to feed me with this excellent brandy.'

Simon turned to Tomas who said nothing, but sat impassive, his hand still at his moustache. Alexandra leaned forward and put her hand on Tomas's knee. 'Please, Tomas,' she said. 'We have to talk.'

He took her hand and looked at her. 'It would be impolite to hasten Mr Lancaster over his brandy,' Tomas said. 'Will you join him in a glass?'

Simon shook his head and walked across the room and ostentatiously began to examine the photograph of General Draža Mihailović.

'Will you, my dear?' Tomas asked Alexandra.

'No,' she said.

250

'Some tea?' She took her head. Tomas was still holding her hand.

'It was a most enlightening afternoon in Court,' said Jumbo shifting his bulk in his small chair. 'How is the great man this evening?' Simon had his back to him. 'I trust he'll be fit to continue on Monday. As one who was never an admirer of His Lordship's political philosophy, I found your cross-examination most entertaining.'

Simon turned back to face him, but remained silent.

'I saw him when they took him to the car,' went on Jumbo imperturbably examining the liquor in his glass and ignoring Simon's pointed silence. 'He didn't look at all well to me and now, I'm told, he's been taken to the London Clinic. A pity, a great pity.'

Simon crossed the room and sat. He looked at his watch. 'It's getting late, Tomas, and Alexandra is very tired.'

Tomas looked at Jumbo, who sighed and emptied his glass. 'And your business,' he said, putting the glass on the table, 'cannot wait. Meanwhile, Counsel does not deign to utter a word to the humble journalist. Lawyers, Colonel Tarnovic, are impossible creatures, as doubtless you're discovering. They flick their fingers and we're all expected to scamper about to do their bidding.' He struggled clumsily to his feet. 'In the earlier part of this century, Mr Harrington, a famous Counsel called Sir Edward Marshall Hall insulted the then Lord Northcliffe and, as a result, his name was never again mentioned in the columns of the Press that Lord Northcliffe controlled. It had a serious effect on his practice. It is rash, Mr Harrington, for ambitious Counsel to get across the Press.'

He turned to Tomas. 'Well, Colonel Tarnovic, I think we've reached a satisfactory understanding and we'll look forward to your contributions to our columns. I'll be in touch next week.'

He lumbered to the door where he turned. 'Good-night, Miss Layton. Good-night, Colonel Tarnovic. I trust that your mysterious business will not keep you up too late.' He ignored Simon and Tomas followed him out into the hall.

251

When Tomas, using his cane, had limped back into the sitting-room and sat himself in his chair, they could hear Lancaster's car as it reversed up the lane. Tomas looked benignly at them. 'Well, my dear friends, this has been a good day.'

'I could not speak in front of your visitor,' said Simon, 'and when you've heard what I have to say you'll understand why.'

Tomas, in his chair, bowed gravely.

'On Sunday evening, Dr Ivan Duric of Santa Barbara will be arriving at Heathrow from New York.'

Tomas tugged at his moustache. 'Well?'

'Tomas,' said Alexandra. 'Tomas.'

'Dr Duric will be accompanied by Eva Janjce. At about the same time, Milovan Leskovic will be arriving from Hong Kong.'

'And what of it?' asked Tomas defiantly.

'Tomas,' repeated Alexandra. 'Don't pretend, Tomas! We know about them – and about you.'

'Did you imagine,' said Simon, 'that Lord Brackley, with all the resources available to him, would not have found them? Why didn't you tell us about them?'

Tomas leaned forward, his cane between his legs, both hands now resting on the silver nob. 'They are irrelevant,' he said.

'Oh, no, Colonel Tarnovic,' replied Simon and Alexandra noted the formal address. 'They're certainly not irrelevant. They'll be the most relevant witnesses in the whole of this trial. The charade is over, Colonel Tarnovic.'

'We know the true story, Tomas,' said Alexandra.

Tomas turned and looked at her. Then he said almost under his breath, 'No. You do not know the whole story. But I admit that the three who are coming will have come too soon.'

'No, they will have come in time. Before you could per-jure yourself,' said Simon.

'It is too soon. A few days too soon.'

'You knew that they would come?'

'Of course I knew that they would come, but not before — '

Simon interrupted him. 'Not before Colonel Tomas Tarnovic had his day and his say in Court. Is that it?'

'Perhaps.'

'Apart from the lies that you have told Alexandra and me and the facts that you have concealed from us, do you admit that you were prepared to go to Court, take an oath and tell lies to blackguard an innocent man?'

Tomas thumped the floor with the ferrule of his cane as he had done in Court. 'He is not an innocent man!'

'What do you mean, not an innocent man? Your story about him was a total invention.'

Simon was very white. There were dark shadows under his eyes. He is very angry, thought Alexandra.

Tomas, his face now flushed, again struck the point of his cane on the floor. 'It was not total invention,' he said fiercely. 'And he is not an innocent man, no more than any of those who were sent to my country fifty years ago were innocent men!' For the third time he struck the floor with the ferrule of his cane. The dog, disturbed, came to him and when Tomas ignored him, wandered out into the dark garden. 'They were all part of a conspiracy of secret Communists to help the cause of their Communist friend, Tito. They lied about my General Draža Mihailović, saying that he was collaborating with the Germans; and they were responsible for his death. They were not innocent men!'

'Colonel Tarnovic,' said Simon wearily, 'may I tell you that I am not concerned with the politics of fifty years ago, nor whether the Allies made the wrong decision in the War when they chose to back your enemy and not your friend? I am concerned with the fact that you wrote deliberate falsehoods about a distinguished Englishman and were prepared to go into a witness-box in an English Court and lie about him.'

'What I wrote and what I would have sworn to was not a lie.'

'It was a lie that you personally witnessed what happened

253

in the mountains when Captain Brackley parachuted in to join that band of Cetniks. Do you think that when the jury have heard the evidence of that doctor, his niece and the man from Hong Kong, they will believe anything you say?'

'I never wrote that I personally was there. Nevertheless, what I described was the truth.'

'How do you know as you were not there?'

'I know. I know, and the world shall hear what I have to say.'

For a moment Simon was silent. Then he said quietly, 'You deliberately provoked Lord Brackley into suing you so that you would have an opportunity to speak about what you call the wrong done to your country by the wartime Allies fifty years ago. All of that has been said many, many times by many, many others.'

'But not by me. When others have said it, no one has listened. But they will listen to me when I speak in Court and expose one of their heroes as a traitor and a coward.' Tomas waved his cane towards the door behind him. 'That man who was here tonight, the journalist, he said that millions would read what I have to tell the Court. He promised to publish in his newspaper anything I wanted to write and then millions more would know the truth.'

'Colonel Tarnovic, that journalist was not interested in the battles and decisions of fifty years ago. He was interested in your blackguarding a former Cabinet Minister and making political capital out of your accusation that he was a fraud. That's what he'll pay you for, not for writing about what happened years ago when the British, you say, backed the wrong side in your civil war. That has nothing to do with the case before the Court.'

'But it has. It has everything to do with this case and your Court.'

'Colonel Tarnovic, you call yourself an honourable man. Yet you were preparing to tell deliberate lies to the Court in the case in which Alexandra and I are engaged as your lawyers.'

'I never wanted lawyers. You know that. You forced yourselves on to me. I told you that I wanted to do this alone. I planned to do it alone. Lawyers are always trouble.'

'You accepted us as your lawyers to defend you in Court and you deceived us.'

'I am sorry to have deceived Sacha. It was chance which brought her here and it was chance that she found those papers on the table when I was sleeping after my fall at the studio. If she had not, I would have done what I planned alone.'

'Let us be quite clear. You deliberately manufactured a case and were prepared to lie on oath and destroy the reputation of a man you'd never met, so that you could have a platform to repeat your accusations about the British liaison officers and the decision to abandon Mihailović and support Tito.'

'I did it to expose a decision which led to fifty years of tyranny and I did it to expose him.'

'Brackley?'

'Yes. I was going to tell the world that those who made that infamous decision were deceived by men like Brackley who lied about my friends and who lied about my leader. So I was prepared to lie a little in return.'

'You intended to go into the witness-box and pretend that you were present at those battles in the mountains, when, in fact, you were hundreds of miles away. That would have been a little lie, would it?'

'Compared to their lies, yes.'

'But you knew that the little lie, as you call it, must, in the end, be exposed. What in God's name was the point?'

Before Tomas could reply, Alexandra said, 'What did you think would happen to you when it was exposed? If you had gone into the witness-box and told that story, it would have been perjury. You could have gone to prison.'

Tomas smiled at her. 'I know all about prisons, Sacha.'

'And to justify what you say was the great lie of the War,' said Simon, 'you were prepared to lie about an innocent man.'

Tomas turned on him. 'I told you. He is not an innocent

255

man! It would have been no lie about Brackley. The only untruth was that I, personally, was there when he betrayed my countrymen. But another was there. When Brackley wrote his lying account in his book, I saw that this was the chance to expose him and to keep a promise.'

'What promise?'

'When he wrote his book, Brackley believed that there had been no survivor from the massacre of the Cetniks by Tito's Partisans, so he thought that he could invent the story of the battle and the ambush by the Germans. But one man did survive the massacre of the Cetniks. He was the Commandant. When Brackley brought the Partisans, he was in the plain, in the village at a Council-of-War with neighbouring commanders. He told me his story when we were in the prison camp in Trondheim in Norway. Later, he died – in my arms. That was the only lie, to pretend that it was my story. It was his story I was telling, not mine.'

There was a silence. Then Tomas went on: 'He told me of the betrayal and the massacre and when I read Brackley's book, I knew that it was he who had been the traitor. So I determined to tell the true story, the Commandant's story. But I knew that no one would pay attention unless I could force Brackley to take me to Court. And that is why I wrote how I did – to force Brackley's hand. And I succeeded.'

No one spoke. Simon broke the silence. 'Earlier this evening you offered me brandy. May I have some now?'

Tomas waved his hand contemptuously. 'If you wish.'

Simon went to the side-table and poured himself a glass. He sipped it and then came back to the table on which he placed the buff folder which Leslie Turner had given him. He bent forward and leaned towards Tomas in his chair. 'So a fellow prisoner in Norway told you the story of a massacre by the Partisans of a band of Cetniks, which had taken place in 1943.'

'He did.'

'What was this man called?'

'Andrejevic, Colonel Trifunovic Andrejevic.'

'At that time, there was much fighting in the civil war

between Mihailović and Tito, apart from the fighting with the Germans?'

'Of course there was. I have told you. Tito destroyed Mihailović with the help of the British. Without them, it would have been Tito who would have been destroyed.'

'Did Colonel Andrejevic tell you where this massacre by the Partisans had taken place?'

'At his command Headquarters in the mountains near to Orgulica.'

'Weren't several of Mihailović's bands then operating around Orgulica?'

'Yes.'

'When was this?'

'In 1943.'

'Did Colonel Andrejevic tell you that a British officer called Brackley had been with his band of Cetniks?'

'He said that there had been a British officer with them. Andrejevic did not know the name.'

'So he never gave you the name Brackley?'

'No. But it was Brackley. I am certain of that.'

'There were many British officers and their wireless operators dropped into the mountains of Yugoslavia. Did Colonel Andrejevic tell you that it was the British officer who had betrayed them to the Partisans?'

'Andrejevic told me that the British officer had failed to fire the charge and could not be found when they attacked the bridge and later had left them. As soon as I read Brackley's book, I knew that he was the man who had been with Andrejevic and his companions.'

'Why?'

'I knew of him. I had heard his name, Brackley. My cousin Stepan at Cambridge had spoken of him as a Communist.'

'Stepan actually spoke the name Brackley and said that he was a Communist?'

'I have told you so.'

'Over fifty years later you remembered that name?'

'Yes.'

Simon moved from the table and again began pacing the

room. 'Why could it not have been another officer and not Brackley?'

'Because Brackley was one of the Communist traitors who were at Cambridge.'

'When did you first learn about the Cambridge traitors? Did you know about them in 1944 in the camp in Norway when Andrejevic told you his story?'

Tomas put his hand to his head. 'So many questions. Why do you ask these questions?'

'To get at the truth. The Cambridge traitors were not exposed until well after the War was over. So how could you know about them when Colonel Andrejevic told you his story in 1944?'

Tomas laid his cane on the floor beside his chair. 'I knew,' he said. 'I knew.'

'When Colonel Andrejevic told you his story, did he give you all the details about what happened, which you describe in your pamphlets?'

'About the operations, yes. As for the liaison officer, I knew what those men sent from Cairo came to do. They wanted Draža to fail.'

Alexandra kept her eyes on the old man. He had begun to look even older than his years. Simon went on inexorably. 'Last year you read Brackley's book, the story of one of those liaison officers whom you blame so bitterly for betraying your leader and your country. In that book, Brackley wrote that he had been at Cambridge. Wasn't that the first you knew of it?'

'No.'

'Are you so sure that when you visited Stepan at Cambridge, you met a student whom Stepan told you was a Communist?'

'Yes, of course I am.'

'Are you so sure Stepan gave you the name Brackley?'
'He did.'

'What did he tell you?'

'I cannot remember his exact words. All I know is that he said that Brackley was one of them.'

258

'One of whom?'

'One of the Cambridge traitors.'

'But that was in 1939. At that time, there were not known to be any Cambridge traitors. Their exposure came years later. So how could he have told you?'

'He may not have called them traitors.'

'But you did, Tomas. When did you start to believe that Brackley was one of the Cambridge traitors?'

Tomas did not reply. Simon leaned closer to him. 'Think, Tomas, think. Was it last year when you first picked up Brackley's book and learnt that Brackley was at Cambridge? Did you then invent what Stepan said to you in Cambridge fifty years ago?'

'No, I did not.'

'You have invented quite a lot, Tomas.'

'No. Stepan spoke to me. He told me that Brackley was a Communist. I cannot now remember his exact words.'

'Try, Tomas, try. You see, when you say that you met or heard the name Brackley from your cousin in 1939, no one then knew anything about traitors at Cambridge.' Tomas did not reply. 'That is right, isn't it?' Simon paused again. 'Colonel Andrejevic never told you that it was the British officer who had betrayed his men, did he? Nor did he tell you that the British officer with those Cetniks was called Brackley, did he?'

'All these questions. Why do you keep on at me? I am tired.'

'We all are, Tomas. Very tired.'

Tomas turned and appealed to Alexandra. 'I cannot be expected to remember everything!'

'In Brackley's book, he wrote about the incompetence of the Cetniks, the superiority of the Partisans and of the collaboration of the Cetniks with the Germans. Did that anger you?'

'Of course it did. It was a lie.'

'How do you know? You were not there.'

'Because I knew their leader, General Mihailović.'

'You knew him before he raised his standard in the mountains. You do not know if what some of the British officers reported was true – that he was collaborating with the Germans.'

'That is a lie.'

'You have set yourself up as the champion of General Mihailović. Brackley was a champion for Tito. You have admitted that it was after you had read his book with his contempt for the Cetniks and their leaders, that you conceived the plan to libel Lord Brackley and provoke him into suing you so that you could have a platform to tell the story of your General's betrayal. That's right, isn't it?'

'Yes. I have told you so.'

'And it was only after you had read that book that you convinced yourself that it was Brackley who had betrayed Colonel Andrejevic.'

'When I read that book, I recognised that it was my friend's story. When Andrejevic was dying in my arms in that hut in the cold and ice of that terrible camp where they starved us and beat us and worked us so that thousands of us died, I promised my friend that I would revenge him. That book proved to me that the traitor had been Brackley, the British Communist sent from Cairo.'

'Colonel Tarnovic, I am going to make some suggestions to you. Please listen carefully.'

'Do what you like.'

'I suggest that Colonel Andrejevic never told you that he and his comrades had been betrayed by a British officer.'

'It was obvious that they had been.'

'I suggest to you that all that he told you was that his band of Cetniks, to whom a British officer had previously parachuted, had been attacked and massacred by the Partisans.'

'He told me of the failure by the British officer to fire the charges.'

'That happened on occasion, did it not?'

'I do not know.'

'No, you do not, because you were never in the mountains.'

'That was not my fault.'

'Of course it was not your fault. I suggest to you that it was when you read Brackley's book and were so angered by what he wrote, that you got it into your head that Brackley was the officer who had been with Colonel Andrejevic.'

'It was Brackley.'

'You have no proof.'

'I tell you, I know.'

'I suggest that it was you and not Colonel Andrejevic who made the British officer into the traitor, because you had come to believe that all the British officers had been sent deliberately to betray the Cetniks.'

'That is what they did. It was my duty to expose Brackley. I had given my promise to my dying friend.' He put his hand to his head. 'You are confusing me. It is very late.'

The old man had begun to shake. Alexandra rose from where she had been sitting and went and stood behind his chair, her hands on his shoulders. He lifted one of his hands and placed it on hers. She thought of her father when she had lunched with him at his club. She had done the same to him and he, like Tomas, had placed his hand over hers. Only her father's hand had been firm and Tomas's was trembling.

Simon took a document from the folder on the table and leaned across and put it under Tomas's eyes.

'Eva Janjce says that you were taken off the street by the Germans and deported from Belgrade in October 1943. Look. Do you see that?'

Alexandra leaned over Tomas's shoulder and pointed to the place on the paper which Simon was holding. 'There, Tomas.'

Tomas slowly took his glasses from his top pocket, unfolded them and put them on his nose. 'I have read it.' He took off his glasses, his fingers fumbling as he put them away. 'What is wrong about that?'

'There is nothing wrong about that, but it is important. She says that in October 1943, she saw you taken.'

'Yes. She is describing what happened to me.'

261

'She is. She cares for you, doesn't she? Eva Janjce is your friend.'

'Yes, she is my friend. She did not want me to come to London, but Stepan's widow wanted me to leave and the money had run out. Eva wanted to care for me.'

Simon placed the statement back into the folder. 'Do you see the importance of that date?'

'Do you think that I can ever forget it?' Tomas looked round at Alexandra and placed his hand once again on hers. 'How much longer are you going on with all these questions?'

'Very little longer,' said Simon quietly. 'When did you first meet Colonel Andrejevic?'

'On the prison train to Trondheim.'

'So you and he were deported together?'

'Yes, I and my friend, Andrejevic, went together and later he died in my arms.'

'So the massacre of Colonel Andrejevic's men must have happened before you were both deported.'

'Of course.'

Simon walked from behind the table and sat in his chair. For a time he was silent. He did not look at Tomas. The dog came in from the garden and went to Simon, who put his hand on the dog's ear, fondling him.

'As you met Colonel Andrejevic on the prison train, which took you from Belgrade to Norway,' said Simon quietly, 'don't you understand, Tomas, that Lord Brackley could not have done what you imagine that he did? For you were arrested and sent away in those cattle trucks in October 1943 and Colonel Andrejevic was with you. Lord Brackley never came to the mountains until November. He could not have been the British officer with Colonel Andrejevic, for by the time he came, Colonel Andrejevic was already a prisoner.'

Tomas stared at Simon. No one spoke. Then Simon said quietly, 'It is all wrong, Tomas. It's all wrong.'

Tomas kept staring at him and then slowly he lowered his head and tears began to roll silently down his cheeks.

Alexandra went from where she had been standing behind his chair and knelt in front of him. She took his old head in both of her hands, while the tears coursed through her fingers.

TWENTY-TWO

It was dawn when they left. Tomas was sleeping with Tito beside him. Simon had taken the dog for a run up the Lane and along the Fulham Road, while Alexandra had stayed with Tomas as he prepared for bed.

'Do you love that young man?' he had asked her.

'I do.'

'He was very fierce with me.'

'He had to be, Tomas. He had to make you understand that it couldn't have been Brackley.' Then she had asked him about Eva Janjce.

'In Belgrade, she was only a young girl and she idolised my Sacha,' Tomas had said. 'She is very motherly now. When we met again in America, she was very good to me. She wanted to care for me. I shall be glad to see her again.'

'Even though she was coming here to prove that you were wrong and that if anyone betrayed your friend, it couldn't have been Brackley?'

He was silent for a moment and then said, 'I was so sure. I so wanted it to be true. You see, Sacha, I failed Draža. I failed to join him in the mountains when he needed me. Even though it was fifty years late, I thought I could make amends here in London.' He took Alexandra's hand in his. 'When Draža Mihailović was condemned to death by the Communist Tito, he said that it was the gales of the world which had blown him away. Now they have blown me away, like they did him.'

He placed his other hand over that which held hers. 'I am very old, Sacha. Very old.'

264

'I'll make you some tea,' she said. 'It'll help to make you sleep.'

When she came back, he was sitting up in bed. She saw that he had begun to weep again, silently, and she sat beside him.

'No,' he said. 'It could not have been Brackley, for Andrejevic and I were prisoners before he came. Eva was right. She was always right.' He took Alexandra's hand once again and pressed it with a strength which surprised her. 'I was so certain, Sacha. I was so certain and I was wrong.'

'It will be all right, Tomas. Simon will make it all right.' But she could not calm him.

'It had all come back into my mind when I read that terrible book. I could only think of my and my country's suffering and of the execution of Draža Mihailović and of the death of Andrejevic in my arms in the camp at Trondheim. And here was this man Brackley accusing them, insulting them. I am sorry. I am so very sorry.'

'Simon,' she repeated, 'will put it right.'

Then the old man's mind began to wander. He was in the prison train with Andrejevic and later friendless in the mines in Siberia; he was in the street in Belgrade with Sacha being torn from his arms. Then he went even further into the past, into the time of his youth when he was at school with the Headmaster who kept the menagerie. The kangaroo, Tomas kept saying to Alexandra, the kangaroo has been killed. He saw that she smiled when he said this and he smiled in return.

By the time Simon had returned with the dog, Tomas had quietened. He would not talk to Simon and Alexandra settled him with the dog lying on the mat by the bed. As she bent to kiss his forehead, Tomas said, 'I am glad that Eva and the Doctor will be here soon. I would like to see them again.'

When she had been making the tea, she had seen a spare front-door key hanging on a nail in the kitchen and as she drew the curtains across the alcove, she promised that she would be back later in the day that had already dawned –

either she or Felix. They waited silently in the sitting-room until they heard by his breathing that he had fallen asleep.

At Onslow Square, they stood together under the shower and afterwards in bed, they lay naked in each other's arms like children. They slept for four hours. Then began the telephoning.

At eleven in the morning they separated; Alexandra to take Tomas's key to Felix, who had agreed to visit him. From the studio she was to drive to Wiltshire, to her father. This time she was expected. Simon left for the home of Leslie Turner in Kensington Square, from where the two of them would drive to Kingston Hill to descend upon the Judge. They, too, were expected.

The Judge's villa on Kingston Hill was meticulously neat, the house as well as the garden. A manicured lawn led from a verandah at the back, between borders of immaculate beds of salvias and geraniums. Like a municipal park, Simon thought. Half-way down the lawn, three deck chairs and a table had been placed beneath a large striped umbrella. It had the appearance of a stage set, carefully prepared and positioned. They were led to it by Blanche, the Judge's wife, a brawny, determined figure with a prominent nose and fierce blue eyes. She escorted them briskly through the house and into the garden.

'Brian will be with you in a moment,' she said. 'He's on the telephone to the Chief. After you called and told him that you both would be coming to see him, Brian assumed your libel action wouldn't be effective on Monday, so they are rearranging his list.'

She sat in one of the chairs. 'I wish they'd send him on circuit – get him away from London and out of the house and stop him fussing around. I've a lot to do at this time of year and he gets in the way.'

A figure appeared from the verandah. It was Mr Justice

266

Tetley immaculately dressed in a white coat over black trousers, on his head a Panama hat with a band in the colours of Merton College, appropriate kit, he felt, for a gentleman to receive visitors at noon on a Saturday in summer. He was approaching unsteadily, for he was bearing a tray on which were three glasses and a bottle in a wine-cooler.

'Go and help the old fool,' Lady Tetley said to Simon. Simon went to the Judge's aid and relieved him of the tray.

'Thank you, Harrington, thank you. Very good of you. I thought that we might enjoy a glass of hock to lighten our deliberations.'

'A delightful idea, Judge,' said Simon, who disliked hock intensely.

'Good morning, Leslie. It's not too early for a glass on this fine summer morning, eh?'

It is far too early, thought Leslie, but the scene had been set as Brian Tetley believed it was set in grand country houses throughout the Realm – and so it should be in the villa on Kingston Hill.

'I'll be off now,' said Blanche. 'I have an NSPCC committee in Surbiton and I shan't be back until the afternoon. I've left your lunch, Brian, in the fridge – a tin of pilchards and salad. It's his favourite,' she said to Leslie.

The Judge winced. He felt it unfortunate that his mundane tastes should be brought to the notice of his visitors.

'Or would you prefer tinned salmon? There's plenty of that.'

'No, no, my dear. Pilchards will do excellently. I hope that you have a good meeting.'

'If we don't, it'll not be my fault. They're all such muddlers, you know,' she confided to Simon. Then to her husband: 'Now don't forget to stay in the shade under the umbrella, Brian. You know how bad the sun is for you. It'll bring you out in splotches and that makes you look so silly under your wig. Well, I'll be going now. Goodbye.' Lady Tetley marched off to the house and her meeting in Surbiton.

267

The Judge poured the wine. He raised his glass. 'I trust you will like the wine.' It came, Simon noticed, from Sainsbury's. 'And now to business. What is the news of your client, Leslie?'

'Very bad, Judge. He's under intensive care in the Clinic. I've spoken this morning with Lady Brackley and I shall have another bulletin this afternoon. But I fear the worst.'

'I am sorry. You know what that means if he should die?'

'Yes, the case will die with him.'

'So we won't be resuming the trial on Monday.'

'We shan't be able to continue with evidence, but there is now no need. Simon and I have come to tell you that the case has been settled.'

Brian Tetley raised his eyebrows. If he had his cambric handkerchief with him, thought Simon, he would have waved it. Instead, the Judge removed his Panama hat and fanned his face.

'Settled! You have settled the case? Well, I am most surprised. I didn't think that this case was capable of compromise after Harrington's, how shall I put it, raking cross-examination of the Plaintiff yesterday afternoon. On what terms, may I ask?'

'The Defendant wishes to withdraw each and every reflection upon Lord Brackley and wholly accepts that what he published about Lord Brackley was incorrect.'

'This is most odd, Leslie. The Defendant alleged acts of cowardice and betrayal, he enters a defence saying that what he wrote is true and now he withdraws that defence and apologises!' Tetley turned to Simon. 'Is your client now admitting that everything he wrote was false?'

'He is, Judge.'

'Then your cross-examination which, as I understand it, was intended to suggest that Lord Brackley was, at the time, a secret Communist sympathiser intent on betraying the guerrillas he had parachuted to join was scarcely —'

Leslie interrupted. 'I know all the circumstances, Judge, and what Simon was putting in cross-examination was strictly in accordance with his then instructions. It was, I assure you, perfectly proper. He only received the further and decisive information last evening.'

'Then what is the explanation of your client's sudden withdrawal of his extraordinary accusations?' Tetley asked Simon.

Simon told him what Gray had discovered and how he, Simon, had confronted Tomas during the night. He recounted the story of Andrejevic.

'Tarnovic had became obsessed over the injustice done to his hero, Draža Mihailović. He had this wild idea to revenge his friends by telling Andrejevic's story and pretending that he had himself been with them in the mountains.'

'And invent lies about Lord Brackley?'

'I fear, yes.'

'That was very wicked. And he deceived you?'

'He did.'

'And last night he confessed to you?'

'Yes. One of the statements which Leslie had obtained was from a woman who'd been with Tarnovic in Belgrade and who had witnessed his arrest by the Germans in October 1943.'

'The importance of the date,' said Leslie, 'is that Tarnovic only met Andrejevic when they were both prisoners. So, the Andrejevic incident of the massacre of his men must have happened in or before October 1943. Lord Brackley never came to Yugoslavia until November 17.'

Mr Justice Tetley replaced his Panama on his head – like the black cap in days gone by, thought Simon.

'It was a terrible plan to have conceived. Is he being taken into care?'

'It is hoped that something can be arranged.'

'The damages to which Lord Brackley is now entitled must be astronomical.'

'As you say, Judge, astronomical,' said Leslie. 'But Simon and I have discussed this. The Defendant has very little money. All we want is a public apology and withdrawal and we need it immediately, lest Lord Brackley die and the case die with him. We accept that the Defendant has suffered appalling experiences, which may have left him unbalanced. Accordingly, once there has been a comprehensive and public withdrawal and apology, we shall let it rest.'

'Without any damages, Leslie? If there are none, the settlement and the apology might be suspect.'

'I agree. There'll be a token payment of five hundred pounds so that we can say, without announcing the exact sum, that the Defendant has offered and the Plaintiff has accepted damages, which the Plaintiff will then devote to charity. Both sides will be bound not to say more.'

'Has the Defendant got five hundred pounds?'

'He will have,' said Simon tersely. 'By Monday.' And the Judge, for once, asked no more. So, Harrington himself is going to pay, he thought.

'Very well,' said Brian Tetley. 'Let us pray that Lord Brackley survives the weekend so that his reputation can be publicly vindicated.'

Leslie and Simon managed to swallow their glasses of sweet hock, Leslie refusing a second glass on the plea that he was driving; Simon on the plea of a headache after his night-long conference.

As they walked to the house, Brian Tetley unexpectedly took Simon by the arm and stopped him, allowing Leslie to go ahead into the verandah.

'I just wanted to say, Simon – may I call you Simon?'

Simon saw to his surprise that Tetley appeared to be embarrassed. 'Of course, Judge.'

'Well, all that I wanted to say is that although your cross-examination has come to nothing and for very good reason, I thought at the time that, professionally, it was first-class.' And Brian Tetley hurried after Leslie into the house.

'What an extraordinary mixture he is,' Simon said in the car as Leslie drove him back to London.

'I know. Despite his absurd manner, he's not a bad judge and underneath the frippery, he has rather a good heart.'

270

'I had not seen that before.'

'He does have to endure that terrible wife.'

'Tell me about Bentall. What was he up to?'

'Far more than he should. Gray says that Bentall was almost paranoid in his determination to win this case. He will not remain Senior Partner of Baker and Turnbull for much longer – or remain on the rolls as a solicitor. He could be struck off, if not more.'

'So there were two men in this case who suffered from an obsession – one on either side.'

In Wiltshire, her father was in the garden when Alexandra arrived. Grace Brackley had kept him informed about her husband. The Admiral had offered to go to London, but Grace had said there was no point – George was unconscious. He could not live long, she had said, but Leslie Turner had told her that on Monday all the allegations about her husband in the libel case would be withdrawn, so he would die the hero that he was. She prayed that he would live long enough.

James Layton watched as Alexandra came across the lawn to where he stood beside the herbaceous border. When she was a few yards from him, she began to run to him and he opened his arms.

Jessica watched them from the house as they walked together towards the beech woods, the Admiral's arm around his daughter. He will have his grandchildren now, she thought. But she would have preferred the merchant banker.

On the Monday morning, the jury were in their places. Neither Tomas, nor Grace Brackley, nor Roger Bentall were in Court. The young juror had been looking forward to the morning. He was hoping for a few more fireworks like those on Friday afternoon. He had enjoyed them. Helen Hunter had not. She thought that the young Counsel

271

had been very rude to the nice old gentleman in the witness-box, although she had to admit that the nice old gentleman had got rather flustered before his fainting fit.

Then the jury heard Leslie Turner read out the long prepared statement – the Defendant's apology and the withdrawal of all the accusations which had been levelled against Lord Brackley. Mr Justice Tetley made a little speech. Lord Brackley's splendid reputation, he said, had been entirely vindicated and after expressing his thanks in suitably flowery language to the jury, he discharged them from further attendance.

As they left the jury-box, the young juror said to Helen, 'Bloody waste of time. The lawyers have carved it up. I bet they keep their fees.'

As the Court emptied, Jumbo Lancaster eased his bulk from the Press-box. Something happened last Friday night, he thought.

His car took him to Pelham Lane. Felix opened the door to him.

'Tomas is ill,' he said when Jumbo enquired. 'He doesn't want to see anyone.'

'Has he seen a doctor?'

'He has.'

'We had in mind a business arrangement. I'll call again later in the week.'

'He'll not be here. He's going away.'

Felix closed the door on him. Later other journalists appeared. Felix repeated what he had said to Jumbo.

On that Monday afternoon at a meeting of the Partners of Turnbull and Baker held not in Bentall's glossy office in Clifford Street, but in the Partners' old room in Lincoln's Inn Fields, Roger Bentall was required to step down as Senior Partner. The Law Society and, indeed, other authorities had been informed about his conduct.

The next day, twenty-four hours after the Court had heard of Tomas Tarnovic's apology and withdrawal of the charges he had levelled, George Brackley died.

Eva Janjce and Dr Duric took Tomas with them back to

California so that he could end his days under their care at the Four Seasons Retirement Home. Tomas had been glad to see them, especially Eva Janjce. They had even taken his dog, Tito, with them.

The flat in Pelham Lane was put on the market and after Tomas had gone, Felix was asked to dispose of the belongings which Tomas had left behind. He sold the furniture and asked Alexandra to help him go through the old man's papers and pack the books for dispatch to Santa Barbara. They sat together in the bare, empty flat placing the books in packing-cases and sifting through a mass of old papers, bills and letters, which they found jumbled together in a cardboard box.

One which Felix came across was a letter from Eva Janjce in California addressed to Tomas when he had first come to London over nine years ago. He sat on a packing-case and read it.

I hope that you've arrived safely and are now settled into your new home in London. You know I never wanted you to go, but that American wife of Stepan's was determined to drive you away. If ever you're in trouble and need me, remember that you can always count on your old friend. I often think back to those days when and you and dear Sacha were living above us in Belgrade. How much has passed since then – all those terrible years when you were a prisoner. Promise me that you will try to forget them and live happily in the land where you spent your youth. Don't brood about the past. Those days are long gone and no one can bring them back. I know, my dear, how bitterly you feel about what happened to Draža, but I beg you to try to forget and live peacefully and happily.

It is, I think, forty years to the very day since, from the upstairs window, I saw you and your dear Sacha taken by the Germans off the street outside our apartment. But I don't want to remember those far-off, terrible times and now that you are gone, I am determined to drive them from my memory. It can do no good to remember. You, like me, must forget, for we are old and I am here with Ivan in California and you in Stepan's flat in London. So you see, all has at last ended happily.

The memories fade, so be at peace, my dear old friend, and write and tell us how you are getting on.

All my fondest love,
Eva

Beneath her signature she had written the date – November 30 1983.

Felix handed it to Alexandra. 'This is an old letter from Eva Janjce. You can tell how fond she is of him. I'm glad she will be looking after him.'

He went on sorting out the papers. It had meant nothing to Felix that in this letter written many years before the libel case, Eva Janjce had then thought that the date of Tomas's deportation from Belgrade was not October 1943 as she had sworn when she had made her statement, but November. Nor did it mean anything to Felix that if the date of Tomas's deportation had been at the end of November, then Lord Brackley could have been in the mountains with Tomas's friend when someone had betrayed the Cetniks and the Partisans had massacred them.

But it did to Alexandra. When she read the date of the letter, she thought back to the night when Simon had so fiercely pressed Tomas until they had finally convinced him that Brackley could never have been the British officer who had been with the Cetniks commanded by Colonel Andrejevic, Tomas's friend, who had died in his arms in the prison camp in Norway. She remembered Tomas's despair and desolation when they had proved to him that he must be wrong and how she had knelt while the tears of the old man ran down his face.

'What is the matter?' Felix asked as he saw her look around the room when she had finished reading. 'Is anything wrong?'

274

'No,' she said. 'Nothing. It's a lovely letter.' She folded it and put it in the pocket of her jeans. 'I'd like to keep it.'

They went on clearing the papers and packing the books and when they had finished, nothing remained of the life which the old man had passed in London.

In the evening, Alexandra showed Eva's letter to Simon. When he had read it, he said, 'So – November 30 1943.' Then he looked again at the letter and quoted, '"It is, I *think*,"' and he emphasised the last word, '"it is, I think, forty years to the very day since, from the upstairs window, I saw you and your dear Sacha taken by the Germans off the street outside our apartment."' He paused and then said, 'But when Eva Janjce was prepared to give evidence in a Court of law, she swore it was October.'

He stood for a moment in silence. Then he walked over to the chimney-piece, took down a box of matches, turned and looked at her.

'It is finished,' he said. 'It is all over – and it is better that it should be. But you and I will never know for certain what was the truth.'

She nodded, and watched as he put a match to the letter and saw the paper burn and blacken into ash.

Two months after his death, a memorial service to honour the life and work of the Right Honourable Lord Brackley of Brandsby was held in Westminster Abbey. The Queen was represented by the Right Honourable Walter Fairchild, the Chancellor of the Duchy of Lancaster. The Prime Minister attended and Admiral Sir James Layton bore the deceased's medals and decorations up the nave.

Lady Layton and Sir Leslie and Lady Turner were among the great number who attended. The Right Honourable the Earl of Cranston, the former Foreign Secretary, gave the address. As he stood high in the pulpit above the vast congregation, he told the story of George Brackley's life of achievement. He concluded with the man himself: 'My friend, George Brackley, was a great public servant and a fine man. To use that old-fashioned phrase, he was straight as a die – loyal to his country; loyal to his friends; and loyal to those beliefs and ideals which he had acquired as a youth and so passionately sustained throughout his long life. There are not many left like him – and the nation is the poorer for his passing.'

Among the hymns Grace had chosen was the old hymn 'To be a Pilgrim' set to the traditional English melody adapted by Vaughan Williams, with words by John Bunyan on the virtue of constancy. She had chosen it because, she said, it evoked so truly her husband's life. The last hymn at the end of the service was the hymn of England.

'Land of Hope and Glory, Mother of the free,' the Prime Minister and Her Majesty's Representative sang from their stalls near to the sanctuary, as the trumpets of Lord Brackley's regiment accompanying the organ blared out under the Abbey's great roof.

'How shall we extol thee, Who are born of thee?'

Then the trumpets were stilled and Grace, escorted by her two sons and their wives and George Brackley's grandchildren, followed the Archbishop and his crozier through the screen, down the long nave, skirting the tomb of the Unknown Warrior let into the stone floor of the Abbey, and went out through the great west door into the mellow sunshine of the English autumn.

As she walked, her face pale, her eyes brimming with tears but her head erect, Grace could think only of the husband she had loved so dearly. Just before he had died, he had opened his eyes and stared up at her as she stood beside his bed. When she bent and took his hand in hers, she thought that he had been trying to tell her something; something more than his love for her, for of that she had no doubt. It was, she had thought, a plea to forgive him for having persisted with the case which had, in the end, killed him, as she had always feared that it would.

But the plea for forgiveness which Grace had sensed in George Brackley's eyes was not what she thought it might be. It was for forgiveness of another kind.

For it had not been the image of Grace which had floated before his eyes in those last moments. It had been images further back into his past – the image of Anthony Blunt, the 'talent-spotter', with the two of them sitting alone together in Anthony's rooms in Trinity, while Anthony had charmed him and taught him and converted him; then the image of the fat, crumpled figure of James Klugman in his baggy uniform, with the cigarette hanging from his lips, sitting in the discreet restaurant in wartime Cairo shortly before George Brackley had entrained for Derna and his parachute descent into the mountains – while Klugman instructed him what he must do when he joined the Cetniks and plotted for him on the map where lay the nearest encampment of the Partisans.

And the last image, the most vivid image of all, of the night when he, Captain George Brackley, had led the Partisans through the snow and up the hidden path to storm the Cetnik camp. As he lay speechless and immobile on the narrow hospital bed in the London Clinic on the point of death, George Brackley lived again the scene of the massacre which he and Klugman had planned – with the sight, but without the sound, as if in an old silent film.